Done and Done

An enemies to lovers, multicultural, plus size romance

Leonor Soliz

Leonor Soliz

Cover Art by Leonor Soliz

Final formatting by Leonor Soliz

First edition

Print ISBN: 978-1-7782872-7-5

Ebook ISBN: 978-1-7782872-8-2

This book is for anyone who has been told they're too much. Don't shrink for anybody. Occupy space unapologetically.

Contents

Author's Note

M Y BOOKS ALWAYS END in a Happily Ever After. My stories are generally low-stakes and fluffy, with a good mix of humor and angst. Nevertheless, I believe it's important to give readers every chance to consent to reading my book. Although I write generally happy romance, if you'd like to access content warnings for this story, check <u>THIS PAGE</u>, or visit leonorsoliz.com/done-and-done.

Chapter 1

I N ALEX'S EXPERIENCE, PEOPLE started bristling within three minutes of being in his presence. His theory was that people couldn't handle his brand of brooding, full of bored and sour looks. It made them uncomfortable at best, angry at worst. If they went away and called him a grump behind his back, it served him well. Alex reveled in being left the hell alone.

People rarely tried to befriend him. No one wanted to understand him. No one invited him to friendly get-togethers. His phone, always on silent, seldom lit up with calls. His texts were typically absent. So why was the phone in his pocket ringing?

Right, because his mom insisted he set her as a priority contact, so her calls would get through the do-not-disturb mode he preferred.

He grabbed his cell from his pocket and stared at the screen as it rang. While Alex blocked most people or sent them to voicemail, he'd not gone as far as fully avoiding his parents. At least, not for very long. Still, he considered ignoring the call, just this one more time... but he'd already avoided his mom's two last calls. And he hadn't talked to anyone outside of work in two weeks.

With a preemptive scoff, he tapped the green button. "Hi, Mom."

"Hello Alex. I'm glad I caught you." Of the few people in Alex's life, Mom's voice was one of the only ones that didn't immediately bring a scowl to his face.

He sighed. "What's up? Everything okay?"

She didn't respond right away, silence heavy on the line. He used as much of a neutral tone as he could muster, but his mother knew him too well. She had almost thirty years of experience, after all. He couldn't hide the bite in his words; maybe he'd forgotten how to speak to people he cared about. Maybe he'd been sullen and annoyed long enough that he'd forgotten how to be anything else.

"Everything's okay," she said, hesitation clear in her inflection. "I wanted to chat with you, that's all. Is this a bad time?"

Even if the answer was simply that he'd been unhappy too long to care much— if at all— about how his behavior made other people miserable... he was still willing to make an exception for his mother, this one time.

"No, it's fine." He rubbed his forehead in hard circles and bit back another sigh.

"I know you're an adult, but I still worry about you."

"Mom, it's fine." The words came out clipped. He pressed his lips together, air hard on his nose as he breathed deeply. "Sorry. Let's... catch up."

Silence filled the call again but, before Alex could stammer a few conciliatory words out, his mom relented and went for neutral territory.

"How's work?"

He dropped his free hand and walked to the big windows of his apartment, doing his best to summon memories of his day but nothing came clear. He barely had a sense of what being at the office had been like. Everything had been tinted gray. He'd just arrived home twenty minutes ago, taken groceries to the kitchen, and started to change into gym clothes when his mom called.

"Boring. Stagnant." He gazed over the dark city below; it had been another long day at work. Every day was a long day at work.

"Have you given some thought to leaving, then?"

"Yeah. Everyday." Having a pretty good idea of what his mom was thinking, he allowed himself a roll of his eyes, since she couldn't see him. "It's fine, mom. You can ask. I know you want to."

She let out a single chuckle. "All right, yes, I want to ask. Liam's your brother, and his job offer could be the change you need, could it not? You'd get to help build a company, make decisions about how things should be run..."

He flexed his free hand in and out of a fist. "It also means moving to LA and working in the film industry, to say nothing about spending a lot more time with him. As an employee."

"C'mon. It's your brother. He's not a bad person."

"We're very different."

And Alex was certain that Liam would want to push Alex in directions he wasn't ready to go.

"Not so different that you can't learn to have a good relationship and work together."

He let the words hang in the call for a moment. "Maybe."

It almost escaped his awareness, but he stole a glance at the empty canvas sitting on one corner of his place. Tucked away in a shadowed angle, as if he were hiding the fact that he hadn't touched a brush in two years. As if he didn't want to see quite clearly that he hadn't put paint to treated cotton in what felt like forever.

"Talk to him." His mom's voice held back the begging, but Alex heard it nevertheless. "Talk to Ana, too. When Liam brought her to meet us you seemed to like her; maybe she can help you understand things better? You don't have to decide until you learn more."

"I know."

Chapter 2

ELY HUGGED ANA SO tight that a couple of ribs must have come close to cracking. Her best friend gave as much back.

They stood somewhere outside of Arrivals in LAX, letting people pass them by. They didn't talk much; after so many years of friendship, they didn't need to. Their hug said it all, heart to heart pouring out how much they had missed each other. Even if they were in touch on the phone every day, either by call or text, living in the same city again shifted the Earth's axis back to its proper place.

"C'mon," Ana said after a while. "I'll drive you home."

They found the car and, soon, they were out of the parkade and into the city.

Ely still found it hard to believe that, upon landing in LA, she now lived here. She had yet to find her own place but no matter. Ana and her boyfriend invited Ely to stay at their house until Ely found a place. Not only were they helping her find a home, but they had hired her to do her dream job: manager of social impact for their production company. It didn't get better than that. She'd be working with youth, helping lower barriers and provide better access to opportunities for them. Perhaps even setting them up with a good career in the film industry! Ely hadn't seemed able to stop smiling since Liam and Ana had made her an offer over the phone; not that she had tried to stop it. Smiling came naturally to her. The golden balloon living in her chest, making her light enough that she could possibly walk as if on the moon— big, long, slow jumps with each step— that was new. And she loved it.

"I can't believe I'm officially living in LA." Ely fixed the seatbelt between her breasts for the second time since leaving LAX. Liam's car, no matter how fancy, was just like any other in that regard: the strap of woven plastic refused to sit nicely between her full boobs. The annoyance wasn't enough to ruin her mood. "It's exhilarating. I love change."

"Ay, Ely. Only you could say something like that." Ana shook her head, baffled as always when Ely talked about enjoying change. "How long do we have to find you a place?"

"My parents should be here with the truck next Thursday and they're taking it right into storage, so I don't have to worry. It'll all be there until I find my place. Unless I've found something, of course, but who knows."

"Your parents are awesome, to be driving your things all the way here."

Ely's eyes kept going from detail to detail of the landscape, noting the first palm trees around them and reading every sign. "Yes they are, and they're very excited about it, actually. They're treating it as a road trip! They left last Saturday; they're following the scenic route. They expect to be here next Tuesday or Wednesday."

"Where are they staying? They may have come up with excuses not to stay with us, but they have to at least accept an invitation for dinner."

"I don't remember the name of the hotel, but that's a good idea." Ely shrugged. "Though you know my mom, she'll want to cook."

"C'mon. She'd be our guest. We can't make her cook."

Ely waved a hand in dismissal. "That's okay. My mom wouldn't know what to do with herself if she wasn't the one hosting the meal. I can get her to send me the shopping list for whatever dish she'd like to make, then we buy and prepare everything around it. Patacón *will* be involved, knowing her... which I'm sure will make you happy."

" Yes, ugh. I haven't had a good patacón in a long time. Probably since the last time your parents had me over. You think your mom will still want to make me some? Isn't she angry with me and renounced me as an adoptive daughter, now that I stole you away from them?"

"No, no." Ely laughed. "They said they've felt like empty nesters for long enough that they've already learned to make the most of it. I already broke their hearts five years ago when I moved out. Me living in LA gives them a reason to travel around more, I think."

Ana slowed the car down as they approached traffic. "Great, because I wouldn't want them to get into a feud with me."

"Don't worry, they won't." Ana's words brought a different kind of conflict to Ely's mind. "Talking about feuds, have you heard from Alex?"

While working on the employment contract between Ana and Liam's company and Ely, they'd let her know they'd offered the Manager of Operations job to Alex. An interesting option, in Ely's opinion; from the little she'd gathered from Ana, Liam changed when his brother was around.

Like a caged animal, Ana had said. *Ready to spring. Hypervigilant. Cranky.*

Considering that Ely had only seen Liam be affable, she had a hard time imagining it. Alex had to be a special kind of someone to cause Liam's preoccupation to flare up.

"No." Ana tsked. "We told him we needed his answer in about a month— that was a month ago. I told Liam last night, we should have given him a firm date. *About a month* gives him too much leeway and now we're in a bit of a limbo."

Ely's eyebrows rode high on her forehead. She grabbed her water bottle. "So when you say you haven't heard from him, you mean nothing at all? Not only no definitive answer but not even a text or anything?"

"That's right. Complete radio silence. Liam is irritated as hell of course, but trying to be true to his word and give Alex time to think. Meanwhile, we started a search for candidates, because we don't want to string our business along just because Alex doesn't want to commit. There's a couple of people who seem like they could be a good fit."

"But if Alex says yes... then it'll be Alex?" Ely gulped half the bottle and watched the people on the sidewalk, the car moving slowly toward the red light.

"Probably. On paper, he is a good fit. It's the other stuff that worries me a bit. When I met him, he was so... unapproachable. A bit antagonizing."

"That's what I don't get. If they don't like each other, how come Liam isn't concerned about it?"

"They don't like each other and Liam *is* worried about it. I'm still not sure what the problem is between them; to be honest I don't think Liam knows, but he wants to change it. I get the feeling he hopes that with the three of us in it, Alex will soften and it'll make it easier for them to solve their issues."

Right. Liam wished for a good relationship with his brother, and counted on Ely to help in making it happen. Even though Liam and Alex weren't Latino, Ely and Ana were. Ely understood the impulse to do anything for family, even if it meant a bit of a rough time at work for the sake of helping someone, or making things better with someone.

Ely took a deep breath. "I'll do my best to aid in this cause. I'm not going to disappoint you or Liam, I promise."

Taking her eyes off the road for a second, Ana winked. "I know you won't."

———

Alex's boss's boss droned on and on about a damn spreadsheet he'd already reviewed. If there was anything that brought the saying *it could have been an email* to life, it was meetings like this.

Alex worked for the subsidiary of a larger parent company, consulting and contracting managerial services for small businesses. The man at the head of the table spoke way louder than necessary, with movements reminiscent of a music conductor. Probably to compensate for his boyish, frat-boy looks. Like his hands could distract from how inadequate he looked in the role, hypnotizing everyone in the room like a fucking snake.

God, Alex was bored out of his skull. No wonder he'd gotten *poetic* there for a second.

It had been barely over a month since Alex's brother, Liam, and his girlfriend— partner— whatever— had offered him a job; and almost ten days since Alex's mom had encouraged him to say yes. On this random Tuesday, stuck in a stuffy office, forced to listen to mediocre top management, he gave it true consideration for the very first time.

"Any questions?" Steve said from the head of the table. He gazed around the group of attendants, but everyone remained quiet. "Good. Now, on a different matter— new client files have been distributed to your desks—"

Alex's every muscle tightened up, first in shock, then in an effort not to slam both hands on the table. Two of his peers groaned, and one of them went as far as to grumble, "Are you serious?"

The boss's boss frowned, lips turning down in irritation at their reaction. "If someone has a problem with this arrangement—"

"You said we weren't getting new client files," John, the peer who'd spoken before, dared to add.

Alex's breathing picked up, and he pressed his hands against the surface in front of him, digging his fingertips into the textured wood.

Top management had also said they were taking steps to fairly distribute the workload, such as hiring more people and creating a new team, but none of that had happened to date. After eighteen months of waiting for it to come to fruition, bowing his head and silently competing for the promised position of team lead of that new department subdivision, Alex admitted to himself that they were never going to do it, no matter how much they promised it was just around the corner. They simply liked to dangle it like a carrot, while chaining them to their spot.

Steve glared in John's direction. "We have to meet this quarter's goals. We count on a percentage of those profits to set up the new team. Without it, say goodbye to your chance at a promotion."

There it was. The same old threat. Alex bit his tongue.

Steve brought the meeting to a close in the heavy silence that followed his statement. Alex took his papers and computer and stomped his way to his office, where he slammed the door closed. He threw his things on his desk, causing the folders with new client information to spread out into a mess of papers. Alex ignored it all and stood by his window, and punched his forehead with a tight fist in frustration. He squeezed his eyes shut.

His heart drummed against his breast bone, and his lungs were in overdrive. Fucking hell. He couldn't do this anymore.

"Fuck it."

He turned and grabbed his possessions, stuffing his pockets with the minimal number of things he bothered to carry around. He opened his door with a wide swing, and stopped by his assistant's desk.

"Jessica," he said. "I'm taking the rest of the day off."

The words sounded weird on his tongue, but he hid the fact as best he could.

Jessica opened her eyes wide. "That's uh... sorry. Right. What should I say if—"

"Did I hear that right?" Steve's voice reached Alex; the man sounded like he was standing somewhere behind Alex. "You're leaving?"

Alex didn't turn and talked to Jessica instead. "Family emergency."

"Can't you tend to them after office hours?" The recriminatory cadence in Alex's boss's boss tone remained. "There's an extraordinary meeting tonight. Didn't you check your calendar?"

Alex closed his eyes and curled his hands into fists on his side. An extraordinary meeting that happened every week wasn't *extraordinary*.

"It's an emergency," he said. There wasn't such a thing going on, but he couldn't take it anymore.

"I wouldn't do it if I were you. You know I like you. I want you around, so I can nominate you for that promotion. I need you to show up for the company. Your family will understand, right?"

"No." Alex turned and marched to the elevator.

"Alex?"

He kept going, ignoring everyone around him. He didn't dare wait for the elevator; he couldn't slow down. He took the stairs at a fast pace. He needed *out*. Now.

The firm he worked for leased two floors in a newish office building in the city where he'd grown up, San Luis Obispo. Alex escaped the place, driving over the speed limit to his apartment.

He stuffed a bag with some of his things, finally reading a text Liam had sent him a couple of days before. Nodding at his brother's words but without responding to the message, Alex got back to his car and drove straight to Los Angeles.

Chapter 3

THE DAY BEFORE, THEY had put Ely's things in the guestroom and she'd *aahhh'ed* and *oooh'ed* at the house, with its balance between cozy and modern, its many paintings on the concrete walls, wooden design elements, a spectacular patio overlooking the ocean and the city from up in the hills, and even a pool. Then they spent the evening on the patio, talking and looking at listings.

They spent the morning showing Ely around. Now up to her chest in Liam's— Ana's pool, leaning back against its wall, Ely cupped cool water in her hands and dropped the refreshing liquid on her shoulders. She lifted her face to the sun and feasted on its warmth.

She sighed. "This is all just... amazing, Ana. Amazing. Have I told you lately that I think you're living the best life? Look at this view!" Ely stretched an arm out to the edge of the patio, then swung it in front of her. "Los Angeles! The ocean! One day, you were signing with TCA and we were celebrating. Next thing I knew, you were introduced to Liam and filming that documentary, and all our lives changed forever."

Liam had been away filming commercials for a brand endorsement contract and was scheduled to arrive that evening, surely tired and carrying many new freebies. Ana and Ely took the afternoon off to relax and wait for him.

Ana floated away in the pool, as if flying. "I know. It *is* amazing. How does that even happen for me? For us?"

"It happened. Real life facts. Now you moved in with your famous actor boyfriend and offered me the best job in the world, and I'm basking in the glow of your sun. As one should."

"That's just California life, my friend."

"No, I mean Liam is the sun and he's making all of this possible for all of us." Ely chuckled.

"He'd *hate* it if you called him the sun."

Ely treaded water with her arms moving in long arches. She smiled. "I know he would. But it was him coming into our lives that changed everything, right?"

Ana shrugged, the movement failing to alter her perfect floating technique, a smile in place as well. "We could argue I came into his life and, and as we are a package deal, it's changing your life, too."

"You know what? I like your version better. *You* came into *his* life and made it amazing. He should be thankful every day."

Ana laughed. "We didn't start Jump Cannon Productions for the purpose of getting you here... but I'm so, so happy it worked out that way."

A ringtone Ely didn't know blared from the nearby lounge chairs. Ana stood in the pool, orienting herself to the noise. A second later, Ana checked on Ely as if hoping she knew what that was about. The ringtone went off again just as Ely shook her head and shrugged.

"Liam wouldn't be ringing the doorbell," Ana said before scrambling up out of the pool and checking her phone.

So she did know what the sound was. It had just been confusing to Ana because they were not expecting anyone.

Ely turned and put her arms on the warm patio tile. Ana mumbled and handled her phone; five seconds later, Ana's eyes opened wide. "Alex?"

Ely's eyebrows arched high. Alex? As in Liam's brother?

"Ana?" A deep voice said from Ana's phone, faint in the space between Ely and her friend. "Hey."

Ana's words came out hesitant. "I didn't know you'd come! Everything okay?"

A pause on the intercom app. "It'd be better if I could come in."

"Crap, yes, of course! Come in, just make sure the gate closes behind you."

Ana grabbed her coverup from one of the sunbathing chairs and put it on, a frown on her face.

"Did I hear that right?" Ely said, still from the pool. "Is Alex here?"

Ana nodded, tying the layer of thin linen around her waist. She shook her head. "I don't even know, Ely."

Ana made her way to the house, tapping furiously on her phone.

Only the sound of water surrounded Ely as she stood still, her head turning sideways to follow her best friend with her eyes. Ana's shoulders curved with tension as she disappeared into the house, clearly surprised by Alex's visit.

Ely's reaction mirrored her best friend's. The man arriving unannounced could end up being Ely's coworker, and Liam and Ana hoped that Ely would help them shape their relationship with him into something better.

After a couple of minutes of indecision, she got out of the pool and put on her cover up. She didn't bother to close it; LA was warm enough that she wanted the breeze on her skin.

Ely pressed her lips together. She had a job. It went beyond the company's mission. She needed a power pose and a deep breath. As far as she knew, Alex could be unfriendly and she would need the full power of her gregariousness to conquer the divide.

"I'm going to make it work." She said the words out loud, hands on her hips, feet wide and grounded. "It's all going to fall into place seamlessly."

She shook her shoulders, arms, and hands, and took a deep breath. She grinned, too— what an adventure, this was going to be.

She walked into the house, relishing the way her cover up floated behind her like a cape.

"Hello," she said to the room, as her eyes focused on the scene in front of her.

Alex and Ana stood in the middle of the big room, at the spot where you could either go to the bedrooms or the living room. They gazed around awkwardly, their bodies angled at ninety degrees as if they couldn't quite face each other. Ana stole glances at Alex, while he looked around the house without stopping at Ana a single time, his arms crossed tight against his body. Ana didn't seem to know what to do with her hands.

Ely didn't let their discomfort break her stride. Emboldened by her pep talk, she smirked at the two people in the room and vowed to make it better. For Ana, for Liam... and for herself, too. This job at Jump Cannon had all the ingredients of her best career life, and she wouldn't let Alex ruin it.

The man occupying her attention turned his head to her, his face impassive, his body still. She raised an eyebrow, and didn't hide her quick perusal of him. Liam had been right, all those months ago; they were clearly related. Alex was a bit shorter and generally slimmer across the chest and arms, and quite attractive. His hair was a few shades darker than Liam's, but the shape of their face held eerily similar lines. Handsome to a fault.

Yum. Her lower belly came to life with appreciation.

Ely reached their general vicinity. It granted her the opportunity to catalog that face in detail: the cold hazel eyes and a mouth that curled down in a sour slant.

"Hi." His deep voice fell flat on the floor.

She straightened her spine. The tingles in her core went into remission. Pity, that Alex was so hot and so evidently bitter.

It was fine. She had enough sparkle for the both of them.

"I'm Ely." She extended a hand. "Ana's best friend. Also known as Elena Castillo, the new Manager of Social Impact for Jump Cannon Productions."

Ely stared at Alex, hand in the air between them, and waited for his response. It came slowly; he peeled his hand away from his body with an angle to his hand that screamed hesitation, the other arm sticking close still to his torso. When his hand finally wrapped around Ely's, his skin was soft and cool to the touch. The strength of it was mild. He didn't say anything.

"You're Liam's brother," Ely added, explaining for him. He nodded once, taking his hand away from hers and tucking his arm right back against his chest. Like he would have rather not engaged in the effort of shaking her hand.

His eyes didn't waver from her face. The only movement she could detect consisted of a newly appearing frown.

Her lips pressed slightly together. Her nostrils wanted to flare but Ely stopped it. She wouldn't give him the satisfaction of irritating her. Well, showing him he irritated her. Truth was, her skin was getting prickly.

"You're staying here, right?" Ana pointed at the travel bag at his feet. "Ely is taking the guest room but we have another room with a bed, it's just not as finished."

"If that's okay," Alex said.

"Of course it's okay. Come this way."

"I'm going to change," Ely announced for Ana's benefit, letting them walk ahead of her.

Ely disappeared into her bedroom.

Whaaaat, she said under her voice once she'd closed the door behind her. When she'd met Liam for the first time, she'd asked him about his brother. Liam told her Alex tended to the side of cranky— her first experience with him made it clear that Alex's personality lacked warmth. More than cranky, he seemed sullen. It got under her skin a minute into having met him. And to think that at the time, making breakfast in Ana's old tiny kitchen, Ely'd been fantasizing about the idea of ending up with Alex...

Yeah, no. She could let go of that wild, passing notion. It didn't even matter that her body had picked up sexy vibes from the meeting— somehow, unbelievably. Good looks wouldn't fix the issue of having opposite personalities. As for work, Ely had to believe she'd find a way to succeed if he ended up becoming her peer. She'd make it work, for Liam, Ana, and above all, herself.

Chapter 4

ALEX KEPT HIS EYES glued to the plate in front of him. Ana, her friend Elena, and Liam sat around him at the table, chatting as they had dinner. While they shared a friendly meal after Liam had arrived home from his trip, Alex focused on keeping his face blank and ignoring them. Fuming.

Liam had six of Alex's paintings hanging on the walls of his home. He had even arranged for proper lighting to showcase the art, with frames that fit both the mood of each piece and the overall decor of his home. Looking at them all turned Alex's stomach. His traitorous eyes kept stealing glances at them, burning his retina each time. Especially the one about Liam and Alex as kids. What had possessed him to paint that, and where and how had Liam gotten it, Alex didn't know.

He wished he could tear them down and burn them. But he remained sitting at the dinner table, moving his food around on the plate.

"Not hungry?" Elena asked.

Elena, dangerous woman that she was, had been the first to talk to him. Alex didn't care for it. He'd have preferred Ana spoke to him instead; as soon as he'd met Elena earlier that day, one thing had been starkly clear: she was magnetic. An electrical field seemed to crackle around her, and he hoped the metallic elements in his blood didn't respond to it. She'd walked into the house with such aplomb, her body swaying and reverberating with each step she took, and those waves broke the quiet in the air like a crack in the time and space continuum. It had been a long time since he'd felt anything remotely similar to attraction and, at this time, it wasn't welcome. He was busy keeping distance from them all. Didn't she know?

Alex put his fork down, avoiding her eyes. "No."

"Would you like to eat something different?" Ana asked.

Great, now she talked, putting Alex firmly at the center of attention. Three pairs of eyes pointed in his direction but he didn't engage. He turned to stare at one of his paintings on the wall, not that it helped dissolve the heavy weight in his stomach.

"No." He also didn't care for Ana's friendly tone. It couldn't be authentic. His words and demeanor were prickly and bound to cause irritation in others. Ana likely managed her annoyance due to a misguided sense of hospitality. He'd much rather she reacted to him as she truly felt; he didn't plan to let it affect his behavior, anyway.

"You're welcome to check the fridge or order something," Liam offered.

"I said I'm fine." Of course Liam had had to insist, not hearing— or choosing to ignore— Alex's first response.

If the silence that followed was heavy, Alex refused to take responsibility for it.

"Do you have any plans... or goals... for your stay in LA?" Ana said, breaking the silence.

"I imagine it's easy to guess why I'm here." Alex was about to cross the line from unpleasant to assholery, and trying to stay on this side of it was as much as he was willing to do.

Elena joined the inquisition. "Something tells me that if we tried to guess it wouldn't go very well, despite that comment."

Alex glanced at Elena to his side. Only his eyes moved. She smirked at him, a glint in her eyes.

His cock twitched. Alex frowned. His cock had no business twitching.

"You know," she added, "you don't seem like you're playful that way."

Fuck. Not good.

Alex turned his eyes to Ana. "I want to learn about your company. I'm... entertaining the offer."

"You made it right on time." Even though Liam responded to him, Alex didn't look at his brother. He went back to playing with his food, staring down to his plate. "Ana and I are leaving for Toronto on Friday morning. We are booked to premiere the documentary at the fest there."

"This week we were planning to look for office space." Ana drank some of her water, the lemon slice in it traveling up and down with the liquid in the glass. "Tomorrow morning I'll be busy helping Ely find a place to live, but in the afternoon you should join us to look at a couple of places with our commercial realtor."

Elena tapped her long nails on the table. "It'd be good to have you there, if you're really considering working for Liam and Ana. If the four of us may be in this together, having you help us choose a place where you and I may end up spending most of our time could be good."

Alex again glanced at Elena. The glint was still there. Like the sparks were coming from within. The sassy slant to her lips screamed a challenge.

Alex turned his eyes away. His gut had forgotten to give him any kind of signals for years, but it was blaring an alarm at the moment. Elena was a menace, especially for a guy like him. She was too beautiful, too alluring, too full of life. He didn't have enough energy inside of him to fight her. He'd burn like a moth drawn to a flame. He scowled, determined to keep himself safe. At a distance. Work. Only. And even that wasn't fully on the table.

"I'll go with you. I'll speak my mind," Alex said. "But don't take it as an agreement to join your venture."

"We'd never dare to make that mistake." Elena's voice vibrated with barely subdued teasing.

He didn't need to look at her to know she was smiling. Or smirking. He wanted to roll his eyes but he didn't. Even that response would be giving her too much power over him. Ignoring her was best. She could tease, he wouldn't engage.

"One thing we need you to know," Ana said, "is that we're in conversations with a few people for your role. They know our timeline; they're expecting an answer early next week."

"I was going to text you tomorrow. Ask for confirmation that you weren't interested," Liam added. "And we were going to hire one of these other people."

Alex nodded, slowly, only once. "Makes sense. I'd disapprove of your business decisions if you'd dropped the ball on this."

From the periphery of his low-cast eyes, Alex watched Liam scrunch a napkin in his hand. Ana placed a hand on his forearm, squeezing the flesh there in what seemed like comfort.

"We were waiting for you." Ana kept her hand on Liam's arm. She squeezed again.

Liam cleared his throat. "Giving you time."

Their tones hit a different note. While Ana had sounded like she clinged onto patience, Liam sounded like he struggled not to explode.

Maybe it would be better if Liam exploded. It'd give Alex a reason to say no to this proposal.

Then again, if he exploded and Alex felt vindicated in rejecting the offer, Alex would keep on being stuck in his job.

Alex closed his eyes and released a strained breath through his nose. "Fine. I am going to give this a fair try."

"I'll give you a copy of the business plan for you to check." Ana got up and put her plate away, while Liam got the rest of the plates. "Anyone want something to drink?"

As Liam and Ana busied themselves, Elena leaned closer to him and spoke to him in a low voice.

"We all will give this a try, I think."

Alex didn't move his eyes. Elena's glass came into his field of vision, clinking against his half-empty one on the table.

Chapter 5

A FTER VISITING THREE APARTMENTS and two offices, Ely wanted to call it a day. Pushing herself to come to the current space paid off. Even though she hadn't made a choice on a place to live yet, this potential working venue seemed promising.

"This looks good! Three offices— one for the operations manager, whomever it ends up being," Ely said without looking at Alex. "One office for me, and an extra one for private meetings or if one of you wants to work from here one day." She waved hand between Ana and Liam.

Ana had taken Ely around to visit prospective living arrangements and, after lunch, Liam and Alex had joined them to check business locations. The grumpy one had barely said a word all afternoon and contented himself with grunting when absolutely necessary, arms crossed most of the time. He sported a slight frown that sometimes went wild and increased to a full frown and a mouth scowl combo. The thought alone of his pretty face setting into such sour gestures made Ely want to roll her eyes. Her mom would have said, *cuidado que la cara se te va a quedar así.*

She wanted to channel her mom each time she saw him: careful or your face will set that way.

"The board room looks good too." Liam entered the space and everyone else followed. "Not a stunning view but decent, and the size is right."

The outside long wall consisted of floor-to-ceiling windows, providing natural light and a city view. The inside wall faced the reception and waiting area, made of glass as well but frosted for privacy. The boardroom side walls, the shorter ones, were made of standard drywall, painted a soft gray. No art decorated the space yet but that was an easy fix.

"Do you think we can fit twenty people here?" Ana asked.

The realtor double checked her papers. "The brochure says it can fit thirty plus people, depending on how it's set up. With the right meeting table, it can sit twenty for sure."

"Do you know how many people you'd host here for the youth program, Elena?" Alex walked to the window and stared out to the city.

Feeling petty, Ely waited a beat, two, before responding to Alex's question. "I think we'll take ten to fifteen young people per cohort. We should have enough room here."

Honestly, if he weren't so stern, they could have had lots of fun running the business together. They could have even become friends. Such a pity that his personality sucked.

The four of them came out of the boardroom and inspected the rest of the place. The three personal offices followed the outside walls in a big L, so that all of them had windows. Thanks to the boardroom's long glass partition, light came in and did a good job illuminating the interior section of the space, where a reception desk and a waiting room completed the area.

Ely and Ana stepped into the first individual space. It was a standard office, again with a big window and enough space for proper furniture and storage.

"This looks good, too," Ana said.

They moved on to the second office, where Alex and Liam already stood. This office had a slightly bigger area, enough that she could fit a small sitting section, perhaps even a sofa.

"Oooh. I call dibs!" Ely exclaimed.

She glanced at Alex, who looked at her with a bored expression and a judgy arch to his eyebrow. Those eyebrows were perfectly shaped and so, so judgy. Such. A. Shame.

"Okay, let's see the third one." Liam led the way.

"This one is a bit smaller," the realtor commented. After checking out the final space, the realtor, Liam, and Ana walked out and met at the reception area, discussing something while Alex and Ely checked out the last office.

"What do you think of this option, Alex?" Ely hid her instinct to wrinkle her nose. The words had escaped her before she could stop them. She finished, only to pretend it had been on purpose. "Do you see yourself working here?"

She didn't let herself put her hands on her hips, though she really wanted to.

A beat, two, before he responded. "Does it matter what I think? You clearly like it, Elena, and Liam and Ana will likely favor that."

She took a deep breath through her nose, hoping it would calm the instant fire in her veins. It didn't help much. The oxygen in her lungs had set her organs ablaze.

"Anything the matter, Elena?"

His eyes glinted in her direction. If she wasn't mistaken, this was Alex's version of poking at her patience. It added to her irritation that he'd been so easily successful at it.

"Why do you insist on calling me Elena?"

"That is your name." He didn't move. His face didn't change. A face like his would look well with the passage of time but, at this rate, he wouldn't get a wrinkle in a decade.

She smirked. "And yours is Alexander. No one calls you that."

"Elena rolls off the tongue easier, considering my name. Alex and Ely— there's something about the two L sounds, so close together."

"That makes no sense. But if it were a problem, there are much better options to manage it, Sandy. Did you think about that?"

He gave her a dirty look. There, she'd gotten him to react, too.

"Never in history has Sandy made sense for Alex—" he spat.

"Scotland. It's a popular version of your name in Scotland. It doesn't have an L and it bugs you, so it's perfect."

"Elena."

"Sandy. Not my fault you're so uncultured."

"You're just doing it to annoy me. Using a name other than my own, because I use your full name."

"You got it." She gave him a once over with her best winning smile and went to find her friends by the main door. Clearly, she'd need to have the last word in all battles of wit with that man, no matter how small.

Chapter 6

L IAM CONSULTED WITH HIS PR team and, on Thursday night, the four of them attended the opening of a new and exclusive LA restaurant. The owner favored Hollywood personalities, creating a great opportunity for Liam to keep his networks fresh and push the Jump Cannon name forward.

The sultry space was gorgeous, with warm yellow lights hitting dark walls in a delicious way, and shining off white and bronze details. The place wasn't packed, but it still took them almost an hour to get acquainted with everyone. Liam made every introduction with one of his million-dollar smiles; Ana held his hand, smiled one of her goddess smiles, too, and helped steer the conversation to all the right places. Alex escaped them within a few minutes of arriving at the event, disappearing into the crowd.

Ely *loved* the buzz she got from meeting new people. Since entering the restaurant, she had smiled as hard as Liam and Ana did, shaken hands, and joked with enough people to electrify her nervous system and make her feel slightly drunk.

She sat down on her chair and grabbed the edge of the table for balance. She took a deep breath and smiled at Ana and Liam, sitting across from her. Alex sat next to Ely, silently scrolling on his phone.

Ely ignored him and talked to her friends. "That was great! I'm so glad to have you as a trailblazer, Liam. Without your contacts this would be a mountain to climb."

He nodded. "Without my contacts, this would be almost impossible. But I do know people, and Ana is amazing at what she does, so I think we have an actual shot at this."

Ana leaned to him and kissed his shoulder. "What you and I do is only half of the equation."

"What I've gathered to date about the structure of the company is a smart strategy, too, I think," Alex said. They all startled at his words, but Alex wouldn't have seen it; his eyes were still on his phone. "You can bring other producers on board or keep it small; either way, it's scalable."

Alex had asked questions of all three of them during the past couple of days, two or three sentences exchanged at random times; clipped and to the point. Efficient. Detached. His latest comment tripled his input to date... and signaled interest.

"They are smart people, Sandy." Ely kept her eyes away from him, winking at Ana, but tracked him from the edge of her field of vision. "I'm so excited for everything we can do with Jump Cannon."

He put his phone on the table and directed his attention to Ana. "Is the Manager of Operations expected to go network, too?"

"Yes, when Liam and I are not available," Ana replied. "Especially in the beginning."

Alex dipped his head once in the smallest nod ever known to humankind. The server approached their tables and took their order.

"So, what's next?" Ely asked.

"Ana and I need to prep for the premiere and events in Toronto," Liam said. "You will stay at our place, of course, until you're ready to move and your parents get here with your stuff. We signed the lease for the office we chose effective tomorrow; Mo will drop off the keys."

"We'll get the place furnished over the weekend, at least with the bare minimum, but you'll have to be on call to help handle that stuff." Ana lifted a shoulder. "You know, handle calls from the movers if they need anything. The way we organized it, they're taking all the stuff into the office on Saturday and, on Sunday, they will be there to move things around according to your directions. They won't do much with the decor, though."

"Sounds good." Ely nodded. "My top priority is to get an assistant. I'll focus on that tomorrow morning and on Monday. I have three finalists for the role, and I'll need someone helping me out next week."

"I'll be able to help you once we're back from Toronto," Ana added.

"I had to pack next week full of meetings, after we return from Canada." Liam reached for Ana's hand on the table. "Mostly virtual, but still a lot of my time is tied up. I can help randomly, here and there, but perhaps it's best if you pretend I won't be there for most of it... but Alex might be."

Silence landed around them. They all turned to Alex. Ely liked to think of herself as a good person, but a part of her enjoyed seeing Alex squirm. Their stare affected even someone like him, who'd mastered the art of acting at the edge of rudeness. He had to know what was on their minds; their unvoiced question. They needed Alex's answer.

"If I say yes..." Alex let his words hang in the air. Ely groaned, her shoulders collapsing with annoyance. He ignored her and continued, "I'd have to sign the contract with your lawyer, then meet with Elena several times, create a few drafts for the way both our departments would interact, and then all of us would get together to finalize the structure, right?"

"Right." Liam stared at his brother, a slight frown on him. It made him look a lot more like Alex. "C'mon. It's a good opportunity for you. I think you'd be great for it... and I'd like to have you around."

"I hate all the Hollywood stuff." Alex tapped an insistent index finger on the white tablecloth. They all waited for him to add more, to relent and give them an answer. He took a deep, strained sigh. "I'm sending in my immediate resignation to my employer tomorrow. If they haven't made it clear they intend to fire me, yet. I've been gone for a few days which I'm sure didn't land well with them."

Liam, Ana, and Ely watched him without a word; she suspected Ana and Liam were as in shock as she was. Even though he'd uttered the words, a part of her continued to question the honesty of his interest. He rarely responded with more than grunts, he barely looked anyone in the eye, and his perma-frown had convinced her he didn't approve of anything he'd seen so far. She had fully expected him to decline the offer. Instead, his words suggested she'd been wrong.

Silence continued around them, growing heavier with every passing second. Alex's response to the quiet was to lift a sardonic eyebrow, appearing to care very little about making it awkward.

"Does that mean you're taking the job?"

Ana had been the first to recover— or at least to pull enough sense together to break the stretched moment— and asked the question they all had in their minds. Alex didn't respond right away; Ely was sure, so sure, he let them squirm on purpose. That the asshat enjoyed it. She pressed her lips not to respond, playing in kind. Having a bit of fun herself, though she'd never admit it.

"I wouldn't be quitting my current job if I didn't have something lined up. Your business plan looks solid. There's a good balance between the for-profit side and the social side. I think there are some things that will need adjusting, but that can come with time. If you still plan to be flexible with it for the first year."

"We still plan for it to be flexible," Ana said. "But I think at this point we also need a concrete answer... tell us you're taking *this* job. With the three of us."

Alex glanced at Ana. She seemed to be the one who got most of his rare direct eye contact. Alex's eyes were pretty, but Ely still preferred not getting Ana's treatment. It'd distract her. She preferred navigating this tension, her teasing and his despondency, rather than the intensity of his eyes on her. The few times he'd looked at her, her body had made it clear it didn't care that she didn't like Alex; a primal desire to have sex with him hummed in her veins, waking up the nerve endings of her skin, just in case. Getting a bit of a thrill every time they actually looked at each other threatened great inconvenience.

If his words meant he accepted the offer, she'd have to put her hopes in all of it fueling healthy competition between them.

The tapping of Alex's finger stopped; he flattened his hand against the white fabric instead. "I'm assuming the plan is to have a strategic meeting per trimester for the first year, at the least. Probably two. You should add that specifically to the plan, so that it doesn't fall through the cracks."

"That was always the plan. Like we've said before—" Ely had been unable to stop herself; bickering seeped out of her at the best of times and, again, Alex made it sour on her tongue. The fact he interrupted her only made it worse.

"But you should have a meeting per month, at least, with your peer. Keeping things on track." He said this to her without giving her his eyes. Thank god. What a douche.

"I'll be sure to keep my peer on track," she responded, "but is that peer going to be you, Sandy? Yes or no answer."

She knew she'd won at least one of their battles when calling him by that nickname caused the curl at the end of his lips to drop lower.

He ignored her and flicked his hand between Liam and Ana. "Unless you've changed your minds, yes, I'm taking the offer."

This time, their silence only lasted three heartbeats.

"Welcome aboard!" Ana said, reacting first once more.

It took a second or two, and Ely wondered if Ana had kicked Liam under the table, but Liam responded too. "Yes. I'm glad. I know you'll be amazing in this role."

Alex didn't look at Ely. Ely didn't look at him. The server arrived with their drinks and the first course.

"I'll make sure to get his contract ready." Ely tasted her drink, the right mix of citrus and sweet. "We can probably sign it on Monday with Alex, and you two can sign when you come back from Toronto. I'll add it quickly to my list, please ignore me."

She hid in her phone and pretended that the idea of working with Alex didn't drop heavy in her stomach. Her irritation with him had had an easy outlet in their mostly-one-sided squabble, when she hadn't been sure he'd take the job. Now that he'd taken it, she doubted bickering was the way to go.

Dangerous, as irritation helped mask her body's reaction to him. She'd have to live with the temptation of it and figure it out; over time, her body was likely to get with the program and smarten up.

At one level, she regretted it— if they had been more compatible in terms of personality, they could have had a bit of fun. If they were friendly, she would have considered keeping it simple and fun and leave it as mutual release in having sex once or twice, given the opportunity. But spending time with him the past few days hadn't only erased the old, brief fantasy of ending up with him and having one happy little family with him, Liam, and Ana, it had also shown her that, if left unchecked, they could fight. Really fight. Impossible to work together, kind of fight.

She needed to find common ground with him, for the sake of a good working environment. Sex was out of the picture. Bickering had to be reigned in. Things couldn't get any worse, if she wanted to protect Ana and Liam's business and her own career. Ely had no interest in a work environment drenched in vinegar. Unresolved sexual intention could be ignored. Irritation had to be subdued.

Chapter 7

A NA AND LIAM LEFT right after noon on Friday. It put Alex out of sorts. It didn't feel right to stay in their place without them. What was he supposed to do with himself?

At the edge of the patio, he rested his arms on the railing and gazed at Los Angeles below. He tried to imagine himself living in the city, while fighting the impulse to second guess his decision.

Alex shook his head to himself and cast his eyes to the ocean. The sun had begun its descent to the horizon, and light broke on the water's surface in a million tiny facets. If he still painted, it would have been a challenge to get the color of it just right— a tone of off-white that hid a hint of yellow and a shadow of blue.

He imagined himself carefully defining the edge of each small light shape with a fine brush and his chest caved in with the force of it. He closed his eyes to block the view.

Hell. He'd been fired from his previous job. He'd read emails from his team mates that morning, that went from panicking that Alex wasn't around to panicking because his accounts were being dropped. It escalated to emails from top management threatening to block his bonuses, then his promised promotion, to finally threaten with the sack. All in the space of two days.

"Hey." Elena's voice cut the silence next to him. Alex opened his eyes at once; he hadn't heard her approach. She leaned with a shoulder against the railing, a folder in her hands.

He didn't shift his position nor respond, but turned his head slightly to her. She took a deep breath that seemed to reach into his own lungs. Despite his best efforts, his body insisted on attuning to hers.

"I have this for you." She offered the folder to him. He'd expected her words to be clipped and dry, but they weren't. Instead, she sounded almost friendly. "It's your copy of the contract. Read it and let me know if you have any comments. We have until Ana and Liam get back to iron out the details; as soon as it's signed, I can call the other contenders and let them know we've made our decision."

He took the blue manila from her hands and placed it against his torso, stealing a glance at her and returning to his position on the railing. A breeze caught on her hair, the thick, wide curl of it shifting against her brown skin. What kind of colors would it take to get the shade of it right?

"Okay, then." Her sigh was clear in the space between them this time. "I'll be in the living room—"

"Why are you doing this busywork for them?"

Fuck, but he'd broken his own rule and interacted with her. Evidence of how hard she was to resist. The night before, when he realized he'd be alone in the house with Elena, he'd hoped for as little interaction as possible, to keep temptation at bay. That should have meant not talking, yet here he was.

"What do you mean?" Her voice sounded almost as friendly as it had over the past few days, when she spoke to Liam or Ana.

During the morning and right after Liam and Ana had left, he'd imagined the days ahead as the quiet before a storm, or like Christmas on a battlefield. In his head, the weekend would involve a lot of orbiting each other, giving each other a wide berth. Asking her this question was a test to the ceasefire... and a risk.

Steeling his spine, he prepared himself to gaze at her some more. If her change in tone was her effort at a truce, he'd have to address her with his eyes. He wished he had sunglasses on.

The brown of her eyes grabbed his attention. He arched an eyebrow, praying for disinterest. "I'm sure handling the paper-work, hiring the assistant, dealing with the movers— that none of it is in your contract."

She pulled her lips to the side. He expected she would have smiled for other people, but there was no hint of humor or tease in her expression.

"Ana and Liam are my friends."

He made his eyes look at hers again. "They could pay for people to do this."

She lifted a shoulder. "They could. So?"

"They asked you to do it."

"No. I offered." She crossed her arms.

"Why."

"Why do your questions sound like a statement?" She frowned. It mostly seemed natural, but he caught the faintest trace of irritation in it.

He didn't respond. He had a feeling she'd break and say something to fill in the void. He was right.

"They're taking a risk hiring us. I know I'm good at my job and Ana knows it, too. Liam thinks you're good. But they're mixing the business with the personal and I don't want to give them a reason to regret it."

Alex cocked his head. "They can't have a problem mixing personal relationships with business. They got together before they got into business together. Do you think they're hypocrites?"

She opened her mouth in a slack, offended *o*. She shook her head and scoffed, and turned to lean on the railing in a mirror image of his body.

"You don't owe them anything, Elena."

Irritation was definitely seeping into her voice now. "Maybe it isn't about feeling like I owe them something, Sandy. Maybe it's about trying to be a good friend."

"Don't tell me you're a people pleaser."

She turned her head to give him a hard glare. "There you go again. Does it hurt to be kind? To use a questioning inflection when asking something? I promise you it doesn't. I'm not a people pleaser. Wanting to help my friends does not equal putting myself at the end of the task list every time."

He shrugged. "Sure."

A minute passed. She pushed away from the railing and took a step away. He assumed she wanted to leave, so he startled when she stopped in her tracks and took a step towards him instead.

"Is this you in a good mood?" she demanded.

He scrambled away from the railing and faced her, if only to track her better and stop her if she came too close. He must have shown his shock on his face, and she must have thought it was funny, because she laughed.

The sound of it tore him in two. A side of him delighted in the melodic sound, the other cowered.

"Oh my god. Relax. I'm not going to attack you." Mirth still etched a smile on her face, and filled her eyes with light.

She had attacked him, though not physically. She glowed when she laughed and, to his horror, his heart leapt to his throat. She'd broken the truce by being unexpected, and it reached too deep into him.

"I'm not in a good mood." If his words had been growled, he didn't care much.

She squinted at him, the smile on her lips diminishing but staying. Teasing.

Her hands hung from her hips, thumbs in the pocket of her jeans. "You asked me a question and we had a bit of a talk."

"I don't know what part of that tells you I'm in a good mood." He crossed his arms.

"Do you hate the idea of being in a good mood? Is that it?"

He shook his head. "Elena."

"Sandy."

He closed his eyes and took a deep breath. He begged his body to return to reality; he wanted his composure back.

She spoke before he could get there. "Look. To use your word from yesterday, we're peers now. We'll be working together. I'm trying to learn how to be... neutral with you, if not amicable."

He stared at her and showed her as much disinterest as he could summon. "We don't need to be friends."

She rolled her eyes. "I know. But I'd rather figure out an armistice."

So he hadn't been making stuff up. They were both feeling each other out and coming out of it on a battlefield.

He snorted. "I can't make any promises."

She looked him up and down. "Evidently I can't, either."

She walked back into the house, wide hips swaying unapologetically.

Yes, she was dangerous, but perhaps he didn't need to stay all the way away from her to be safe. She was the first person to crack his despondency in a long time... maybe amicable was fine.

Or maybe the startle response had shaken his brain into utter confusion, and he was only fooling himself.

———

Alex's world shifted later that day. Turned itself around. Seeing his name on a clickbait title had proven to be too hard to resist, and the sad excuse of an article slashed his chest open five words in.

Liam McMillan betrays his brother Alex! You won't believe what the star of Space Bureau did to his own family!

Lying on his bed, a bottomless pit opened in his gut, bile shooting up to his esophagus. Scrolling to read more, he skimmed the spammy page, finding pieces of the story among many ads and external links. The words crammed into the raw, exposed hole in him.

Liam McMillan has a brother, and there's no love lost between them!

Alex McMillan, businessman, was secure in his job at Burton & Robinson Financial. Living most of his life away from the spotlight, he risked leaving his job after his brother promised him an opportunity he couldn't refuse. Liam McMillan's new partner in life and crime, documentary director and filmmaker Ana Lira, got her famous and rich boyfriend to invest in her company, fully revamping it and rebranding it in the process. They invited poor Alex in, only to turn their backs on him!

We have it from a good source close to the brothers that Liam McMillan never planned to hire his brother as business director. He offered the job to someone else, leaving Alex lost at sea. This betrayal cost Alex his job and his dignity, only because Liam is blind to his girlfriend's machinations. Look below for a picture of Ana Lira and Liam McMillan talking to their chosen CEO, happily discussing business plans while leaving Alex in a lurch!

Tell us in the comments what you think of this horrible situation.

Alex navigated out of the page, locked the phone, and put it on his bed face down. He closed his eyes and focused on slowing down his breathing. Maybe it would help tame the nausea building inside.

Alex could have a lot of differences with Liam, but he doubted his brother would double cross him. He was too damn optimistic for Alex, but reliable. Liam might try to drag Alex into new situations, get stubborn about it, forcing Alex to dig his heels and growl, and they might fight for it, but Liam was honorable.

Still, Alex didn't like that Liam hadn't told him about this meeting, whatever the reason, whenever it had happened. Sure, it might be a picture completely unrelated from the article, that they used as evidence when it was all a lie, anyway. Even so, it told a story that filled Alex with dread.

He could see it so clearly in his mind. A long road full of trying to get to agreements with Liam and Ana and Ely, trying to make things work, putting so much effort into it... effort and energy he wasn't sure he had. The three of them were already such a unit, and Alex would be the odd one out in every discussion. As much as it was an escape from his old job, he was still jumping into a hell of a new situation. One that left him feeling inadequate and unmasked. Everyone would be looking at him, his brother and journalists alike, searching to uncover the truth inside, one he wasn't ready to face. Vulnerability tasted metallic in his mouth.

Even if they found a way to have a successful professional environment, the world wouldn't believe it. His name would be added more and more to the rags alongside his brother's, where faceless people would decide a myriad of lies sounded fun enough to pretend they were the truth. He'd be stuck hating the same things; doing work someone else wanted from him, and him biting his tongue to maintain an image. Never doing what he wanted to do for himself.

He couldn't do it. He had to escape before it began. Even if it meant finding another grueling, faceless job in a corporation somewhere. He had savings, he could live off them until he found a new job to hide in.

He didn't sleep until the sun had made its appearance over the city.

Chapter 8

E LY HAD TO ADMIT mild surprise that Alex had slept in that Saturday morning. Or so she guessed, as he didn't come out of his room until noon. She worked on her computer on the outside table, enjoying the perfect weather, when he appeared in the living room. Wearing a white shirt and light gray pajama bottoms.

If he weren't a bit of a douche, she'd let herself appreciate his appearance much more. As it was, she noticed how attractive he looked in such simple clothing— not to say anything of the almost-pornographic appearance of those pants— and pressed her lips tight, lest she found herself whistling.

He didn't look at her. He got fruit out of the fridge and, grabbing his laptop from where he'd left it on the kitchen island, he plopped himself on the sofa and worked— or browsed, who knew— for a few hours. She lifted her eyebrows the fifth time she caught him running his fingers through his hair or rubbing his face, and forced her eyes away.

When Ely finished her work and got back in the house, their hello came brief and tart. Awkward.

Ely got into her room and prepared to take a long, relaxing shower. Her thoughts were full of Alex, of trying to come up with a plan to get things into amicable territory. The idea came to her while she slathered moisturizer all over.

She found one of her favorite dresses and did her hair and make up. She picked heels and a going-out purse, and came out of her bedroom with resolution and courage tied tight around her ribcage.

Alex still sat on the sofa, the same clothes on and hair the messiest she'd ever seen. He leaned back against the plush pillows, arms splayed on the back of the couch, eyes fixed on his screen. After a brief nod, he clicked the mouse pad twice and placed the laptop on the coffee table, releasing a sigh.

"Working hard?" she asked. He turned his face to her, a rare look up and down her body betraying his mild interest. The look was the only sign of it, for his face barely moved.

Shame, that they were in the place they were. That she aimed to come up with the terms of their treaty, rather than enjoy each other's company.

His eyes locked on hers. "Done working. Going out?"

"Thinking about it." She made her way to the sofa and sat down at the other end of it. She gazed at him, studying his form. His mood.

He dropped his head on the back of the couch and closed his eyes. He yawned. "Have fun."

She smirked. "God, Sandy. Don't fall asleep on the couch or that's where you'll spend the night. I don't care enough to wake you up gently or even tuck you in with the blanket."

His voice came deep and rumbly, and tired. "I wouldn't expect any less from you but complete disregard for my wellbeing."

She scoffed.

"I quit, by the way," Alex added. He barely moved, except for his mouth. "We won't be working together, after all. I just sent Ana and Liam the email."

Time stopped in its tracks. A record scratched to a stop in her mind. A second later, warmth infused her face.

It couldn't be true. Here she was, trying to build a working foundation with him, and Alex was already planning to leave.

Ely collapsed against the sofa pillows. "This is a trick, right? You can't be serious."

It took him some time to respond. When he did, his words were monotone. "Very serious."

"What... you... argh!" She threw her bag on the floor and ran her hands through her hair, pulling at the strands. "You just accepted the offer, after *days* of stringing Liam and Ana along! You can't leave them hanging like this."

There was no inkling of remorse in his posture. No change to signal discomfort. "I don't owe them anything. They knew I was here to make up my mind."

"And you supposedly did!"

"I get to change my decision." He didn't have the decency to shrug.

"Gah! You're so infuriating, Sandy. They're not even here to try to deal with things."

He rolled his eyes, so much was clear despite his eyes being closed. "Then you do it. I thought you wanted to help your friends."

So handsome and such a dick. How could anyone be so self-centered? He wouldn't even engage properly with her! The fact that he wasn't angry made things worse. He wasn't even looking at her. Like the inside of his skull was the most important thing to him.

"Do you have to be so selfish?!" she spat out.

That got him to react. He opened his eyes and twisted on the couch, facing her, a fire lit up in his eyes.

The hazel of his irises burned with the energy of his rage. "Making sure I take care of myself and my interests is not selfish."

"It is when you do it at the expense of others, all the time." She met fire with fire. "And let me tell you, in the short while I've had the dubious pleasure of knowing you, I certainly have never seen you prioritizing someone else."

He scowled. "You've known me for less than a week. Don't flatter yourself and think that's enough to make up your mind about me. You don't know me."

"I definitely don't feel anything as positive as flattered in anything related to you. I'm so glad I don't have to work with you. You may seem smart, you may be attractive, you may have a great brother... but you're also so clearly an asshole." Air consumed her lungs from within, her rage caustic.

He shook his head and leaned forward to close his laptop. "None of that matters, Elena. None of that says much about me as a person. Fuck's sake. Sure, you may seem smart, you may be gorgeous, but you clearly jump to conclusions way earlier than anyone with an iota of wisdom would. That is something about you that matters."

"How dare you!" She jumped off the couch to look down at him, her hands fisted at her sides, her body rigid. "I've seen enough to know that you're bitter and dreary. I can't believe I had planned to invite you for a drink, give you the chance to prove me wrong and get started on a good note. I guess there is an insult I deserve: too forgiving."

"You were going to invite me for a drink?" His tone was filled with suspicion, an eyebrow high on his forehead as he looked up at her. "Sure. Ah-ha. Great friends, from now on."

"I can't believe it myself." She took a deep breath and had to forcefully unclench her jaw. "Look. I thought we were going to work together. I wanted to see if we could find a friendly working relationship. There's no point, now, is there?" She picked her bag and stood up. "And to think that for a minute I thought we could get along."

She gave him a scornful look. She could feel the way her face had set into a gesture of deep distaste. She walked away, head held high.

She made her way around the sofa toward the door. She wanted the hell out, go forget herself in finding someone to flirt with, maybe sleep with. Someone who'd help her feel alive in her body, so that she didn't have to let her brain ruminate on this mess.

"Goodbye, Sandy." *And good riddance.*

He rubbed his face hard with both hands. She was almost to the door, leaving for somewhere, anywhere, when he stopped her.

"Elena. Wait."

She hesitated. She went as far as grabbing the door handle, but stopped. Curling her hands into fists again, she turned to him. He walked to her, all rigid, long and lean muscles wrapped in thin fabric, all shifty eyes.

"Listen." Alex jarred his arms, hands low on his narrow hips, fingers splayed. He studied her from under the ridge of his eyebrows. "You know Ana best. They look solid. Do you think they're going to last?"

She scoffed. "What does that have to do with anything?"

"Humor me." He stared at her with steady determination.

She opened her eyes wide. "Why would I humor— ugh. Fine." She threw her hands up in the air. "Yes. I think they'll last. You know Liam. What do you think?"

"Yeah, he's into it. So, chances are you and I are going to cross paths at some point."

She arched an eyebrow. "Are you staying in LA?"

He shook his head. "I'm not sure. Probably not."

"Then I don't think we'll ever see each other enough to make a big deal of it."

"True. But maybe it's the mature thing to do, to try."

Her laugh came out dry and unbelieving. "Mature, huh?"

"That's the word I'm using, yes."

They stood face to face, her in her pretty dress and him still in his pajamas, assessing, waiting. She was on high heels, he was barefoot. Even so, she had to look up to look him in the eye.

Two competing forces warred in her. Alex was the kind of guy she had no tolerance for. The kind of man she had no problems abandoning in the middle of a date, or calling out in the middle of a meeting because they had talked over her again. On the other hand... this was Liam's brother. Ely *would* see Alex again. And it was part of her nature to give people a chance.

"Fine," she relented. Unsure if she was doing the right thing. "Go change. We'll go somewhere. See if we can... fix... this."

"Nah." He released a breath and turned, his steps quiet. Alex opened cabinet doors near the kitchen until he found alcohol. "I'm sure Liam has the good stuff."

Ely hesitated. With a fortifying deep breath, she let go of the fight; she kicked her heels off her feet and made her way to the sofa. She left her bag on the coffee table and settled in the same spot on the couch, waiting for Alex, and readying herself to discover who he was, when there was no job with Liam and Ana on the line. When he was trying to do the mature thing.

It was the first time Alex took any kind of conciliatory step with anyone, and curiosity sprung up inside of her as to where it might lead.

Chapter 9

ELENA SAT STILL ON the couch, eyes on the dark window. Silence enveloped them, only interrupted by the clinking of glass on stone, the slosh of alcohol as Alex poured it, mixed it.

Something had possessed him to try and end his relationship with Ely on a decent note. He'd trapped himself in it, now. Perhaps her allure had finally dazzled him, or perhaps her indignation had cracked something in him and he hadn't wanted her to remember him as a complete jerk. Either way, now he would have to risk it and see what happened when he actually entertained conversing with Elena.

Whatever reaction she'd sparked in him felt new, it had been absent for so long. Maybe it was okay to want her to have a different memory of him than a fight. He was leaving the next day, at least. Whatever happened, it would be over by Sunday morning. And he could claim peace, that he'd shown he cared enough about how his behavior had affected someone else, for once.

He gave her a drink— he'd barely noticed more than the fact he'd found gin in a cupboard and had mixed it with something—

and sat on the same spot he'd been using all day. A bit lost and dreading the silence, he reached for his phone and, connecting it to the speakers wirelessly, put on music.

"Tell me about your painting," Elena said.

Great. Just a great starting point. He stared at her. "I don't want to talk about that."

"They're good."

They squinted at each other. He shook his head.

"Okay, then, choose something for us to talk about," she conceded with a hand flair.

"When are you starting work?"

"This Monday next. The next few days are all about setting up. It's going to be good."

"You are actually happy about it all, then." He took a sip of his drink. Huh, he'd added something fruity to it.

She arched an eyebrow; they had a great shape to them. Now that he was actually looking at her, he was noticing details that made it very clear: he'd been right to keep his distance from her.

"Yes, I am very happy. It's a great opportunity; Ana and Liam are smart, and I am good at my job. Ana may love me as a friend, and Liam respects me and we like each other... none of that interferes with their goal with this company. You were right about that. Passing on someone like me because we're friends doesn't make sense."

Alex moved the ice in his drink, noting the clink of it against the glass. "I can't believe you admitted I was right about something."

She smiled, bright and open. "Don't get used to it."

"How's it going, looking for your own place?"

She ran a hand through her curls, fluffing her hair. "It's going. I hope I get a place soon. It's such a different market from where I used to live that I think I need to adjust my expectations. At least I didn't keep much of my furniture; I don't think I'll get a place that will have a lot of extra room. Single people living on a single income seem to have a hard time here, but I don't think I can have a roommate. We'll see what happens in a year, but for now I'm happy with just finding a comfortable place, even if it's small."

Her hand still played with her hair. Alex followed the line of her arm down to her shoulder, down the thick strap of her dress... to her tempting cleavage.

He took his eyes away. "Yeah. I have to admit I'm happy I don't have to deal with that now."

She left her hair and tasted her drink. "Mh. It's good. Where are you going next?"

He lifted his eyes to the ceiling, tracking the modern stucco pattern on it. Hopefully it'd distract him from Elena's magnetism, and the way he wanted to let his eyes wander down her body.

Yet he was making an effort, so he gazed at her face again. "I wrote to my parents earlier; I'll drive back home early tomorrow."

"Did you tell them you quit?" A spark appeared behind the brown irises. The woman couldn't seem to help herself.

He allowed himself a smirk. "Not yet."

The gleam remained, but she pushed her lips to the side to not add a smile to it. "Liam mentioned your parents had wanted you to take this job."

"I'm not sure I like this— that Liam tells you things about me."

"We're friends. We talk about stuff sometimes. And Ana tells me things, too."

Fuck, what was that... shine she exuded? It wasn't even really directed at him; she always had that shimmer around— it actually tended to dim when interacting with him— but she cast some of it in his direction, having a peace-making drink together, and it disrupted his synapsis.

He fought it with a shrug. "Sure, that's your guys' friendship. Doesn't mean I like it."

"Is that why you quit?" She leaned toward him, seeking to know more, like she didn't understand the waves the movement produced, or their effect on him. "You don't want to work among people who have close relationships?"

Or maybe she knew, the evil woman.

He stared at his lap, to take a break from it all. "Well, no. How close the three of you are was only a small factor in my decision. That was still there when I said yes, originally. The main factor when I decided to join was that I liked how the business was planned. I agree that they're making good decisions and projections are level-headed and good."

"Then, why? Why are you leaving?" She pushed a hand toward him in the space between them, sliding over the sofa's fabric, and intruding into his field of vision.

He lifted his eyes to her, and wished he didn't see her genuine interest. "It's messy in other ways."

"Is this about your relationship with Liam? I swear, you guys are like teenagers together."

"You and I haven't been much better before right now." He drank from his glass and shook his head. "Not all siblings have great relationships."

"I guess." She scoffed. "I wouldn't know. I'm a single child, like Ana."

"Maybe that's why you two got close. Had the good stuff without the bad."

She took her hand away and shrugged. "I don't know, I thought Liam offered you the job because he believes you were good at what you do… but also because he wanted to mend fences."

What would have happened if he'd reached out for her hand? If he'd followed the faded instinct that appeared in him with her gesture?

Problems, for sure.

… or, wait. Was that accurate?

Right. They were talking about Liam. He pursed his lips. "There are no fences to mend. We haven't done anything particularly bad to each other. We just never got along."

"I think he wants to change that. Make the effort to have a different relationship with you."

Alex took a good look at her again. "Do you know him this well after so little time?"

"I think I know him better than you do, because I've been open to seeing who he is."

Hell, Elena knew how to push his buttons. Every one of them, even the ones that had been dormant for years.

He shook his head at her. "You and I are supposedly trying to give each other a chance, and yet you're bugging me about my brother?"

That stole a smile out of her. It punched him in the gut. "It's what I'd do for a friend. You and I— we're not friendly, but I care about Liam. So maybe I'm doing this for him."

The corner of his mouth pulled up with a mild sneer. Perhaps the seed of a smile. He wasn't sure. "Sounds like you're the loyal sort."

"I am, therefore I'm at a complete loss as to why you're leaving. It does not compute, for someone like me."

He'd forgotten what curiosity felt like, but he was filled with it that night. He couldn't imagine what it'd be like to have someone be loyal to him that way, to have that kind of passion directed at him. Or what it would be like to have Elena feel those things for him.

And it was so, so tempting to get a glimpse of it, just for the next few hours. If only to avoid explaining to her that staying made him vulnerable, that he didn't know how to be Liam's brother, and to distract from the part of him whispering that he was self-sabotaging.

"You baffle me, Elena."

She startled, a mild, almost-not-there gesture. His honesty got to her; he could see it in the way her eyes sparkled.

"I baffle you?" A surprised chuckle came out of her. "You baffle me!"

He raised an eyebrow. "I do. I baffle you."

"Of course you do, Sandy." She covered her mouth with a hand, like she wanted to stop herself from laughing. But the mirth escaped through her eyes anyway. "There's an ocean of... of *something* inside of you that you hide from everyone. You protect it from prying eyes with such... zeal. Like a growling dog."

Her words slammed his chest. His lungs convulsed and released the air within in a mighty scoff. It left nothing inside to voice a response. Not that he knew what the fuck to say to that. It proved he'd been right; staying would mean having everyone inspecting him.

"And it's a pity, really," Elena continued. "I bet there are people who'd love to know what's there."

He shook his head. "Don't. Not tonight, satan."

"Satan?!" That loosened her laughter. It filled the space with its loud, magical sound. "You can't be serious."

"I wasn't altogether serious. It's as close to joking as I get. Don't you know that by now?"

She moved her head from side to side, unbelieving. Her lips took on a gleeful slant, and her eyes sparkled with mischief.

She curled her legs under herself, taking on a more relaxed position toward him on the couch. "Okay, then. So getting to know you is a no-no. Which is ironic, considering the whole purpose of this conversation. It makes me *satan*, in your eyes. Got it. May I ask what else you think of me, then? I know you think I'm smart, you admitted to that earlier in a fit of sincerity and growling."

He scoffed. "Sure. You're also very confident... verging on annoyingly so, perhaps."

She laughed again. "You also think I'm gorgeous. You admitted to that, too."

She clunk her glass against his.

He rolled his eyes, ignoring the twist taking a hold of his stomach. "My eyesight is good. I'm also smart enough to know that's not all there is to a person. You and I? Would never work. For work... or for other things."

He definitely needed to stop looking at her. Catching so many details that wanted to make their way into his brain. His gut. And below.

It was bringing something dangerous out of him.

"Oh, I fully agree." There was a change in her voice. A challenge. "You're attractive, but a grump like you and a firecracker like me? Not a good mix."

Despite the truth in her words, temptation pushed his heart to a faster pace, effervescence in his blood.

"Sounds like you've been thinking about it." The words escaped him with a thrill.

She grinned. "Clearly, so have you."

He'd been right. So right. Looking at her, actually paying attention to her, was enough to undo him.

He let his eyes roam down her body. "I tried not to. I did my best to avoid thinking about it."

Her dress was short. It gave him a good sight of her legs, the line of her thighs, and the curve of her full calf.

"I've tried, too. You're so crabby, Sandy. Not clicking with you helped. The tension of it all— well, I told myself it'd fuel some healthy competition at work." She took a sip of her drink and added, "Since we could never sleep together as coworkers— talk about things getting messy, since we don't like each other as people— that we'd pour that into work and we'd build a strong, successful business. If we managed not to throttle each other."

He'd never said he didn't like her, but admitting to that would make her ask what he felt instead. He would never confess she scared him.

"I was planning to do my best to ignore you," he finally said.

He checked his glass; Alex hadn't drunk a third of it. Neither had Ely. Alcohol didn't explain the heat making an appearance in his veins, warming up his skin. The way she looked at him explained it so much better.

It had been a long time since he'd felt anything like this.

He couldn't admit to his feelings but... maybe he could do something about the blood that kept wanting to rush to a long-unused organ.

She licked her bottom lip. "I told myself I was annoyed at you, every time I noticed my physical attraction to you."

She was flirting with him. Maybe. Probably. He could tell himself he was simply being honest, but his last few statements could be construed as flirting on his part, too.

He sipped his drink. "We're not going to be working together, now."

His words and his body did not seem to care what he knew intellectually. Couldn't be surprised; this feeling was primal, and Elena triggered a response in him he thought had disappeared. It seemed he had been wrong.

He could still want.

She looked him up and down, assessing. She dropped her head to the side. "Are you proposing something?"

He wanted her. What a treat.

He approached her on the sofa and took her glass from her hand. He put both his and her drink on the coffee table, his heart beating strong enough to create its own electromagnetic field. Pretending to be sure of himself, he moved to the space between them. She gazed at him with that damn sparkle in her eyes, that confident curve to her lips.

His voice came out from deep in his chest. "One night, mutual... company. We could keep it simple."

Whatever her answer, the dam broke in him. Blood flooded his cock. He gave up resisting his body's response to her.

He hoped she could see the courage it took for him to show her.

She wrapped her neck in her hand. "No complications, since you're leaving."

He swallowed. "And one day we meet at, don't know, Liam and Ana's wedding—"

"— How patriarchal—" her hand moved down to her cleavage, but it seemed unstudied.

He ignored her and continued, "We'll be polite and *amicable*, no need to talk about that night we had all that time ago."

She took her hand away from her body but bit her lip. "It's still likely to be a bad idea."

"We're just choosing not to resist something that was already there. It's just lust."

Chapter 10

E LY'S SKIN TINGLED FROM head to toe. A deep bass drummed in her lower belly.

She wanted to have sex with Alex.

He'd shown a different side to him during their conversation. He gazed at her; not so much her eyes but right next to them, as if her eyebrows or her temple were as close as he could get. Except when his eyes burned a path down her body. And he didn't quite open up, but he was chatting with her like they were two people who tolerated each other.

In the process, she discovered that tolerating one another was enough to spark desire for this man. To the point that it had only taken fifteen minutes for them to confess they lusted for each other.

She gulped and hid it with a smile. The purr of desire thrummed in her belly, her body reminding her that yes, she liked sex, and yes, Alex was appealing to her at that level. Very much so. She hadn't meant to flirt but sitting next to him, talking to him, knowing he was leaving, had made it feel inevitable. Like it had given her permission to press pause on everything else.

Alex wasn't her peer anymore. This night was a random night with an attractive guy, and her body really wanted to have its way with him. The change in circumstance was a gift. Maybe.

She needed to make a decision before her attraction to him took over.

"It's only worth it if you're good at it. If we're a good fit," she said. Testing. Begging for time.

But he responded calmly, directly, not even phased that she'd challenged him.

"We won't really know until we get going." He touched her forearm with the tip of his index finger, his eyes following the gesture. She followed the movement, too. It woke up every nerve ending under the gentle pressure of his touch.

Oh, yeah. Her body wanted him. Badly. Now that she didn't need to keep her distance. "Then I reserve my right to stop it or redirect, if I don't like what's happening."

A smirk appeared on his lips. "Of course. That's always the case."

She could stop everything else. The irritation, the annoyance over his personality. He'd taken the step to find a real truce, now that he'd be gone... and it showed her she could let go of it all. For the sake of wanting him.

Ely stared at his wide shoulders, the way they tapered down to his waist. To his narrow hips.

It was the erection in his thin gray pants that melted all her questions and worries.

"Look at me," she asked.

He did. The hazel of his eyes burnt her.

She jumped him. Kneeling next to him on the couch, she kissed him. Despite all the bickering and the whisper of hesitation in her, his lips felt right on hers. Hard, wanting her as much as she wanted him.

Her conflicted feelings about his personality, the fight they'd had half an hour before... it all disappeared when he grabbed her head to change the angle of the kiss, his tongue seeking hers.

Not a minute had passed when he grabbed her and pulled her to him, leading her to his lap. The skirt of her dress scrunched up her legs, allowing her to position her sex right on his hardness.

She undulated her hips and they both moaned into each others' mouths.

"Thanks for quitting." She kept her sinuous movement on him. "Just don't tell Liam I said that."

"Don't talk about my brother." He bit on her lip. "Tell me more about how you've felt this pull between us."

He kissed her jaw, down her neck, licking the point where she knew he'd feel her pulse.

"Dammit, Alex. When you came out of your room today wearing this—" she grabbed his shirt in her hands, ran them down his torso, and briefly hooked her fingers on the waist of his pajama pants— "I wanted to curse your name."

He nibbled on her clavicles. "You're so hard to resist."

"I didn't even want your attention— that much."

His hands mapped her body. They gripped her thighs, then tested the weight of her breasts.

"I hate this dress. The material is too thick." His breath tickled the sensitive skin of her neck. "Where's the damn zipper?"

She smiled. She pushed his hands down to her thighs, and encouraged him to slide the dress up her body.

"It's a slip on." She lifted her arms above her head. "Take it off me."

A pained expression took over his face, and his eyes almost closed. "Changed my mind. I love this dress."

He pulled it off her with a swift movement of his arm. The dress followed a wide arch through the air, until Alex dropped it somewhere near them.

"Fuck." His eyes took inventory of every detail of her underwear, seeming to catch on the way pink lace contrasted with coral soft mesh. "Delightful."

Ely smiled. It was the first time he said anything like that, and the power of having it directed at her swirled over her skin. She leaned back and placed her hands on his knees, giving him access to her torso.

He frowned in concentration. He placed both hands on her shoulders. Warmth seeped into her from them, causing a sigh to hitch. He drove his fingers down her body, with enough pressure to make her feel thoroughly explored. She changed the movement of her hips to circle over his hard cock.

His eyes shuttered, his lips going slack. One of his hands closed around a breast; his thumb teased her nipple through the thin fabric, while his other hand latched to the soft rounds of her belly and hips. His fingers dug into her flesh, pleasurable pain sparking from each touch point.

Ely's arousal bloomed inside of her. "More, Alex."

His name on her lips lit a fire in his eyes— they fastened to hers. He wet his bottom lip and brought his hand from her breast to her face. There was no gentleness in the way he cupped her cheek, with his thumb carving a hard path under her jaw. Ely's breathing picked up, just as Alex lowered his hand to curve around her neck. Could he feel her fast pulse under his fingers?

His hold on her neck tightened. Ely's pulse sped up. He pushed her back, and she had to let go of his knees. The vague image of the coffee table she remembered behind her guided her hands, and she hiccuped her relief when she found its surface to lean on.

His hand left her neck and it made her feel naked, despite her underwear remaining in place. She almost asked him to collar her throat again, but his devouring gaze down her body halted her intention. His hands seemed to follow the same path his eyes did.

Alex grabbed two handfuls of her belly, his teeth clenching. Ely's breath sped up even further; she melted under the heat of his want.

He lifted his eyes to stare at her from under the ridge of his eyebrows. "More, you said?"

"More, I said."

His chest expanded and contracted with his own breathing, his white shirt stretching with each inhale. His hands traveled down to her thighs, until he reached her knees. He hooked his hands there, and guided her legs to open wide for him. Ely planted her feet on the sofa, giving him what he wanted. She was spread out for him on his lap.

Alex ran his fingers down the inside of her thighs in an electrifying light touch. Ely's back arched in pleasure. His cock nestled between them, and the pressure of her ass and thigh against it pulled a wince out of him.

With the same ghosting stroke he'd used on her thighs, he teased her through the crotch of her panties. "Can't say I'm surprised you're greedy."

Her body screamed for even more, but she only lifted an eyebrow. "If you're going to have me on display like this, you better make it worth it."

A smirk appeared on his lips. His thumb pressed against her entrance and followed a hard pass up the seam of her sex, to end with a rough circle on her clit. All above the fabric of her panties, not quite fully touching her how she needed him to.

Ely's body loosened with the intensity of sensation. Her head fell back. "Alex."

"More." He snatched the crotch of her panties to the side and did the same, his thumb now fully nestled in between her labia.

Ely's moan filled the room when he rubbed her clit with an unrelenting thumb.

"Right there," he added, the circles on such a sensitive spot perfectly timed. Her mind blurred, her lungs overworked, her throat raspy as she moaned again. "Yes. I knew you'd be a feast to watch."

Tension built in her, and Ely grinded her hips against him, seeking his touch.

"More." His voice rumbled, deep and as mindless as she felt. The thumb he used on her barely lost its rhythm as he pressed a tip of a finger against her opening. He fingered the area with complete disregard for her encouraging whimpers. "Fuck. You're so wet."

Alex pushed two fingers inside of her. Ely's elbows buckled.

"Hold up," he commanded. "I want more out of you before you come."

He hooked his fingers and rubbed her G-spot.

Her body jerked in a wave of lightning. "Alex. You're going to make me come."

He stopped the motion of his thumb and slowed down inside of her. "Can't have that."

"Dammit." Ely came back to rest on his knees with one hand, while the other grabbed him from the nape and brought him for a kiss. She bit on his lip and pulled, eyes locked on his, her fingers in his hair. "You either fuck me now or make me come at least once. I'm not your toy."

Alex's smirk had no humor in it. "I'm gonna fuck you. But I don't want you to come until you're coming around my cock."

"Alex—"

He unceremoniously removed his fingers from inside of her and surrounded her back with his free arm. He pulled her to him as he got up; she would have fallen, had he not held her tight to him. She found her balance again with feet firmly on the ground and her hands on his chest.

His hands closed around her arms. "Condoms?"

Hell. He hadn't said it in as many words, but he wanted what he wanted out of her, and she hated that it was such a turn on.

He pulled his shirt off and dropped it behind him.

Ely ran her fingers down his torso. "In my purse."

He pushed away from her to take down his pants. His black boxers tented with his erection when he stood again.

Alex grabbed her purse from the coffee table and walked away without a care. "I'm not fucking you here."

"Alex!"

At least he went into her room.

After a brief hesitation— she wished she didn't want him so much— she reached him there. He stood naked, rolling a condom on. He'd turned on the light.

"Alex." She paused, unable to avoid a long admiring gaze down his body.

"I'd like you naked, wide open for me, on the bed." His voice had devolved to a grumble.

The intensity of his eyes traced fire on her skin. She grabbed her breast over her bra and teased her nipple. This was as close to asking as he got, telling her he'd like to do something.

"What do you plan to do?" With her free hand, she lowered a strap to her bra down her arm until it looped loose.

Alex grabbed his cock and cupped himself, hand moving in a lazy stroke. "I want to watch you undress, get on the bed and open your legs for me. Then I want to eat you out until you're dripping wet. Only then I'll bury myself in you until you clench around me and I forget my name."

Her legs and her brain both turned to jelly.

Ely reached back to undo the clasps of her bra. She wanted to forget her name, too. Forget that this dry talking that slipped into their one night stand was the same that made them fight any other time. Because, right now? It intoxicated her.

She took off her bra and dangled it from her hand for a second, then dropped it on the floor.

"Your panties, now." He twisted his hand around the head of his cock.

She obeyed.

"Now get on the bed and spread your legs for me."

Something deep in a corner of her soul resisted the order, but it got dismissed by her dazed body. She climbed on the mattress, let her knees drop to the sides, and waited for him.

He wet his bottom lip with hungry eyes. He got on the bed but, instead of diving for her clit with his tongue, he hovered over her to get his lips on hers again.

The kiss was deep, venturing, lighting up her body in a more sensual way. He rubbed his cock on her core a couple of times, until he stopped to change the angle; he nibbled at the base of her throat.

Alex licked a path down to her breasts, sucking on her nipples, teasing the other with his fingers. He nipped at the base of her breasts, before rubbing his face on her plump belly. The scratch of his stubble stole a hiss out of her.

"Fucking indulgent," he growled. He lowered on the bed until his face was suspended above her sex. He inhaled deeply. "Hell, I can smell how wet you are."

Ely closed her eyes as her bones liquified. Her blood turned to a simmer in her veins when he parted her labia and flicked her clit with his tongue. It went to full boil when he stroked her once, twice— lost count of the times he flattened his tongue against her in long and slow passes.

He sucked on her clit and put two of his fingers inside of her. He repeated the move from earlier, fingertips against the nerve endings of her G-spot, until she moaned and groaned and buckled under his ministrations.

"Alex. Sandy. I'm gonna come."

He took his fingers out and put both hands on her pillowy hips to stop her movements. He swirled his tongue on her clit once more, bracing her instinctive jolt to a stop.

Ely fluttered her eyes open. He climbed on top of her.

"You got me humping the bed," he panted. "You have that kind of hold over me."

One of his hands dipped the mattress next to her shoulder. He held himself high above her, eyes open and warm hazel on hers. She wrapped her hand around his forearm and meant to use her free hand to guide him, but he took hold of himself and plunged into her.

Her sensitized body almost exploded in pleasure at it, but he held his thrust back.

"Stop teasing me and fuck me, Alex."

He started moving slowly. His second arm joined next to her other shoulder; both locked to keep him high over her.

She caressed his chest, teased a nipple.

"Faster," she asked.

He picked up the pace. She played with her breasts; his eyes followed the movement but returned to her eyes. His mouth hung open, his breathing labored. His eyebrows knotted together in concentration.

Alex rested his weight on only one arm, and used the free one to caress her face. He clenched his jaw and changed the tone of his touch. His hand slid off her face and grabbed at her hair.

His eyes became even more fervent. Something happened, Ely wasn't sure what, but her heart flickered in recognition. He dropped his mask. He didn't hide. This moment was one of connection.

He pumped into her in rolls of his hips that managed to tease every sensitive spot.

"Yes. God." She fought her eyes to keep them open. A thrilling mix of butterflies and lust filled her chest; something about how he looked at her erasing all thoughts and irritation from her consciousness. "Just like this. This."

He sped up.

She moaned. "That's good."

"Touch me," he asked. She did, running her fingertips and nails on his skin. Softly scratching his flat belly. A hand grabbed his ass and the other went to rub her clit. "Yes."

"More." Her eyes kept wanting to close, get lost in the pleasure of it... but she didn't want to miss a thing. She wanted to see him. He was letting her in, this was a secret place, one she could enter just this one night, this one time, just for fun.

"Fuck, Ely. There. That's the spot."

She didn't know what he'd seen, but he was right. She rocked her hips as he continued to thrust, hitting exactly where she wanted him. She rubbed her clit and it took only two touches from her fingertips to create a mind-bursting, shattering climax that ricocheted through her.

He groaned, the sound of it barely making it into her awareness. He kept his rhythm but it cost him; the first thing she saw upon opening her eyes was his frown.

"God." He rocked back to his knees and grabbed one of her legs. He maneuvered it to drop on top of the other one, so now she lay on her side as he fucked her.

She twisted her torso at the waist, she wanted to see him, film the look on his face with her mind, to never forget.

His eyes were closed. She lifted a hand to his face. He grabbed her by the soft flesh of her hips and thighs, two hands clinging to her for purchase as he thrust into her.

With her free hand, she brought one of his to her breast. "Alex."

He opened his eyes. They shone. He rubbed a nipple with his thumb, and she caressed his cheek.

A long moan from deep in him filled the room as he came. He let go of her breast and her thigh, pulled away from her and sat in his haunches. He dropped his head, chin to chest, as he recovered.

The connection between them gone, her breathing returning to her and her mind back online, she came down from the high of it all.

She slid her hands under her head and stared at him. Neither talked.

Now that it was done... what? At least she'd enjoyed it, even if it had turned out to be more intimate than she'd been prepared for, somehow.

Acknowledging the closeness it had involved sent a chill down her spine.

She had to joke to break the tension building inside of her. "Well, I'd say compatible enough."

He didn't immediately respond. A minute or so later, he got up and turned away from her, sitting at the end of the bed. She guessed his movements were about him disposing of the condom, then he found his underwear and put it on.

He straightened and turned to her. "I knew it would be good."

She bit her lip, but hid her discomfort in a grin. "In a year or two, when I see you again... I'll smile at you. You'll know why."

He scoffed. "I'll smile at you, too."

Her grin turned into a smirk. "Don't make promises you can't keep."

He studied her shape on the bed. As confident as she was in her body, she wished she could cover up. She didn't.

He stared at her eyes again. "I don't know if I'll see you in the morning."

"Then this is goodbye?"

He nodded. "Bye, Ely."

The use of her nickname was a gift, poor as it was.

"Bye, Alex."

Chapter 11

E LY WOKE UP WITH a smile, her body rested and energized. Good sex typically had that effect on her. And today she had all of this wonderful house to herself. Because Alex had left. Probably. Likely.

He'd surprised her. The way he'd looked at her. The way he'd touched her, like he couldn't get enough. Like he'd craved her, too. Like he was letting her see something within him, something that didn't need words. That alone made her grateful she'd decided to have sex with him. It'd help to have those memories, when she saw him again someday.

With a sigh, she stretched, sat up on the bed and reached for her phone. She needed to get ready; she was scheduled to go to the office soon to organize the furniture. She found a text from Ana, and Ely tapped to read it.

> **Ana:** did you hear what Alex did?!!!
> He QUIT
> **Ana:** Poor Liam is furious. I think he's
> feeling betrayed

The memories of sex with Alex were good, and she was happy to have them, but she still had a rock anchored to her stomach at what his departure did to Ana and Liam. Ely would help them, and do what she could to make it better for them. She nodded and typed a response.

> **Ely**: Yeah, he told me last night.
> He left LA already I think

The texts had come through an hour earlier so Ely didn't expect a reply, but she saw the three dots appearing to let her know Ana was writing something back. Ely criss-crossed her legs on the bed and prepared to text with her best friend.

> **Ana**: did you bite his head off when he
> told you? Pls tell me you did

Ely smirked. She didn't give Alex oral so she couldn't even make a joke about that. Not that she planned to share any details about anything. Thank god, she and Ana never talked much about Ely's one night stands. She'd rather keep certain events private.

> **Ely**: I was very angry at first
> and we fought about it, but
> then we decided to be mature

and talk it out. We ended on a

good note.

Ely pushed her lips to the side. There was no chance Ana'd guess exactly on what note they'd ended the night.

Ana: too bad, I feel like he
deserves war

Ely: I know you're exaggerating

Some time went by without a response. Ely killed time by checking some of her notifications. That's when she saw a head-line she wanted to read.

Ever since the big Hollywood debacle of the year before, Ely kept a watch on what people said about her best friend and her beau online, but rarely shared it with Ana. With a reduced number of notifications, Ely didn't read everything, either, but did make a point to keep an eye for things that seemed a bit more important. Like the headline she'd just read.

A new text symbol appeared on the top bar, but Ely finished reading the article before replying.

Ana: only a bit. I am angry, but
Liam is hurt

Ely: Poor Liam. Tell him we'll figure
it out. I'll reach out to the old
shortlist tomorrow

Ana: I think we want to reach out
to Michael, so give us a couple of days

Ely: sure thing

With a big sigh, Ely typed the news.

Ely: So I know you told me you're
tired of the social media gossip
around you guys, but I think you
might want to know about this one.
You don't want to be surprised during
an interview or something.

Ely sent her the relevant screenshot, a blurry picture of them the night before, followed by a title: *Ana Lira doesn't think her relationship with Liam McMillan will last. Trouble in Paradise?*
It took Ana a minute to respond.

Ana: yeah, I don't want to be surprised
if someone asks me about it. Thanks.

                          Ely: I'm sorry :(

Ana: This isn't shaping up to be a
good day

                          Ely: I love you anyway

Ana: I love you too
Ana: Gtg. I need to get ready now or
we'll be late to the interviews.

                          Ely: Good luck :heart emoji:

When Ely finally got out of her room she confirmed it: Alex
had left. He'd even picked up her dress from where it had landed
the night before, folded it, and left it on the back of the couch.

She smiled. She put her dress away and prepared for a good
day.

Monday echoed the easy vibes from Ely's long, productive Sunday. She prepared for the official workweek by setting up the critical parts of her office and hiring an assistant, Celeste. She'd start working on Wednesday, helping to get things ready and giving Ely an opportunity to get to know her more.

The new hire kicked off what was building up to a great week. Ana and Liam were scheduled to arrive from Toronto that evening, and Ely was planning to see an apartment on Thursday morning that looked promising. That day in the evening, her parents were arriving with her stuff and their warmth, which they'd show at dinner on Friday at Liam and Ana's place. Ely couldn't wait. Her mom had sent her a shopping list that hinted she wanted to make her famous Colombian Ropa Vieja dish. Just the thought of it made Ely want to moan in anticipatory pleasure.

Ely left the office, got back to her temporary LA base, and killed time by picking furniture for her future apartment, imagining the place she would go to see on Thursday. She'd started to make dinner when she heard the garage door open in the back.

Ely put the food to cook on low and went to find Ana, who maneuvered a couple of suitcases into the house.

Ely took one of them from Ana and helped her roll it across the floor. "Hi!"

"Hey, Ely." They paused the suitcase arrangement to hug for two seconds, before they continued to carry everything to Ana's room.

"How was the festival?" Ely asked, placing the piece of baggage she'd grabbed at the foot of the bed.

Ana sighed. "I'll tell you over dinner."

"Where's Liam?"

Ana arranged the two suitcases she'd carried at the foot of the bed, too. She straightened and turned to Ely with a half incredulous, half humorous look.

Ana chuckled through a grin. "You'll never guess. He went back home to talk to Alex."

"Is he going for the battle royale, then?" Ely lifted both eyebrows, a smile creeping to her face.

"Nope. He's going to try to change his mind. Try to get him to come back and work for Jump Cannon, after all."

Ely's smile cracked at the corner of her mouth. This was not good news.

She opened her eyes wide. "He is?! Why?!"

Ana hooked an arm around Ely's and guided her out of the room. "Because he wants a relationship with his brother. I think it's sweet."

"But Alex... he... Ana, Sandy quit and, well..." The words got stuck in her throat. Ely wasn't even sure what she wanted to say but maybe it didn't matter, it didn't want to come out, anyway.

"I know. This is the last time Liam tries and if Alex comes back I don't expect things to go smoothly, all of a sudden but... we'll try, right?"

Shit. Sure, sleeping with Alex had suddenly become more complicated than a simple one night stand, but that couldn't be more important than actually getting Jump Cannon Productions off the ground and running straight into success.

"Right." Ely pressed her lips together. "Things might be a bit complicated..."

Her throat closed up to the words again. It wasn't sharing about the sex part that worried Ely; Ana wouldn't expect Ely to share that kind of thing. But they did have the kind of friendship that made Ely want to warn her friend that things could turn out to be a bit dicey between her and Alex.

But they didn't have to be. If Ely and Alex invoked doing things for the sake of maturity again, they could very well find a good working relationship, after all.

Upon reaching the kitchen, Ana let go of Ely to take the lid off one of the pots; she leaned forward and inspected the food.

Ana inhaled the smell of ajiaco de pollo deep into her lungs. "Gah. I love you Ely. What a welcome home." She sighed and put the lid back on. Ana leaned onto the counter, resting her hip against it. She crossed her arms. "We'll be fine, Ely. We'll make it work, with or without Alex."

Ely smiled and let Ana's reassuring words reach into her skull. She could figure it out. She would.

Chapter 12

ALEX HAD ARRIVED AT his apartment in San Luis Obispo around noon on Sunday, and had spent the following twenty-eight hours looking for a job. The only break had been the few hours of sleep he'd gotten late in the morning. If his first in-depth search was any indication, he faced slim pickings for his next job. He might end up having to relocate, after all.

Later that Monday, he'd taken a call from his mom and ended up agreeing to join them for dinner. He wouldn't have answered, but the call had interrupted the third daydream he'd fallen into, all of them featuring Elena. The woman wouldn't stay off his mind, so the ringing of his phone had seemed like the perfect interruption to be free of the memories of her.

He wouldn't have minded the mental images of the amazing time he'd spent with Elena, but they brought up regret each time, and he *hated* regret. It's not that he wished he hadn't slept with her. His issue was that, for a moment, swimming in her perfume and hands full of her lush body, he'd been able to forget about the ton of lead in his chest, the feeling of being lost. He'd been in the moment and he'd enjoyed it. Connecting with her had been powerful, and an opportunity to remember not everything was shit.

And that was the problem. For a brief hour he'd remembered what it could be like to be content. Involved. To flow. Like he used to feel when he painted, but hot. The brief joy of it threatened to break his heart all over again. It made him want to look into the hole in his chest, and that was supposed to be a no-no. He needed to figure out a way out of it. Stat.

So now he sat at his parents' kitchen island half chatting with them, half trying to come up with any reasonable next steps, while they made dinner.

The doorbell disrupted the comforting routine of food-making at home.

"I'll get it," Alex said.

When he opened the door to see Liam standing on the darkened porch, his stomach dropped to the floor.

Neither said anything, they simply stared at each other. Liam frowned, a traveling bag in his hand. Alex held his brother's gaze, unmoving.

"Who is it?" asked their dad behind Alex; he knew without looking that his dad approached them. "Oh, Liam— this is a surprise. Come in. Will you be staying the night?"

"I'm not sure." Liam dropped his bag on the ground and crossed his arms. Alex smirked.

"He's here to fight with me, I think." Alex turned and walked to the living room, hoping it seemed like he didn't care. "Come in, then. Let's have it."

He turned back around in time to see Liam stomping into the house, coming to stand in front of Alex.

"Why, Alex? Why are you like this? Why did you change your mind at the last minute? Why is it so easy for you?"

Alex crossed his arms and sat on the back of the sofa, noting Liam's scowl and tense fingers on his hips. Alex's eyes came up to confront Liam, holding his raging gaze.

"Why do you assume things are easy for me?" His voice sounded thinly controlled to his own ears.

Dad had grabbed Liam's bag and now stood next to them, letting them argue but keeping an eye on them. Mom came to monitor their fight as well, ready to intervene like when Alex and Liam were teenagers.

"What's going on?" Mom asked.

"You didn't tell them, did you?" Liam's accusatory stare left Alex; he focused on his mom and dad. "Not only did Alex take his sweet time agreeing to work for Ana and my company, but once he'd said yes, he changed his damn mind. He sent me an email to quit— then he left!" Liam turned to Alex again. "You toyed with us."

Alex pressed his lips together and tried to control his breathing. "I hadn't signed anything yet."

"Is that your excuse?" Liam scoffed. "Your word means nothing to you?"

"Oh, Alex." The disappointment in his dad's voice dropped on Alex's shoulders like a boulder.

"You told us it didn't work out," his mom added.

"It didn't," Alex tried. He closed his eyes and did his best to control the swarm of emotions reeling inside of him.

Liam took a step away, two, then turned and returned to Alex. He closed his eyes and ran his fingers through his unstyled curls, messing them up.

Alex's brother opened his eyes and shook his head, eyes glassy. He dropped his arms to his sides.

"Tell me what happened." Liam's voice had changed, Alex didn't know why. "I really want to understand... and I'm trying, Alex. I'm really trying."

There was something disarming about Liam's voice changing. It wasn't kind, it wasn't inviting... but it was measured. Perhaps even hopeful. And there was clear hurt in it.

Waves of emotions crashed against the old walls he'd built around his heart, building quays out of his guts. The familiar ton of lead in his chest multiplied in mass, until the top of his lungs stopped working altogether. It pushed the salt water of his feelings around, sloshing and battering against his edges. Whatever had opened up that door inside of him, it had forgotten to close it. It had been easier when he felt nothing.

He loosened his arms around himself, keeping them crossed over his chest, but hoping the lessened pressure would help him breathe easier. "You met with someone while on your trip to the festival, didn't you?"

Liam arched a sarcastic eyebrow. "I met with many people; you'll need to be a bit more specific."

Alex didn't smile, but he heard the mix of humor and irritation in Liam's words. He took a deep breath. "A column said you were betraying me and that you were already thinking of firing me—"

"What?!"

"I know it wasn't true—"

"Fucks' sake— no, it wasn't true." Liam looked just about to stomp his foot on the ground, like when they were kids and got into an argument. "I did have a conversation with him— if they were talking about Michael— I talked to him in person to let him know we wouldn't be offering the position to him— you know, because you'd taken it. He was great and I thought he deserved to be told face to face."

Alex clenched his jaw. "I didn't ask for an explanation. I knew you weren't doing stuff behind my back but..."

He let it hang in there, unsure of the words, how far to go.

"But?" Liam pressed. "Alex, you can't trust those rags that call themselves magazines— "

"I didn't! I just..." Alex released a hand from the shield he'd set up around his chest, and he rubbed his forehead with hard fingers. "It was a lot to deal with, and I hadn't even started working for you yet. My name everywhere, doing work for someone else, the responsibility of it because it would be your company... what happens when I refuse to say what someone wants to hear during business meetings, and they take it out on you or the company? Having to constantly deal with things you didn't tell me that show up and are twisted online—"

Liam shook his head. "C'mon. Don't make decisions about your future based on the trash that gets written online. This is about us, and about Jump Cannon, and the choices you make about your own damn future. This job is meant to be a vehicle— don't ruin it."

"Don't you see? That's part of the problem!" Alex's skin crawled. He got back onto his feet, leaving his perch on the back of the sofa and stood there, surrounded by his family. "I can't find my way out of stuff like this. Jobs that take things out of me until there's nothing left. You say don't ruin it— who am I ruining it for? You can find someone else for my role but I... I need something different. I'm done. I'm... tired."

"Is this about painting?" Liam said. "I promise, I can do better at telling you what I'm up to and, honestly, in this job you'll have time to do your art—"

Alex shot an arm forward, up in the air in a frustrating shake. "What is even the point? I can't paint! And I'm stuck doing work I don't care about!"

"I can't fix that!" Liam matched Alex's volume. "I can just try and make things easier for you. I'm trying to give us a chance to finally have a brotherly relationship—"

Alex jutted a finger forward. "And you don't think I'm trying in my own way?"

"Of course you're not! You just ran away." Liam scoffed, his lips curling down in almost disgust.

It sparked derision in him; it swirled in his stomach. "Changing my mind doesn't mean I'm hiding—"

"Alex, I think you're depressed," his mom interrupted.

Alex whipped his face to her, his eyes sharp on her. He barely registered that Liam and his dad stared at her in a similar way.

Liam was the first to turn to Alex, then his dad. Now all three studied Alex and he wanted to be small, to hide. A wave of nausea built inside of him, making him dizzy.

"I knew you were unhappy," His dad said. Alex had to close his eyes. "I thought you were angry."

"I am angry," Alex managed to say through tight vocal cords. The words rasped their way out of him, leaving a sore throat behind. "All the time."

His mom put a hand on his arm. "I've been reading and I think depression looks like that, sometimes."

"I don't know." Alex shook his head. "I just feel... stuck. I don't know where to go... how to get there. And perhaps I'm just a grump."

"A grump who's depressed, maybe." His dad cleared his throat. "They're not mutually exclusive."

Alex crossed his arms, twisting from side to side as if looking for an escape route. The only light in the living room came from the kitchen. He forced his body still, and fixed his eyes on one of his mother's paintings, as if he could get lost in it rather than being in his present situation.

"The corporate world burnt you." Liam took a step towards him and Alex tried to get away, keeping his distance, but his brother put his hand on Alex's arm to stop him. His mom's hand was still on the other arm. "I get that."

"Do you?" He couldn't stop the bitterness in his voice.

"You're an artist," his mom said.

Alex cast his eyes down to his shoes. Even his mom's work reflected the lack of art in his life.

He bit on the inside of his cheek until it hurt. "Working for Liam won't fix anything. Even if he decided to use his millions to be my patron— I'd never accept it."

"I'm not offering that." Liam's hand rested heavy on Alex's arm. "I'm offering something else and I'm hoping it'll help, too. There are things that can't be fixed. When that happens, all we can do is to keep trying to find a different road."

"What do you know about it?" Alex scoffed. He lifted his head to challenge Liam again, and he had to forcibly stop himself from jerking his arms away. "One day this offer of acting fell in your lap and it was so easy for you to take it. Just because you jump and things work out doesn't mean the same is true for me."

Liam's eyes remained steady on Alex. "It's not like that for me, either. I've been in therapy for almost two years to help me find my center in my career. In my life, really. My work also almost did me in."

Alex stared at his brother, breathing through the surprise of his words. His body went still as he processed Liam's words.

Liam took his hand away and crossed his arms, but he kept his clear green eyes on Alex.

"We didn't know that." Dad placed a hand on Liam's shoulder. The care in his words put a knot in Alex's throat.

"Maybe that's not totally accurate." Liam pressed his lips together. Mom put her free hand on Liam's arm. They were all connected, now. "My job— the acting, that's fine. I like it. A lot. But I met people in this industry who burnt me out and..." Liam lifted a shoulder. "At first I didn't want to worry you. Then things were better, so it made even less sense to burden you with it."

"But we'd've liked to have known, because it was about you," their mom said. Then, turning to Alex, "And the same goes for you. We don't like seeing you miserable."

"Perhaps, if you work for Liam, things could be different." His dad put his hand on Alex' shoulder.

Alex forbade himself from rolling his eyes at the way his parents expressed their support in a hand-to-body chain. A secret, faraway part of him found comfort in it.

"How?" He asked, eyes on the textured ceiling.

It sounded like Liam took a deep breath. "No one will expect you to work extra hours. There'll be no need to fight for that raise, or for that promotion. And the social aspect of the company... well, it might give you a small sense of purpose."

"Maybe, then, you could find your way out of depression... maybe one day paint again," Mom said.

"Maybe," Alex conceded, but it was hard to imagine. "If this is, in fact, depression."

"Please." Liam's tone was pleading. Alex rarely if ever heard that from him, and it drew his eyes to Liam's. "Let me do this with you. Leading this company together, with Ana and Ely. Being your brother."

Alex teetered at the edge of a big jump again, hovering at the edge of a cliff, not knowing what he'd find if he let himself fall. It was dark and foggy beneath and whether he'd land on his feet or crash on rocks or water, he didn't know.

He tore his eyes from the green of his brother's, and studied Mom and Dad. They all seemed supportive, but Liam's eyes held a hint of patience Alex had never seen. It was confusing, but it turned out to be the gentle push he needed to take a leap of faith. Perhaps he could give this all a try, after all.

"I can't say this makes me hopeful," Alex finally said. "But I'm going to give it a chance."

They returned to LA together the next morning, each driving a car with a trunk-load of Alex's things.

Chapter 13

E LY FRETTED ALL DAY at work, knowing that Liam and Alex were on their way back to LA. She spent a chunk of the morning trying to decide how to approach things, her worry increasing each time she hammered a nail into place, hung a painting, or placed a vase in the right spot.

Light faded around Ely as she said goodbye to Celeste, who went home at a decent time, while Ely stayed and continued to prep the space for the following week. She checked her watch; it was getting late. She wouldn't be able to procrastinate going home for much longer.

Ely sighed. She had expected to leave all things Sandy in the past but, as soon as she returned to Ana and Liam's house, he'd be there. Now the memory of him touching her, kissing her, wasn't a nice memory to look at fondly as months went by; it was memories of her professional peer doing these things to her, and she wasn't sure how to handle the situation.

She shook her head clear of the images of Alex and her on the sofa and closed up the office. She took a cab and attempted to look for a car to buy online, but the rising levels of anxiety in her stomach distracted her. What was Ely meant to do when she saw Alex again? And would it mean that Ana and Liam would learn of what had happened?

Ely didn't think that Ana would be angry. Would Liam? Ely hoped not. But she'd decided to have sex with Alex under the assumption she'd never see him again, and that wasn't the case anymore.

Maybe that was the point. Ely needed to be clear with Alex, asap. If he promised to be professional and followed through the promise, they could really move on and let bygones be bygones.

She'd prepared so much for the evening that coming home to find Alex and Liam were gone actually deflated her. She kept Ana company as she cooked dinner, time during which she let Ely know they'd gone out to find Alex a place.

"I personally think something else is going on." Ana stirred the sauce currently bubbling in a pot. "But Liam hasn't had a chance yet to explain. When we talked he was relaxed and, dare I say, optimistic about it all? So it must be okay."

They arrived just in time to eat dinner.

Liam and Alex came into the house from the garage. Liam gave Ely a bright grin that she returned and, while hugging him, her eyes sought Alex's over Liam's shoulder. Ely let go of Liam with awareness heavy in her stomach, that last time she'd seen Sandy she'd been fully naked on the bed, and he'd only been wearing his underwear.

Liam stepped to the side and went to greet Ana. Ely and Alex stared at each other in silence, not even a nod in hello. Ely turned away and helped Ana finish making dinner, and didn't glance or talk to Alex again until dinner was done.

"How do you feel about a nightcap at the patio?" Ely suggested to Ana and Liam. "Go enjoy a drink, Sandy and I will clear this up."

"Come join us when you're done." Liam made a quick drink for himself and Ana, and they stepped outside.

"So I'm helping you, now?" Alex opened the dishwasher and began adding dishes to it.

"It's obviously a ruse." Ely kept her voice low. She grabbed everyone's water glasses and brought them close to Alex. "Did you tell Liam we slept together?"

Alex brushed food remnants off a plate. He turned his face to Ely and arched an eyebrow. "No."

"Good. Don't." Ely walked around him to collect the pots.

He went back to the dishes in the sink with a mild scoff. "It's not a big deal, it was just sex."

"Exactly." She placed both pots on the granite next to him with barely constrained force, the sharp clank of it clear in the space. She leaned on the stone counter, hips against hard stone. She was close to his side, that way. Her words wouldn't carry. "And it was a one-time kinda deal. Done— " she pointed at him— "and done." She flicked her hand in dismissal. "I'm not in the habit of letting people walk over me. So don't you think you have a green light with me just because you returned. From now on, all we have between us is work."

Again, he only turned his head to her, plates now abandoned as he looked her up and down. His hazel eyes stared deeply into hers. "You're not the reason I came back. I came back for me."

His words stabbed her chest, a wound opening through flesh and bone that narrowly missed her heart. Her and her feelings had been so low in his priorities that he didn't even consider her for a hot second.

"Such an asshole." The contempt in her voice made her feel a bit better, like it could compensate for the way his words made her feel. "You know what I mean. I don't want things to get messy. We're coworkers now."

"Leave it alone, Elena. I'm not looking to be anything else— "

She poked him in the shoulder with a stiff finger. "I'm setting boundaries, and you'll follow them."

"Won't be an effort." He turned back to the plates and continued brushing away debris like he didn't notice or care about the few broken pieces that had fallen from her emotions.

She huffed and turned away, clearing the remaining dinner paraphernalia in quiet anger.

She left him alone, filling up the dishwasher as soon as she was done.

They didn't talk again that night.

Chapter 14

LAUGHTER TRICKLED INTO ALEX'S room from the common areas in Liam's house, disrupting his reading. Apparently, Elena's parents, who'd arrived in Los Angeles the night prior, had come to the house to make food for everyone. From the hum of chatting and continuing guffaws, the meal would be a party. Alex didn't feel like a party. Hence why he hid in his bedroom, tucked away in the back of the house.

A deep, unknown, rumbling voice reached Alex's bedroom. Likely Elena's father. Curiosity about the kind of man that could raise a spirited daughter like her spluttered to life inside of Alex, but it died almost instantly. Its disappearance didn't stop his train of thought, and he caught himself wondering if Elena was the kind of person to ask for her mom and dad's advice for things all the time. She seemed like the type; maybe that's why Elena had finally found a place, and why she was ready to move in there within a few days.

Elena hadn't asked Alex for help moving into her new apartment during the upcoming weekend. Alex didn't offer. It's not like they were friends, or on the best of terms. He was fine with that.

The taste in his mouth soured. She'd said she was done with him. She'd looked at him with resentment that he'd returned. He hadn't known what to do with it, and they'd fought again. Only this time he couldn't use the excuse of maturity to change things.

A knock on the door stopped him from mindlessly staring at the same book page for any longer.

"Yes?" he called.

Liam came in and closed the door behind him. "Hey. You okay?"

Alex resisted the urge to roll his eyes. "Yes."

Something in the tension around Liam's eyes told Alex perhaps his brother was also resisting the urge. "Dinner will be ready soon. It smells delicious; you don't want to miss it."

Alex closed his book and left it to his side on the bed. "I suppose it would be rude if I ask you to bring me some food to my room?"

The corner of Liam's mouth went up in a hint of humor. "I think they already think you're rude, not coming out to spend time with them."

Alex scoffed. "Well, I'm glad you're being honest. Does it mean I can ask you to bring me food here, then?"

"C'mon." Liam jerked his head towards the living room. "Come spend time with us."

Alex allowed himself an eyeroll, this time. He got up from the bed. "Fine."

"Did you reach out to any of the people Linda recommended?" Liam opened the door, but didn't get out of the room.

Liam had offered to get him some referrals from his own therapist; three names now glared at him every time Alex checked his inbox. He still wasn't sure if his mom was right, but now his parents and Liam seemed convinced he had depression. He didn't know what to make of it; he didn't think he could be objective about the possibility, and it could be different when you're the person going through it. Maybe it was less obvious. So yeah, it could be true. The part that worried him was how much of his personality would be tied in with depression, if he had it. What people would expect of him if he met the criteria and got treatment for it.

Alex cleared his throat. "Yeah. I called and left a voicemail at one of their offices."

"Sounds good."

At least Liam wasn't pushing. Much.

They got out of his room and followed the call of laughter.

Liam motioned Alex into the kitchen. "Mónica, Jorge— this is my brother, Alex."

Elena's parents stood by the stove and turned to gaze at Alex. They had the same energy field around them as their daughter. The three of them were also all the same height, just below average, and had the same warm tawny skin.

The palms of Alex's hands tingled with the memory of Elena's supple skin.

Alex pushed the thought as far away as he could.

"Hello." Jorge approached Alex and shook his hand. Alex gulped. "Nice to meet you."

The man had great curls and a beard with hair mostly gone white.

"Hello, Alex. Are you doing okay?" Mónica turned from the stove for a second, only to give him a quick up and down, before returning to the pot in front of her. Elena stood next to her, hip popped against the counter, arms crossed. She also gave him glance and, though her eyes shone as always, she didn't seem to get much joy out of his presence.

Alex had to hide a smirk. Elena knew how to hold grudges, it seemed. "Yes, I'm well, thank you. You?"

"Good, good." Mónica put the lid she held in her hand in the sink and turned to her daughter. "Okay, Ely. Is the table set? Dinner will be ready in five minutes."

"C'mon," Liam said to Alex's side. "Help me get it ready."

They were in the middle of putting down plates when Jorge and Mónica switched to Spanish to talk to each other. Alex knew three common words in the language and didn't follow, but Elena and Ana evidently did. The four of them laughed again, the sound filling the space.

Liam shook his head. "I don't know when the last time was that there was so much... life... in my house."

"Is that... good?" Alex arched an eyebrow as he set the final plate down in its place.

The smile on Liam's face grew soft. "Yeah."

They worked together, their backs to the room, as the conversation around them continued.

"Since Ely is leaving tomorrow," Liam said, "you can move into her room on Sunday if you like."

Elena in her underwear, shifting her stance as he admired her body, and told her to get in bed so he could devour her. Her room would be full of memories.

Alex pushed the images away for the thousandth time and gulped. "I'm good where I am. Hopefully I'll find a place soon."

"You don't have to rush."

Alex didn't say anything, but he took note of the mild change in their ways.

Ana appeared between them, putting a heat mat in the middle of the table.

"Make way!" she exclaimed.

Ana moved out of the way and Elena replaced her, carrying a pot full of food. After placing it down on the heat mat, she remained bent down for a second, visibly taking in a deep breath.

She moaned. "That's good."

She turned and for a second or two, they stared at each other. He didn't realize his eyes were fixated on her until she gave him a look and raised an eyebrow with so much sass, a close call to derision, that it stole a micro smile from him. And he felt it— a tiny, unfamiliar spark eroding a dark corner inside of him. It was gone in an instant, the negative impression of a film left in its place— like such a small source of light had been enough to overexpose the film. The shock of it drew a chilling path down his back.

He must have made some kind of weird gesture. He couldn't gauge what it told her, exactly, but it couldn't have been a good thing, because she rolled her eyes at him and gave him a warning glare. She walked away and helped her mom bring more things to the table.

There was no spark this time, but the tiny smile made a reappearance.

Chapter 15

ELY WALKED INTO THE office on Monday happy and exhausted, after a long weekend of setting up her new place and visiting with her parents. It was Celeste's first full day on the job, too. Ely's brand new assistant smiled as she entered the office and Ely was happy to return her grin.

"Good morning, Ms. Castillo," Celeste said. She'd set up at the reception desk already, and Ely admired the work they had both done with the general waiting space over the previous week.

"Good morning! So glad to have you. And I told you to call me Ely. Do you need anything to get started?"

"Not at all. The package you prepared has everything I need."

"Excellent." Ely walked slowly away, backwards, so she could continue to engage with Celeste. "I'm leaving early today, but we're still meeting at 1, right?"

She nodded. "For sure. Also, Mr. McMillan is in his office and he would like to see you."

That stopped Ely in her tracks. "Which one? Which Mr. McMillan?"

Please. Please. Pleeease.

"Alex."

Crap.

"Okay. Thanks, Celeste!"

To get to her office, Ely had to walk past his. She slowed down and finally stopped by his door, hesitating.

"Who's there?" Came from the office and, caught, she grabbed the handle and opened the door.

She closed it behind her as she walked into his office, slightly irritated at the impossibility of hiding when the door featured a top half of frosted glass.

"Morning, Sandy. Surprised to see you here." She sat on a chair across from him and crossed her legs. Shoulders low, neck long, and back straight, she stared at him, challenging.

While Ely had chosen to dress casual, he had too; he was wearing gray slacks and a light blue shirt, no tie. Her pencil skirt was tight and had ridden up as she sat down, but she did not fix it or show discomfort.

He leaned back on his chair and crossed his arms, raising an eyebrow. "That's a good start to our working relationship. I feel very welcome, Elena."

Ely mirrored him on her chair. She put as much confidence as she could to the arch of her eyebrow. "You're not quite the prodigal son, if that's what you're imagining."

They sat in silence for a minute, assessing each other.

Ely was the first to crack. "Celeste said you wanted to see me?"

"Yes. I wanted to set a meeting with you to discuss the budget."

Ely frowned. "You could have asked Celeste to look at my calendar."

Alex's lips pressed together and his eyes shifted to the painting on the wall. "I arrived before she did. I startled her— it was awkward having to explain to her who I am. I thought I'd give her some room this morning."

"Neither of us knew you were starting today." Ely suppressed a smile. "It might have helped if you'd let us know."

"Yes." The long way he pronounced the syllable held three different gravelly notes. He didn't add anything to it.

"You'll do better next time." She winked at him, hoping it'd annoy him.

"What does that even mean? There won't be a next time."

It did. She smiled. "Good. Now, I'll be leaving early today— my parents are still in town. I have a meeting at one with Celeste; you should probably be there. We can meet tomorrow about the budget."

"I look forward to it."

Nothing about his voice indicated that that was true.

Who knew what working with Alex would be like. It was time to discover it.

Chapter 16

TWO WEEKS LATER, WORKING with Elena proved to be a test to Alex's already-thin patience. The woman argued with him about everything, and he was sure she ignored his calls on purpose. Like just then, when he'd called her for the third time to no avail.

He hung up the phone and rubbed his eyebrows— hard. He clenched his jaw until his teeth hurt, but what was the worst that could happen? Cracking a molar was worth it, for the sake of not exploding in rage at Elena. He was angry, but he didn't know what would happen if he didn't hold back even a little.

She might never know he tried, really tried to hold back; she might believe that what she saw was the full extent of his temper. But it wasn't, and knowing it for himself was enough. He wasn't doing it for her, anyway; this was to feel in control in a small way, and not to risk being booted from the job now that he'd decided to stay. Jump Cannon had good benefits, after all.

He scoffed and stood, stomping to his door. He opened it in a forceful move, hoping it'd release a chunk of his irritation, but Celeste had been walking in front of his office. She jumped and the papers she carried rained to the floor.

"Ah!" She yelped.

Alex closed his eyes and released a hard gust of air through his nose. "Celeste. Please stop being scared of me."

"It wasn't you— it was the door."

"Everything okay?" Elena appeared through the door to her own office. Her voice was strained. "What did you do, Sandy?"

He stood still in the doorway. He crossed his arms, indignant. "What did I do? I opened my door. How is that reproachable?"

"It was an accident." Celeste kneeled, the movement a blur at the edge of his field of vision. She collected the papers strewn all over the floor, but his eyes were drawn to Elena instead.

The infuriating woman shook her head and stomped to Celeste, where she dropped to the floor as well and helped their assistant collect the papers.

"The very least you could do is help." Elena lifted her eyes to him as she organized a few papers in her hand. "*That* is reproachable."

He clenched his jaw again. That was true, but he hated to admit it.

Fuck, it was true, regardless.

He lowered himself to his knees and did his share.

"Is this the document I asked you to print, Celeste?" Elena asked, her voice open and friendly.

"Yes," the sweeter person replied. "I was taking it all to you when Alex came out of his office and startled me."

"It's the perma-frown, isn't it?" Elena added, humor in her voice.

He didn't say anything only because it probably let Celeste calm down.

Alex directed his voice to his colleague. "I was coming to see you too, Elena. I called you three times. Too busy to answer?"

She didn't respond right away. He gazed at her, but his eyes got caught in her neckline; in this position, he had a great view of her breasts. It was easy to imagine what they felt like in his hands, because he'd had them in his hands. And in his mouth.

He gave the papers he'd collected to Celeste and stood fast enough to make himself dizzy.

The two women stood as well, and Elena took all the papers from Celeste.

"I'll put them in order, don't worry about it." Elena brought her eyes to him. "Come to my office, then. Since you have to speak to me so urgently."

"Thanks, Ely." Celeste smiled— an assured grin to Elena, and a more tremulous one to Alex— and turned around toward her desk.

Elena turned as well, and sprinted back to her office. Alex followed, leaving the door slightly ajar behind him.

"Not that I need to explain myself to you, but I was busy all morning following up with offers for program placements. Doesn't your phone tell you when my line is busy?"

She sat behind her desk, and put her focus on flipping through pages and re-ordering them. She didn't offer a chair to Alex, but he took one anyway.

He put an ankle over his knee. "Maybe. I didn't check. I just called you."

"I'm not on call for you. You should check."

"I didn't expect you to be so busy." He shrugged, dismissive, his eyes over her shoulder to the window and the city behind.

"Of course I was busy." Her voice was strained, and it brought his attention back to her expressive face. "I was working. I do not spend my mornings doing my nails."

"Stop it, Elena. I know that."

"Okay, then." She frowned. "What do you want to talk about?"

"I can't go to the party tomorrow night."

Her hands froze; her whole body did. The only thing to move were her eyes, which pinned him with invisible daggers.

"Why not?"

"I have an important meeting after work. The times don't work."

"A meeting *after* work? That sounds like an excuse."

Alex shrugged again, and spoke through the smirk on his lips. "Believe whatever you want. It's personal stuff."

"Just say you have a hot date and deliver me from your reasons."

"Not a date. And I don't have to explain it to you."

She went back to organizing her papers, her lips pursed in annoyance. "You have to go to one of these things soon. You can't keep avoiding it."

"When's the next one?"

"In about ten days. It is in your calendar already."

"We'll talk closer to the date. I may have another commitment."

Elena put all papers in a neat pile on her desk and slammed her hand on top of them, as if they were about to fly away in a random breeze... or like she wanted to slap him, instead.

"Seriously? That's definitely an excuse."

"Not an excuse."

"You're insufferable."

"And you're pushy."

"Argh! Fine." She jerked open her drawer and rummaged through it; she took a big binder clip. She didn't use it right away; she opened it in her hand like she was pinching a stress ball. "Let me know if you're going to the one in your calendar."

Alex stood and pursed his own lips. "It'll be my pleasure."

"Next time send me an email."

Alex gave her a military salute and left her office. An email might be the better choice, because it might mean he didn't have to see her indignation written all over her glass face.

Chapter 17

A MONTH LATER, ELY tapped her fingers on the board-room table. Ana and Liam sat across from her, casually chatting as Ely silently fumed.

"Where have you been?" Ely demanded as soon as Alex entered the boardroom.

He was five minutes late, plenty of reason to irritate her. She tried to hide the accusation in her words, but she wasn't sure she'd succeeded.

"Phone call." Alex sat next to Ely without acknowledging her or anyone else, and put his computer and papers in front of him.

Like Alex predicted, that first brief meeting in his office a few weeks ago had set the tone for his and Ely's working environment.

Ely turned to Liam and Ana, but talked to him. She surrounded her mug of warm coffee with both hands and used it as a bit of an anchor. "You've been out all morning."

"Yes." After some indecision, he talked to Liam, adding, "Charles."

Ely would rather faint than show curiosity. She wanted to be angry at him— everything he did poked at her patience— but, as usual, she bit most of it down.

Since starting to work together, they'd done their job, done it well, and argued every single time they met. It wore her down, but keeping at it was a point of pride for her at this point. She still hid most of her reaction to him because, otherwise, she feared they'd escalate each other and explode. Then things would really go awry.

"So, now that he's here, we can get started." Ely made herself smile for Ana and Liam's sake.

"How are things going?" Ana asked. "It's been a few weeks since you both started working together."

"It's going well." Ely rotated her mug on the table, still with both hands on it. "I put up a call for applications for the program. I'm in the process of securing placements— "

"We'll get to that," Ana interrupted. She put a hand on Liam's knee. "Let's check in about the flow of things between the two... departments. We also want to know everything is going well with the two of you."

"Oh." Ely didn't look at Alex. She took a sip of her coffee. "We have meetings. We make decisions. It works."

Liam laughed and Ana smirked. "Sounds efficient."

"Does it?" Alex organized his papers on top of his laptop.

"So, yeah, we bicker," Ely admitted, "and our disagreements can get heated, sure, but there's never screaming. Ask Celeste."

Ana understood Ely's words best, able to read between the lines. She arched an eyebrow at Ely and Ely pressed her lips together, letting her best friend know the conversation wasn't for this meeting.

Ana seemed to get it; she squinted at Ely but let it go.

"Is this conversation important?" Alex leaned back on his chair and crossed his arms. "I've sent the first report. Everything seems to be in order, right? Our short-term plan is solid."

"Initial numbers and projections look good," Liam said. "We were wondering about the other part of it. Do you need someone else to help handle the production side of things? Do you have a hard time working through the bickering?"

Ely's face grew warm. Her embarrassment wouldn't be visible on her skin, but she felt it nevertheless. "We cope."

"We don't need an intermediary." Alex moved his papers to the table and opened his laptop. "Nor anyone else at the time. I can handle all that work. I'm finishing up a summary of the contacts we've gotten for production, and proactively looking for things that could be produced is something that comes from both of you."

"Our eyes are open." Liam pursed his lips and set an arm around Ana's back, over the chair.

"As we get more familiar with the industry and get to know more people, we can bring in projects to the table as well." Ely put a wild curl of hair behind her ear. "I've been dropping hints to anyone that will listen that we're looking for ideas and open to investors."

"How's that going? Networking and such?" Ana's hand left Liam's knee to drink some of her water.

"That's going well, too. I'm trying not to overbook myself," Ely said. "I'm only booking two or three big public things a month. Create a sense of scarcity... like we're exactly where we want to be—"

"Which is true." Alex leaned forward and started typing on his computer. "The priority right now is to get the youth program set up."

Ely side eyed him. "As I also need to balance networking with the other side of my role, I need to keep in mind pacing. The speed we're going at is sustainable, I think."

"The application window starts on Wednesday and, within a month, we'll be meeting to go through the first selection of participants." Alex fingers continued to fly over the keyboard, each keystroke needling into Ely's brain.

"Have you been to these networking things, Alex?" Liam asked.

Alex didn't respond right away. "Not to date."

"He's always had a... good reason... not to go." Ely smirked, but it faltered when Ana frowned.

The typing stopped. "What are you implying, Elena?"

"That you're avoiding going, Sandy."

Alex lifted a dismissive shoulder. "I have no problem admitting that. Yes, I'm avoiding it."

"But it's part of the job!" Ely turned to him on her chair. "People need to get to know you, too. There's barely any paparazzi, either. We're not the famous people they seek."

"Paparazzi are not even the worst part of it." He shook his head as he gazed out the window behind Liam. "Being social on command? That's what I can't stand."

Ely hated when he didn't look at her. "Not surprised, but going is part of your job. You're not doing everything in your role if you're not going."

That got him to give her his eyes, even if it was with a glare. "I'm doing my job fine—"

"C'mon, guys. Really?" Ana interrupted. "It's been five minutes and you're bickering again. Be honest. Is this going to be a problem? Can we help?"

"No." Ely clenched her jaw. "We're grown ups that put down some strong boundaries. We can keep this animosity contained."

"We're professional." Alex's tone was monotone.

"What about going to events?" Liam asked.

Ely let out a quick release of air through tight lips. "We may not be on each other's team, but we're on your guys' team— we're on the youth's team."

"Our bickering shouldn't affect you." Alex returned to his laptop. He typed fast. Couldn't he get to his emails or whatever later?

Ely shook her head at him, drank more coffee, and stared at the ceiling. "And I make sure to protect Celeste from it."

"I mean, we always knew you two didn't quite hit it off," Liam said. "But this is the first time we see you actually working together and we need to make sure this is doable for you two. We'd rather this whole thing doesn't torment you both."

"Don't worry, Liam." Ely rotated her cup again, this time more forcefully. She watched the coffee create tiny waves in its container. "Totally doable. Think about it as lighting a fire under us so we are more productive. You know, because we're trying to one-up each other."

She refused to acknowledge that she'd used the same excuse before.

"I'm not in competition with you, Elena." Alex's voice came clipped.

"No, you're just Stern Supreme."

Liam sighed. "We truly believe in what each of you can do and, because we care about you, we want to make sure this is a good working environment. Productivity isn't the utmost priority."

"We also care about you two as people," Ana added.

"We're fine. We will be better," Ely assured them. "We just need to find our rhythm."

"You need to attend a few events, Alex." Liam stared at his brother with a steady gaze. "People need to know you to make it easier to navigate work."

Alex scoffed. A sigh followed. "Fine. I'll go."

"There's an event this Thursday. You'll have to come," Elena said. She wasn't pleased but Liam and Ana were right. In the adrenaline rush of fully starting this new job, she'd forgotten how important finding a fair playing field with Alex was.

Chapter 18

ALEX HAD FALLEN INTO Elena's trap. She'd told him they should arrive at the party together, and to go to her place to get a cab from there. He'd arrived on time— he wasn't going to give her a reason to start criticizing him— but, when she let him in, she wasn't quite ready.

"I just need to finish a couple of things with my hair. Come with me."

He entered her space with a minor spike of suspicion. She left him standing at the door and walked away; he closed the door behind him.

Her apartment was small, but that wasn't surprising. From what he'd seen during his own search, this was quite standard. To one side, a kitchen and small dining area, with a few boxes lying around and only one painting up, framing the table. He would have imagined that she'd favor colorful and eclectic decor, and the sparse walls drew the corners of his mouth down with mild shock.

To the other side of the place he could see her bedroom through an open door. She disappeared through it and he followed. Her bedspread was a soft cream, somewhere between a pink and a beige, and she'd added a deep green blanket at its feet. She'd folded the top edge of the sheets, which were a pink of a more intense tone than the undertone of the bedspread and contrasting to the green.

More color here— he forbade himself from connecting any dots regarding how her bed was the place holding her personality, lest it brought memories he did not welcome at this time.

The lack of decor had to be all about slowly settling into her apartment, taking her time to make it hers, for sure. Her bed was not the point of anything.

There were two doors in the room, aside from the one where he stood. She called him from the farthest one.

"Alex?"

He walked through her bedroom, hesitating. He found her in the bathroom; he hovered at the door, gingerly.

She looked at him in the mirror. "What?"

"This is awkward."

"Why?" Her sassy high eyebrow made an appearance.

He crossed his arms. "We were bickering again this morning. Now I'm in your place. It's too... intimate."

She laughed. "Are you real? We've had sex."

He stared at her reflection. Her grin stretched free on her face, as her hands busied herself with a shiny metal pen-type thing he assumed was mascara.

"What does that have to do with anything?" He asked.

She waved the mascara wand in the air once. "You'll have sex with someone, but feel weird about being in their place?"

"You don't think this is weird." He echoed her gesture, but infused his high eyebrow with incredulity, like she was the weird one.

She shrugged, leaned towards the mirror, and applied mascara on her long lashes. "I'm comfortable in my skin."

"I remember."

The words escaped him. He didn't want her knowing just how clearly he remembered that hour they'd shared. He studied her reaction, tracking any piece of data that gave away her thoughts.

She stopped her movement and stared at him through the reflection in the mirror again. Serious. "What I mean is that I don't get all prickly about having someone around."

Alex pursed his lips. "And you think I'm prickly."

Both her eyebrows reached high on her forehead this time. "Am I wrong?"

He broke the staring contest. From the corner of his eyes he saw her continue applying mascara, then twisting the wand back into its holder.

Alex shifted his weight on his feet and crossed his arms. "I'm surprised you're not ready."

"We'll be there fashionably late. We don't want to be there on time." She scavenged for something in a plastic container on the vanity.

"All that posturing nonsense... don't you hate it?"

"I don't care. It's just a thing." She didn't find what she'd been looking for and opened a drawer, continuing her rummaging.

"So if you were planning on us being there fashionably late, why ask me to be here early?"

"So that we can prepare." She found what she'd been looking for— two pins of some sort, apparently— and placed the two things on the vanity.

"Prepare what."

She sighed. "Remember we need to pretend to like each other."

"I don't dislike you, Elena."

She scoffed and lifted a hand to her hair. She played with her curls, moving them around. "Then you're a great actor. Maybe it runs in the family."

"It's not an act, either way. I'm neutral about you."

She laughed, her hand dropping to wrap around the white porcelain of the sink edge. "That's just delightful. Then why do we argue so much?"

"Because I take you seriously and I'm not easily swayed by your charm. If I disagree with something, I'll tell you."

She turned and leaned on the vanity. "You take me seriously."

"Of course. God, Elena. I work with you. I wouldn't have come back to Jump Cannon if I didn't respect you."

She tsked. "Then I suppose I don't get you."

Alex shook his head. What was there to get? "I take you at face value. Well, not face value. I don't let your face— or your shine— distract me. But I listen to what you say."

"You just happen to disagree with a lot of what I say."

"And when I don't, I keep my mouth shut."

Elena shook her head and turned to the mirror again. She picked one of her curls with both hands and pinned it back, twisting it in such a way it looked modern rather than romantic.

She wore a black and white dress, where the black looked like twisted fabric tightly patterned over the white. It was tight, it was short, and it rode up on her legs as she leaned forward closer to the mirror.

There was a red strip of fabric following along her back, right at the center of the dress. Curving around her delicious ass.

"Right. Never distracted," she teased, distracting him.

Caught. He wasn't going to admit it. Or how it was the small birthmark near her nipple that would intrude in his mind out of nowhere, making him lose a train of thought. Irritating him.

She turned again and stepped toward him; he turned to the side to let her walk past. She went into her closet and came out with two earrings.

"Anyway." Her fingers worked on each earlobe to put on the long, dangling things. "You can call the cab. I'll be done by the time it arrives."

He took his phone out of the pocket and pulled up the right app.

"Are you taking time in lieu tomorrow?" she asked. "I am, so I can sleep in."

He kept his eyes on the screen, tapping away the request for a cab. "Then it'd be a short day on a Friday."

She stared at him like he had two heads. "Yes."

Right. This wasn't like his old job. He wasn't being asked to simply add time to his work day because he needed to prove himself.

But he hated the party nevertheless. He felt like he followed Elena everywhere like a lost puppy. She hadn't enjoyed it, either, by the way her looks had kept on getting harder and harder as the night went by.

When she announced she was leaving, he left with her. They waited for their cabs together.

"I can see you're angry. Let it out," Alex said.

"All day. All day I've been trying to be more amicable with you. Did you even notice?"

He hadn't. He didn't respond.

She kept herself held tight, shoulders and arm tense. "You make it so hard, sometimes."

He kept quiet.

"Is there something the matter?" Elena's words came hard out of her throat, shot at him at high speed. She turned to him on the sidewalk, their cabs nowhere in sight. "Is there anything going on that helps explain— that would help me understand— You followed me around all night and you said nothing. Nothing. You helped me in no way. You might as well have been a lamp post. The whole point of you being here was for people to get to know you. People won't think twice of a wall, Sandy."

Alex clenched his jaw. "Maybe there's nothing wrong— "

"If there's nothing wrong, then you're just an asshole." Her chin lifted in defiance.

Rage built inside of him, magma erupting through his diaphragm. "I'm an asshole? For not being all smiles and small talk and charisma?

"You're an asshole for not trying, leaving me alone to carry the whole night."

He sneered. She got so quickly, so deeply on his nerves. "You're just angry with me because you don't like my personality."

"No, I'm angry with you because you don't think of other people, like, ever."

He jerked back. Her words hit something in his brain, clanking against a memory, and not one of the sexy kind for once. "Is this about me returning? About the fight we had? You're angry because I returned."

"No, I'm angry because you didn't even consider how it would affect me that you returned." She scoffed and crossed her arms. "And it doesn't even matter. You're here, I can deal with that. You're grumpy, I can learn to deal with it. We have to live with the regret of having had sex—"

"I don't regret having sex with you." If nothing else, he wouldn't let her put words in his mouth he would never say.

She scrunched up her face. "Agh! Neither do I. It was a fine idea at the time. I even liked you, that evening, after we decided to be mature. You tried that night, but you're not anymore."

He had to fist his hands not to reach for his phone and check how long until the cars picked them up. "Does it really matter that much to you? It can't really affect you."

"I work with you! I don't want my day to feel like a battle. And Ana and Liam are worried—"

Alex rolled his eyes. "You don't have to care so much about what they think— "

"Of course I care about what they think! Sure, they're our bosses but, above all— they're my friends. I care about them. I care about what they think. That's not the problem here."

"Right." He shook his head. He would have liked to look elsewhere, but he couldn't seem to get away from the fire in her. "I'm the problem, I'm going to guess?"

"Why are you like this?"

"Like what? Serious? Direct?"

"Such a— so— sour!"

He scowled. "Maybe I have my reasons."

"Like what?" Her voice turned softer, like the fire had suddenly run out of fuel. "That's what I'm trying to understand because, I swear, Sandy— you make it hard to be patient with you sometimes."

He couldn't take her change of tone in, or what might have hid beneath it. "Okay, let's pretend you're actually being curious and this is not just masked criticism. I'll tell you this. My life is far from perfect; it's nothing like I had imagined. Nothing like I wanted for myself."

"C'mon. There has to be something good in your life. Everyone faces challenges, and life has its ups and downs but at the end of the day—"

Her cab came and parked by the curb behind her.

"Not all of us live life looking through sparkly rainbow lenses, Elena."

She ignored the car and pressed an angry index finger to his chest. "Don't presume you understand my lens. You've never made an attempt to get it and I assure you, you don't. You didn't even let me finish what I was going to say! You decided you disagreed with it and erased the value of my words. Don't forget I work with folks that face multiple barriers put in front of them by an unjust system. I have faced some of them, myself. I'm not naive. I also know that despondency and bitter people keep the problem going because they take no steps to help change things. You need hope to make things change."

"I can't change the world enough—"

"Of fucking course you can't. No one can. But we can all help a bit somewhere and, to find those little corners where we can do something, you need to look for them. You need to believe things can change. Have you asked that question for yourself? Do you want things to change? We all have agency somewhere, Sandy. Have you looked for your own?"

She got in the cab and, damn her, she didn't have the decency of slamming the door closed. She did it calmly.

It was him who was craving the energy and aggression of it.

———

Alex had a terrible night. He slept on and off, restless.

Unable to sleep in, he called in to his therapist's office and asked to be put on his cancellation list for the next few days. Then he did homework.

He sat in front of an empty canvas and prepared the materials for some horrible attempt at art. Scowling, hating the feeling twisting his gut, he worked blue and yellow into the exact shade of green he had on his mind and, saturating the brush thick with paint, he moved it against the canvas in an angled stroke.

He repeated the process trying to capture a soft blush, and a deeper pink.

When he checked his email at work later that day, he had an email from Elena.

> *Alex,*
>
> *Let's not talk today. Let's take some time to breathe.*
> *We need to reset.*
> *We need to put the fights behind us. Accept each other in our differences. If we can't be friendly, let's aim for neutrality. You'll feel neutral about me, I'll feel neutral about you.*
>
> *Let's make it work.*
>
> *Elena*

He wasn't sure why, but it felt like defeat.

Chapter 19

A LEX GOT IN TO see his therapist Saturday morning. He'd been to the office a few times by now, and was finally getting used to the space, with its worn leather sofa, bookshelves lining a wall, and a simple desk against a window. Alex could imagine Charles, messy curly hair and all, sitting at it and looking out the window, thinking about whatever therapists thought about, hands stapled in concentration.

Alex settled on the sofa and gazed at the desk, not ready to fully glance at Charles, who sat in front of him in a comfortable-looking armchair. When Alex finally turned to his counselor, the man smiled.

"So. Hi." Charles accommodated his glasses on the bridge of his nose. Alex tracked every one of his therapist's movements, now that he'd finally turned to the guy. "What's been on your mind today?"

"I've been thinking about how to answer that question. This is our fourth session and now I'm expecting it each time." He dropped his eyes to a glass of water Charles had left for him on the small coffee table between them.

"Nice. It's why I always start with it. I want you to think about what you're thinking."

"Explain again why."

It wasn't a question but a demand. While most people seemed to respond defensively to Alex's tendency to forgo a questioning tone, Charles didn't seem to care.

"Sure. I want you to think about what you think, because it means you'll become more aware of what happens in your head as you go through life. You need to be aware before you can change anything."

"I'm sure people change all the time without being aware of it." Alex lifted his eyes to gaze at Charles.

"True." A glint danced in Charles' eyes. "But I'd argue that change without awareness is something that happens to you, not something you do. There's less agency in that, isn't there? If you want to make an active decision about where you want to go, you need to know where you are."

"Agency." Alex didn't bother hiding his scowl at the word. Not that he would have bothered very often, anyway. "You're the second person to talk about that in half as many days."

"Oh, yeah? Someone talked to you about agency?" Charles was what Alex imagined as the standard therapist, with a notepad balancing on the arm of his chair. He didn't seem to take a lot of notes, but would write a few things every once in a while. At this time, though, he played with a pen between thumb and forefinger.

"Yes. Elena," Alex bit out.

"Oh." A beat passed, another. "You've mentioned her once or twice."

"I work with her. She's in my face all the time."

"Right. And she told you something about agency? Anything relevant?"

"Relevant to what?"

Charle's smile showed up cheeky. "To your therapeutic goals, Alex. That's why we're here."

"Of course." If there was a hint of sarcasm to his words, they were confirmed by the brief arch of his eyebrow. "What else could it be referring to."

"Do you want to talk about it?" Charles put pen down to paper. "You don't seem very willing."

"Actually, I do want to talk about it." Alex crossed his arms. He felt much more grounded with the shield of them around his chest. "She said that bitterness keeps people stuck because you need to believe things can change for them to change. That we all have agency somewhere."

"Okay."

"Is that all you're going to say?"

Charles shrugged. "I'm more interested in what you have to say about that."

"I want you to answer the question."

"You didn't ask anything, Alex."

"Fuck, it's clear—"

Charles stopped him with a broad palm up in the air between them. "Wait— wait. Let's take a moment to bring the intensity of this down. I don't care if you curse, you know that by now... but I see you going up and up. From one to ten, where are you in the intensity scale we discussed?"

Alex closed his eyes, red shining behind his eyelids, fire in his chest. He wasn't sure where he was but, looking inwards, it changed a bit. It went down a smidge.

"Six."

"Okay, then breathe. Like we practiced."

Alex did, several deep breaths followed by a few normal ones. He opened his eyes. "Okay. I'm at a four."

"Good. Let's try this again. I'm assuming you want to hear my opinion of what Elena said?"

"Yes."

"I think she's right."

"That takes me back to a five, Charles," Alex mumbled. He shook his leg.

Charles laughed. "Fair. It's frustrating when people tell us challenging things."

"You've said depression isn't something I did. So how is it true that I need to get myself out of it by *finding my agency*?"

"Both things are true. I can't speak to what Elena meant when she said those words, so don't take this as an opinion of that. But what those words mean to me is the same stuff I was talking about. That you need to be active in what you choose for yourself to get things to change. The places where you have agency are the places where you can be purposeful. Active. Bitterness means you don't think things can change."

"Depression isn't the same as bitterness."

Charles wrote something on his notepad again, but continued the conversation through his note-taking. "Absolutely! I agree. We talked about this. You may always be a bit terse. Maybe it's part of your personality. It doesn't mean you have to live depressed."

"Grumpy and bitter are also different."

"Again, agreed." Charles lifted his eyes to Alex and adjusted his glasses again. "But how are you going to figure out what's depression and what's you if you don't inspect it? If you don't work on depression, where you can?"

Alex pursed his lips to the side and forced his leg to stop the jiggling. "Where I can. That's the agency piece."

"Correct. Remember, there's no one cause of depression, not one presentation— I mean, depression looks different for every-one. That's why coming out of it— how long it takes, what com-ing out of it looks like, et cetera— will look different for people too. And there's always a community piece, too. Self-agency and community care are the two sides of it."

"And you think mine is treatable."

Charles lifted one shoulder in a half-shrug. "As far as I can tell in four sessions, yes."

"Okay."

Charles nodded. "Excellent. So let's keep at it and tell me, do you have any theories about what brought this on for you?"

———

Alex considered waiting before sending Elena a reply email, to see how things were on Monday. He changed his mind when he recognized that he was trying to avoid the vulnerability of it. So on Saturday evening, with a full day ahead to give them time to breathe and process, it was really the best time.

Ely,

I thought about what you said. Yes, let's leave the fights behind. I'll work on it.

Alex

Chapter 20

"Okay," Ely said. "Are you good with the finalists list?"

She gazed at Alex sitting at the head of the boardroom table. He nodded as he continued to type on his laptop. Sandy *loved* his laptop. He took it everywhere in the office, the screen and relevant papers went everywhere with him, and his eyes rarely left them to acknowledge her or anyone else in the room. The boardroom had become a sort of neutral territory; they avoided being in each other's offices. When she let herself question why, she imagined it was their way to avoid getting too close to the other's domain, lest it send the wrong message.

Considering that when he deigned to look at someone or talk to them, he did so in flat tones— a huge improvement apparent over the past month— she did not complain.

"Great," she added, pretending his nod was a full sentence. When she put everything in a balance, this was so much better than before. They'd both committed to their agreement, when they'd fought after that party a few weeks before. "I'll get Celeste to send the emails today and put the physical letters on the mail."

He nodded again. She sighed, but didn't push. Equilibrium was fragile.

She got up. "Good meeting. I'll see you tonight."

He glanced at her in response, blank face at first. When she froze, waiting for his question or comment, he lifted a single eyebrow.

"What?" she asked.

"Tonight."

She straightened, ignoring the tone of his non-question. "Yes. Dinner with your parents?"

"You said yes."

"Why wouldn't I?" She frowned. She didn't let the stab of his tone of voice reach any critical organ.

"Liam mentioned you might go, but I thought it'd be too much time around me."

She cocked her head and squinted at him. "Is this your way of telling me you need a break from me?"

He crossed his arms over his chest and cast his eyes to the ceiling. "No. I meant what I said. I thought you might want a break from me."

"Well, don't worry about that. Both Liam and Ana want me to meet them. I want to meet them, too."

He dropped his gaze and stared at her a second longer, before returning to his laptop. "Okay."

She didn't roll her eyes, but allowed herself a tightening of her lips as she left the room.

When Alex made it to Liam's house, he was welcomed by laughter. It tickled something in him.

Liam opened the door for Alex and gave him a cursory nod of hello. His mom's voice reached him from behind his brother.

"Alex! I'm so glad you made it." She hugged Alex close.

"Of course I'd come, Mom."

"Son." Alex hugged his dad, too, then nodded at Ana.

"Come in," Ana said. She indicated the sofa with a casual hand gesture. "Get comfortable. Do you want something to drink?"

There were snacks and finger food out, and several wine glasses full of deep burgundy liquid.

Alex sat down next to his mom. "I'm good, thanks."

"How was your day?" His dad asked.

"Good."

"C'mon." Dad reached forward from his place on the L-shaped sofa and slapped Alex's knee. "Tell us more."

Alex held back a sigh. "I sent emails. I talked on the phone. Analyzed some spreadsheets." Then, because they were all staring at him with tension around their eyes, he added, "We sent invitation letters to the first youth group for our social program."

"Oh! That's exciting!" His mom exclaimed. "What's this group about?"

"We connect underprivileged young people with mentoring and casual experience in the film industry, in any of the areas related to it."

"Gosh, that's amazing." She sipped from her wine.

"Isn't it?" Liam sat on a single seat kitty-corner from the couch. "It was a project Ana had hoped to develop in the future but, after creating Jump Cannon together, we wanted to make it a core part of it."

"And Alex and Ely are doing so well with it," Ana added. The doorbell rang. "Speak of the devil. That must be her."

Alex's parents stood, politely waiting for Ely to greet her properly. He remained sitting, while everyone else approached the door. He had a direct line of vision to the entrance and he watched the scene from under the ridge of his eyebrows.

"Hey!" Elena's voice resonated through the room. She hugged Ana and gave her a bottle of wine. She then hugged Liam and gave him a second bottle.

"Here, come meet my parents." Liam took the bottle and encouraged Elena forward with a hand on her back.

She wore the same clothes from the day at work, but she'd either done something with her hair or *something*, because she looked wonderful. Her smile was bright and her eyes sparkled and—

"Mom, Dad... Ely is— amazing," Liam said. "She's our friend and Manager of Social Impact for Jump Cannon Productions. Ely, these are my parents, John and Kate."

Elena's smile seemed to grow even brighter. "Hello! So excited to meet you. And happy."

They shook hands, and both his parents grinned back at her.

"You're excited *and* happy to meet us?" Mom asked.

"Yes! I love meeting cool people and, knowing Liam, I'm pretty sure you're cool." They laughed. "He told me you're here before flying out tomorrow?"

"C'mon, sit, everybody," Liam interrupted. "I'll bring you some wine, Ely."

They all sat around Alex, but no one paid him attention. They were all focused on Ely.

"Where are you going?" Ely asked, and they all fell back into conversation.

"We're going to Japan." His dad swirled his wine in his glass before taking a whiff of it.

His mom nodded. "It's our thirty-fifth anniversary and Liam and Alex gifted us this trip."

"Thirty-fifth? Wow, congratulations. You know," Elena said, taking a glass of wine from Liam, "my parents have been together just as long but I can't imagine it. I can't even get a decent date!"

They all laughed again. Alex didn't care for the comment about dating.

"He's out there, Ely." Ana leaned toward her friend and squeezed her with an arm around her shoulders. "It's just that he has to be so great and special to deserve you that he's taking a bit longer to appear. Like nice warm bread that takes longer to bake."

Ely laughed. "You're comparing my future person to bread? Or a brisket that needs slow cooking?!"

Ana grinned and gave Elena a formal blink and a nod. "Only the best for my friend."

"You're so biased." Elena winked at Ana, playfulness and joy sparkling all through her magnetic field.

"We love you," Liam said. "Of course we're biased."

Ely stared at Liam, her gesture softening. "Aw, Liam. It's the first time you tell me you love me."

Alex's brother frowned, but he gazed at Elena with humor on his face. "Is it?"

Alex frowned, too.

"Yeah." Elena smiled at Liam with such abandon it twisted something in Alex's guts.

"Well, I do." Liam lifted a shoulder, completely unaware of Alex and his hidden reactions to everything. "That's why I wanted you to meet my parents."

Elena's lips took on that angle that forbode teasing. Alex wondered if Liam knew what was coming. She glanced at his mom and dad, a sense of playfulness emitting from her. "I'm so honored you'd want me to meet them. Especially because I know it took you one full year to introduce Ana to your parents after you told *her* you loved her."

Ana laughed and high-fived Ely, while Liam groaned. "Really?"

Mom and Dad were laughing, too.

Ely reached and rubbed Liam's knee. "I tease you because I love you, too."

Liam patted Elena's hand on his knee, before Mom joined in the conversation.

"And you and Alex work together, right?"

Ely stole a glance at him, quiet and observant on the sofa, the grin she'd given Liam a touch hardened.

"Yes. We run Jump Cannon." Her hand shot forward to grab a vibrant red slice of bell pepper from the food sitting on the coffee table.

The same coffee table where he'd displayed her to himself.

No.

His dad's hand fell heavy on Alex's shoulder. "We were so glad when he decided to return and take the job. You're liking it, right, son?"

Alex nodded, eyes on one of his paintings on the wall. The mixed feelings that came with it helped cool his blood down.

"Glad to hear it," Liam said. "I know you're doing a good job— I see the results of it— but I don't know much about enjoying it."

"It's good." Alex got up and went for a glass of water.

His mom chuckled. "Do you ever get more words out of him, Ely? How do you even coordinate with one word answers?"

"I use a lot of closed questions— try to make it so that he doesn't have to give me more than a yes or a no."

"Gosh, really?" Mom said.

"No, no, it's okay," Ely insisted. "I don't need more from him."

Mom didn't seem to want to let it go. "When you said you'd sent acceptance letters for the youth program, it made it sound like you were more involved than that."

Alex pursed his lips. He returned to his place, gaining time by gulping half the glass down. "I may have let you jump to conclusions. Ely is the brain behind the program, really. She just— she seems to prefer to check with me about some things."

Elena shook her head at him. "This is how we designed things, Sandy."

Alex's dad choked on his drink. Liam, who sat between him and Ana on the big sectional, slapped his back.

His mom smirked. "Sandy?"

"It's Elena's... term of endearment for me."

"Yep, that's what it is," she said, an eyebrow arched high.

"You are adorable," his mom said to Elena with a chuckle.

Great. They'd fallen in love with her like every other person on earth. Soon Alex might be the only warm-blooded being in the world not utterly devoted to her, head over heels for her.

It made her just as dangerous as he'd first thought. They may have been working to find neutrality, but he could do well by remembering that he needed to keep her tempting ways at bay.

———

Two hours later, Ely stood by the door again, this time with her belly full of delicious food and wine. Ana and all of Liam's family stood around her as she prepared to leave.

"Thanks for dinner." Ely looked at Liam and Ana, and John and Kate in the eye in turn. "And John, Kate— it was so lovely to meet you!"

"You, too," Kate said. "You're lovely. I get why Liam and Ana like you so much."

"Aw, that's so sweet! Your art is amazing, by the way. So— so— heart-grabbing. It makes me happy that Liam has so many of them up on the walls so I can admire them."

"Thank you." Kate grinned. "It's a point of pride as a mom that my sons got an artistic side from me."

"And the green of your eyes!" She gushed in full honesty. "You're stunning."

"You flatterer." Kate dismissed Ely's words with a wave of her hand, but Ely suspected she'd loved the compliment anyway.

"I mean it!" Ely insisted. "I never lie. And you're very handsome, John."

They both laughed. John added, "it was great meeting you."

"Enjoy your trip! And take many pictures. I'll get Liam to show me some."

Ely hugged them, then Liam and Ana. She reached Alex and startled. He stood there, immobile, staring at her. Maybe she was imagining it, but there was a hint of a challenge in his eyes. Was she going to make it awkward by hugging him, considering their history, or by not hugging him, and setting him apart?

"Well— bye, Sandy. See you tomorrow." She put one arm around his shoulders and squeezed swiftly once. He'd kept his hands and arms to himself, but he'd leaned down to give her access.

"See you, Elena." His voice rumbled next to her ear.

She didn't stop to think about it until she was in the safety of her car, driving home.

Chapter 21

S EVERAL DAYS LATER, ELY drove to Liam and Ana's house early in the morning, in her brand-new-to-her car. Liam had a meeting with people in a time zone much further ahead, so coming here for a quick check-in meeting would help him save some time. Ely had no problem doing that and, to her surprise, Alex hadn't complained at all.

He'd moved out to his own place over the weekend and had also gotten his own car, which now was parked in Liam and Ana's front yard. Ely got out of her car and closed the door with a mild slam, still somewhat surprised at how things had improved over the past several weeks. To the point that she was tentatively optimistic.

Ana opened the door to her home and stood on the stone steps at its feet, waiting for Ely.

She reached her friend and hugged her. "Hey! You have editing hair. Have you been editing?"

Ana laughed. "What is editing hair?"

"It's up in a messy bun."

They went into the house, directly to the kitchen.

Ana raised his hands to undo the bun, tease her long hair free of knots, and tie it up in a ponytail. "I put it up in a bun for other reasons. Coffee?"

What reasons? Giving Liam a BJ? Maybe, but Ely knew her friend well. "Am I wrong about editing? And yes to the coffee."

"Fine. You're not wrong."

Ely sat at the kitchen island and Ana busied herself with their fancy espresso machine. "Where's Liam?"

Ely looked out to the patio and saw the swimming body in the pool, so she was surprised to hear Ana's answer.

"He's in the office; he should be done in a bit."

Ely squinted at the broad shoulders and shapely arms keeping a dependable rhythm in and out of the water. "Then..."

After all the years of knowing each other, Ana understood immediately. "Alex."

Ely whipped her eyes away from him and turned to Ana. "Sandy?"

"Yep. So he moved to his own place, right? Well, he'd gotten used to working out in the morning, so he and Liam had a conversation and Alex will keep coming here to use the gym for a while, until he finds a more convenient place. Apparently, it's something he's doing for mental health."

Ana pushed a mug with two shots of espresso and foamed milk toward Ely, having known her favored drink without asking.

Ely grabbed the mug and breathed in the smell of it, deep into her lungs. "Really," she breathed out.

Maybe it was okay for her to believe things had actually improved, then. Sure, they still had disagreements, but that wasn't the same as bickering. His tone had changed, he looked at her more, and she'd stopped taking small digs at him. It wasn't only the emails they had exchanged; they were investing in making things better between them. Looking out to the pool again, she could see he was taking things seriously, and perhaps for more than the work environment alone.

Alex stood in the pool and took off his swimming goggles. With eyes closed, he ran his fingers through his drenching-wet hair, clearing it off his face and messing it up. With two long steps, he pulled himself out of the pool, his shorts sticking to him and nothing more than a strip of soaked fabric covering some of the goods... and leaving many others open to any interested parties: his long legs with defined thighs, flat belly and narrow hips, a chest with muscles that echoed every one of his movements.

Ely coerced her sight away from him and gazed at Ana, forcefully stopping her brain from continuing to catalog Alex's physique. "Can I get an extra shot of espresso?"

"Sure."

Maybe it wasn't a good idea to have extra caffeine, but she hoped it'd help her blame her fast-beating heart on something other than her reaction to Alex.

"Hello, Elena. Ana." Alex had come into the house and nodded his greeting to them. He held a towel in his hand, and his appearance was mostly dry, enough not to drip anymore.

Ely gave him a small smile, making sure she didn't look below the neck. "Hi."

"I'll be right back, just need a quick shower." He disappeared into the house; Ely turned back to Ana and received the mug back from her.

"Things are better with you two, it seems?" Ana's hands flew over the espresso machine again, continuing to make more coffee. "Like there's less tension."

She tasted her drink and sighed. "Yes, I'd say that's true. We agreed to it and... it's working."

"That's so good! I'm glad. I know he's not the most cheerful person but I think he's a good guy. And you're the best; I hoped you two would hit it off enough that you'd enjoy working together."

Ely stared at the ceiling. "We might still get there."

"Hi, Ely." Liam appeared to her side, giving her a quick one arm squeeze. He then reached Ana, putting an arm around her shoulders and kissing her temple. "Can I get one of those?"

She gave him her mug and he drank from it. "I'll make another."

Ely's heart softened at seeing her best friend and her beau's casual show of love and intimacy. Their affection, and Sandy and her neutrality, were all in the small things; she needed to do better at noticing it.

It didn't take long for Alex to appear. He walked past her toward the coffee machine, and the smell of his shampoo or soap or whatever reached her nose, melting one of the last icicles lodged behind her sternum. He made himself a drink.

"Okay, let's do this," he said, and they all moved to the dinner table.

Alex's infamous laptop lay closed on the smooth wooden surface, and he sipped from his mug and opened the lid to his computer.

"I forwarded you three scripts yesterday, did you see them?" Ana asked.

"I did." Alex used his free hand, the one not holding the mug to his sexy— to his *very normal* mouth, to type on the keyboard. "Later today I'll get Celeste to schedule the pitch meetings; I do have video conferences with a couple line producer options. One of them is the one you connected me with, Liam."

"Good," Liam replied. "For us, Ana and I filmed a tease for our conversational project; Ana is editing it right now."

"I have to decide how much of his flirting I'm leaving in," Ana joked. Liam laughed. "He just won't stop."

Ely smiled. "Leave all of it. Fans will love that."

"I guess they will." Ana chuckled. "In any case, we'll need to get more editors soon, and another production head, depending on whether we take one or two scripts."

"Sure." Alex sipped his coffee, continuing to rest the mug on his bottom lip.

Ely hated him a bit for it, even if the irritation of it seemed to come from an altogether different source than it used to, in the beginning of their rocky relationship.

"When does the first group start the youth program?" Ana asked.

"The deadline for them to confirm they're joining the first round ends today, and the first day is next Monday." Ely wrapped her hands around the warm ceramic in her hands.

"I think they're going to get a lot out of it." Alex finally placed the mug on the table, releasing a bit of the tension that had built in Ely's belly. The fact that he now used both hands for typing helped clear all of it. "From what I could see, the activities Elena prepared are going to teach them a lot."

"Yeah, we got a lot of things planned." She replaced visions of Alex's lips with those of everything she'd planned for their program participants. She smiled. "Panels, preparation classes, and a handful of visits to relevant places. It's going to be great."

"The final group activity is at the picnic. Elena and I will do the final selection for the second stage after that."

Ely nodded. "It's all going smoothly to date."

Very smoothly.

"Perfect. I'm looking forward to the picnic," Liam said.

It seemed clear: Ely and Alex had figured some stuff out.

Chapter 22

ALEX SAT AT HIS desk, one hand curled around the phone handset he kept at his ear, the other squeezing a stress ball shaped like a brain. Apparently, Charles kept a bag of them in his office, and gave them out for clients to use as fidget toys. In Alex's case, it helped him not crush the phone in annoyance until it cracked. The guy on the phone was busy giving him excuses as to why there was a paperwork delay for one of the projects, and Alex— often happy to remain quiet— could not find a second to chime in, throw down a deadline, and hang up. The sigh that Alex let escape through his tense lips was slow and deliberate.

Ever since making the move to LA, time had gone by fast. Work, therapy, workouts, it all filled up his time. It was a rare thing these days for time to slow down, but the call he was stuck in did a good job of reminding Alex that time was a relative concept.

The past two weeks had gone by in a flash, especially. Getting everything set up for the youth program had sped up time even faster and, before they knew it, they had a group of young people coming in and out of their office every day. Alex wasn't as involved with the youth, but he'd met most of them for a group interview and would nod and say hi to them when in the office. Whenever he'd crossed paths with Elena, she'd glowed.

It seemed easier, these days, to coast on neutrality where she was involved. Perhaps it was the medication, perhaps the therapy, but he didn't feel in the dumps anymore. They had made it work. While they bickered, they did not fight. And though things moved past in a blur, nothing seemed gray anymore.

The guy on the phone took a deep breath, Alex guessed to go on his next diatribe.

He jumped in with his own fast sentence. "Sure, I can wait for that document, but not much longer. If there's anything you need to discuss further, then we need to book something for another time—" A knock on his door interrupted him. "Give me a second. Yes?"

Celeste opened the door. "You told me to come find you if you were late to the meeting with the youth?"

"Yes, thanks. I'll be out in a sec." Holding his phone handle between ear and shoulder, he unplugged his laptop to take it with him to the board room. "Listen, I really have to go. I'll have my assistant call you to book something. Bye."

Without waiting for more than a whisper of a goodbye on the phone, he hung up and made his way to the boardroom.

"There he is!" Elena called when he entered through the glass doors.

"He's wearing jeans?!" Rodrigo, one of the participants, exclaimed.

"I know, right?" Elena said. Alex allowed his lips to take on a tiny upward slant at the corners. For the youths' benefit. "You'd guess he only owned perfectly pressed trousers, from the look of him."

Alex may still be learning the line between what was him and what was a temporary state of his brain, but that did not ruin his sense of fashion. Not that he'd ever admit anything like that out loud. "I'm also wearing a t-shirt. Don't let it fool you."

The group of young people laughed. The slant of his lips remained.

"A baseball shirt and jeans is the perfect attire for today, Mr. McMillan," Elena teased. "Though I evidently prefer a boat neck shirt myself."

"Did you two coordinate?" Tania, another one of the kids, asked. "You're both wearing a kind of burgundy."

Elena's shirt was of a similar color to his, the line of the neck wide from shoulder to shoulder. Her clavicles, visible only as a subtle curve under her plush skin, drew his eyes. He could bite those— he had.

Alex removed his eyes from her by sheer strength of will, only to find Elena stared at his neck and shoulders herself.

"We did not coordinate," Elena finally said. She left it at that and clapped once. "Who's ready to go? We have a big van— small bus? Waiting for us in the parking lot downstairs. Pick up your things and let's go!"

Alex stood by Elena at one of the picnic tables they'd set up for the day. She'd found a park that allowed for some privacy, necessary as Liam and one of his Hollywood colleagues were in charge of leading most of the activities. Apparently, it would benefit them if some paparazzi or other bystander took pictures of the event, so they had prepared for it rather than tried to hide.

They even had a couple of the participants with a social media placement taking pictures, too, so they had their own photographic evidence in case it was needed, and to use on the Jump Cannon accounts.

Elena took a look around the large space the group occupied. While he faced the table, she faced the crowd. "Some people are taking pictures from afar. As long as they don't get close, I'm happy."

He gave her a nod and reached for the folder with the schedule for the day. "Should we get the next task started?"

She put chin to shoulder to reply. With her hands on her hips, it gave her a sassy look. Her eyes sparkled as she stared at him, but that was nothing new. "I think so. They're finishing up lunch. We can get them to drop their things here and then they can move onto the next activity."

"I'll go tell them." He walked to a central place among the small groups eating on blankets on the grass. "Listen up! In five minutes, clean up after yourselves— don't forget to put your used stuff in the right bags, they're labeled for recycling, organics, trash— and come to Elena and I for the details of the next activity. How was the meal?"

"Good!" A choir of voices responded.

"Excellent. You're going to need the fuel for the next bit. After the next activity is done, one more and we'll call it a day."

"Noooo," the same choir said.

"Any complaints please direct them to the person behind this operation." He put his hands up in defense, and pointed at Elena with his chin. "You'll receive a feedback form in your inbox tomorrow morning, conveniently speaking."

They laughed. Alex inadvertently sought Liam's eyes, who smiled at him.

Alex returned to stand next to Elena, and helped her check that the batch of documents needed for the next activity were properly set up.

"I'd be annoyed at your comment if you hadn't used it to engage with them," Elena said without looking at him, hands busy on the paperwork. "If anyone had asked me two weeks ago, I would've said that you preferred to communicate things with a group like that in monosyllables. Robotic instructions and such."

"I'm not a robot, despite what you tell yourself. Probably still too stern for them." He stole a glance at her. "I know myself enough to admit to that."

"Oh, absolutely. Still, though. You're good with them."

He shrugged. "They barely know me and we both know you're the social one. I'm sure the kids would rather come to you for things."

She smiled at him. "Likely."

He shook his head after a humorless half-chuckle.

"*Still.* I'm glad to see you don't share your brand of grump with them." She fake punched him on the shoulder.

"They're young and, sure, they can be annoying but... they're young. I'm not so old I've forgotten what that's like. I like them more than I thought I would."

She laughed, and the fact he'd caused it sent a shiver down his spine. Even if it was at his expense. "Sandy. We're not even thirty yet."

"I'm just a few months away and, at this age, that's still a century worth of experience compared to them."

A few of the young people came to them and soon they swarmed Alex and Elena. As they needed to give documents individually to each participant, things got messy fast.

Elena got up on a bench to see them all better and distribute papers. After everything had been given away, Liam and his friend shepherded everyone back to the blankets. Alex had turned away to check the agenda when he heard Elena's big yelp.

"Ow!"

Alex jumped close to her. She sat down on the same bench where she'd been standing and, curling down, gingerly held her ankle.

"You okay?" Alex asked.

"Yeah, yeah. I'm fine."

There were traces of pain on her face, and her shoulders seemed wound tight.

"The way you're wincing suggests otherwise." The urge to put a hand on her shoulder to squeeze and soothe didn't escape him.

Liam approached as well, worry on his frown. "What happened?"

Ely stared up at Liam, a rare hint of embarrassment in her eyes. She hid it well under a dismissive smirk. "I felt athletic and jumped down from the bench. I twisted my ankle."

"How bad is it? Do you need to have it checked?" Alex asked.

"No, no. I'm fine." She stretched her leg and tried to rotate her foot. She jerked.

"I think you should have it checked," Liam said.

"Help me stand?" She put her hand out, and both Alex and Liam responded with their own hands.

Ely lifted her eyes to Alex for an instant, but took Liam's hand and stood up carefully. Alex jammed his hand in his pocket as she tried to put weight on her foot. She moved slowly, but it seemed she could do it without much more pain marring her face.

"I'm okay." Elena let go of Liam's hand and took an extra couple of steps. "Thanks. Go back to the kids, Liam. I'm good."

"Are you sure?" He placed a hand on Elena's upper back.

"Yes. Go." She shooed him away with a hand.

Liam went back to working with the kids. Alex tracked Elena from his spot.

"You're not okay," he said after noticing how she winced each time she took a step on her way back to the table.

She shook her head. "I just need to take it easy for a bit."

She wobbled. He reached forward to help her balance. She gave him a look.

He didn't let go of her but returned the glare. "Don't be stubborn, Elena. I'll take you to have that looked at."

"I'll be fine!"

He continued to hold her, one arm around her back and the other holding her bent arm. "Lean on me."

He said it because he had to, though he paid for it almost instantly. Her perfume reached him, the same one that had intoxicated him that night all those weeks ago. It carved its way down to his lungs, burning the oxygen he breathed in a thousand tiny bursts of air.

She softened in his arms, but her lips pressed tight as she shook her head at him. "Fine, okay. You can help me."

He guided her to sit at the same picnic table bench from which she'd jumped and, until the end of the day, he managed to keep her there.

―

Alex stood by the mini bus door, collecting teens and corralling them up the steps into the vehicle.

"Is Ely going to be okay?" Clarissa, one of their brightest students, asked.

Alex stole a glance at Elena. She made her way slowly to them, with Liam helping her walk on her bruised ankle. She laughed at something he said, but continued to wince as she walked.

He tore his eyes away and nodded to Clarissa.

"Let's go home," Travis, another kid, said. "She has Liam helping her."

It churned in Alex's stomach to see, but of course she was more comfortable with Liam.

Alex ticked his list as the last teen went up on the bus. He joined them and organized them in their seats, before exiting the minibus to find Liam and Ely discussing her injury.

Liam stared down at her, arms crossed. "Ely, you really should have that checked."

"Fine." She rolled her eyes. "I'll have it checked."

"I can ask Ana to come. She's busy with that meeting— "

"No, no." Elena waved a hand in a strong negative. "Don't bother her. I twisted my left ankle, I can still drive—"

"Nonsense," Alex said.

Liam hid a smile.

"I can still drive!" Elena complained, angry eyes pointed at Alex.

Even though Liam had arrived in his own car, both Alex and Elena had left theirs at the office.

"Alex is right, Ely." Liam shook his head and played with the car keys in his hand. "Don't take the risk until you know what's going on. Until you get some meds and a wrap at least. I'd take you but I have to go to that thing..."

"I can take her," Alex interrupted. "We'll take her car once we're back at the office and I'll drive her to the doctor, then back to her place. It's Saturday so she can rest tomorrow and hopefully she'll be better by Monday."

She gave them both a look. "I'm. Fine."

"You're not," both brothers said at the same time and in the same tone.

Elena put on a reluctant smile. "I guess I can't fight you both on this."

"It's decided, then." Alex nodded. "Let's go. The driver's waiting."

She sighed, rolled her eyes, and turned to the vehicle. She did her best to climb the steps but, at her third soft *ow*, he grabbed her by the waist and hoisted her up the stairs.

"Alex!" Her voice seemed indignant.

He raised his eyebrows, returning her bewildered look with one of impatience. "I had to help. You're hurt."

Some of the kids laughed at them from their seats. When Alex turned to say bye to Liam still standing behind him, his brother smirked.

"What?" Alex challenged.

"I'm glad to see you two are not at each other's throats anymore."

Alex was the last to join with his own reluctant smile.

Ely leaned against the wall outside of her apartment, watching Alex unlock her door and open it wide. With calm and purposeful movements, he wrapped her shoulders with an arm and held her hand with his free one, like he had in the park. Insisting she leaned on him.

Like, what. She was flabbergasted, but she wouldn't let it show.

"Thanks, Alex."

"C'mon. I'll take you to the sofa."

He closed the door without completely letting go of her and walked her slowly into her place. He smelled good. The vague idea of sleuthing the brand of shampoo, soap, or even cologne he used reached her mind, carried by the scent molecules in the air. If she knew the name, she could buy it and potentially—

Nope, she wouldn't think about that. This was the closest they'd ever been physically... except for the time they'd had sex, of course. It made sense she got confused by that, and the day they'd had.

Better to start wrapping it up.

"You know, I know the doctor said to rest—"

"And rest it you will." His words were short and direct.

The annoyance they caused helped her create a bit of psychological distance with him. "Why do you have to be so... instructional in the way you talk to me?"

She let him help her down to the sofa. His hand slid from her back to hold her free hand, as she lowered herself into a comfortable position. If she was not mistaken, he gave her hand a small squeeze before letting go.

She reached for a pillow to put under her foot on the coffee table, but he took it from her. He carefully wrapped his hand around her calf and lifted her ankle and, after placing the cushion on the wooden surface, rested her wrapped foot there.

He left his warm hand on her ankle and gazed at her. "I know it irritates you. The way I speak. I don't do it on purpose."

His hand left her; he straightened and watched her down on the couch, thumbs hooked in his jean pockets. His baseball shirt made his shoulders look wider, more solid somehow, and she'd found it comforting when he'd let her lean on him.

She sighed. "Well, I don't want to be irritated at you today. You've been super helpful."

He arched an eyebrow. "We're exploring new horizons today, aren't we?"

She pursed her lips to hide a smile.

"Listen," he said. "I'm going to go out for a sec. Fill up your prescription. Do you need anything else from the drugstore?"

"Tampons."

His eyebrows knotted in amusement, his lips even curled up a little. "Are you trying to shock me, Elena? It's not going to work."

She shrugged. "It's fine. I use a cup, anyway."

"Do you need one?" His eyes widened to assert his words, the mildest sign of exasperation concealing the humor in them.

She broke and grinned at him. "No, they're reusable. I have mine in place."

"Then, not a cup. Or tampons, or pads. Which I'd have no problem buying, just so you know."

Her belly rolled in response to his suppressed mirth. "Okay, okay. You're a modern, aware man."

"Do you actually need anything?"

She shook her head.

"Okay, be right back. I checked online while you were with the doctor and I saw there's one just a couple blocks away. Be back soon." He pointed at her with a finger. "Don't move."

He took her keys and stepped out, leaving her as discombobulated as ever.

She didn't think onlookers would think they disliked each other anymore; they'd found neutrality. The tingling behind her breastbone was the newest addition and his sudden helpfulness was to blame. He had no business shaking the ground under her with unexpected kindness.

An image flashed into her mind, of him on top of her, looking into her eyes with an intensity she had not expected.

"Nope!"

She reached for the remote and turned on the TV. She chose a show about a pawn shop; it was the least sexy show she could find on short notice.

Less than half an hour had passed when he returned carrying a bag bigger than she'd expected. The domesticity of him entering her place as if he did it every other day shook her again, a sort of aftershock to the day.

She ignored the sensations it brought up. "I'd offer to help but I feel you'd yell at me to stay sitting."

"Damn right."

He closed the door and came to sit next to her on the sofa. After leaving the white plastic bag between them, he unhooked a metal rod of some sort from his elbow, which she hadn't seen before. He held it in the air in front of her.

"A frigging cane?!" she exclaimed, crossing her arms in an effort to refuse it.

"Yes. It'll help."

"It's leopard print! I just have a sprain! It's tightly wrapped, I promise."

"S'all they had." He shrugged and pushed the cane closer to Ely.

The same mirth from before lived in his hazel eyes.

She squinted at him. "I don't know that I believe you."

"C'mon, try it out. No shame in mobility aids."

She leaned back on the cushion behind her. "I refuse."

"I won't leave until you try it out."

"What's in the bag?"

"I'll tell you in a second. What's the problem with a cane?"

"I am *fine*." When he didn't move, she continued, "it's yellow and black and... animal print. I don't do animal prints."

"Oh, interesting. I thought I smelled the faint signs of internalized ableism."

She closed her eyes. "Sandy, I swear..."

"Come. On." He wiggled the cane between them. "Unless you want me to spend the night and hover to make sure you don't fall and hurt yourself again..."

She grabbed the aid from him. "Internalized ableism, he says. Since when are you so aware of these issues?" She scoffed. "Fine. But only because you threatened me with staying."

"Good thing your insults slide off my skin at this point."

She got herself up on one foot, then balanced herself against the cane. She took a few steps to the kitchen and, turning back, walked back to the sofa.

"I bet I look like that doctor from that show," she said. "The cynical one addicted to Vicodin."

She sat back down with a huff, putting her foot back on the pillow.

Alex reached forward and puffed the cushion for her. "Maybe a bit younger than him."

She glared at him. He remained impassive, except for dropping his head to the side a notch.

"Shorter," he added.

Ely took a deep, slow breath. When she looked back at him, she was certain he was hiding the tiniest smile in the world.

She rolled her eyes. "Anyway. What's in the bag? That looks like more than a couple of pill bottles."

"You're right." He rummaged through the bag and took a small, round, orange plastic bottle full of pills. "They did not prescribe opioids, which I'm thinking now is probably a good idea."

"Har har."

"But these are still painkillers so make sure to read the pamphlet." He gave it to her. "There's a warning on the bottle—don't drive for two hours after you've taken the pill, in case it makes you drowsy."

"Yes, mama hen."

He ignored her. "You should have one now. I got us food, too—we didn't get to eat much at the picnic and then we waited for a couple of hours to have you seen. You must be hungry. And in pain." He took a loaf of bread and packaged sandwich fillings. "I didn't know what you had and the pre-made stuff they had looked gross, so I got this instead. And this to drink," he added, taking two bottles out; green tea with jasmine and the other iced tea with lemon.

He collected all the things on the coffee table and made a knot out of the bag. Ely stared at everything together on the wooden surface, each one evidence of how much he thought things through. Like he really cared, and really, genuinely wanted to help.

She gazed at him. "Thank you, Alex."

"You are welcome." He stared at her in that intense way of his. "Are you okay drinking from the bottle, or should I bring glasses?"

"Bottle is fine."

He nodded, grabbed the food, and escaped to the kitchen.

Ely's eyes got blurry as she stared out of the window, until her phone dinged with a notification.

Ana: You ok??? Liam told me
you got hurt

Ely: Yes. Just a bad sprain. Got
painkillers. Alex is helping me.

Then, because it made her uneasy to let herself fall into the knowledge of it, she made a joke of the situation.

Ely: he got me an effing leopard
print cane [angry emoji]

Ana: [laughing emoji]
Ana: nice of him tho.

Yes, nice, and it still shook her to see.

Ana: Can I bring you some yummy
food tomorrow after lunch? We'll have
a nice girls' cozy afternoon.

Ely: yes! Can you bring buñuelos
from that place we went to the
other day? I need comfort food
[sad emoji]

Ana: I'll bring café campesino, too.
Love you!

Ely: love you too

She sighed, relieved over the idea she'd spend time with her best friend the next day. It dissolved her conflicted feelings, so that when Alex returned to the living room with food, her heart kept an even keel.

———

They'd eaten mostly in silence, watching TV together.

The blinds were open and night was falling. There was something intimate in the moment. It made her nervous.

Good thing he got up, took their plates and bottles and cleaned everything up.

"I'm going." He stood in the middle of the room, hands in his pockets. "Please use the cane and take it easy."

"I will."

"You can text me if you need anything but hopefully a good night's sleep will help."

The light from the TV was all that illuminated the room; a change in scene shifted the light, a series of flashes reflecting off him.

"Hope so, too." She watched him turn; the hook in her stomach told her she wouldn't be able to sleep if she let him go like that. "Hey!"

He turned back to her.

"Alex…" Words formed slowly in her mind. Her breathing got stuck in her lungs, until she gave up and told him what she needed him to hear. "Thank you, really. You were amazing today."

He gave her a single nod. "Glad you think so."

"I mean it. You really made me feel like I could count on you today. Like we're a team."

"Yeah." There was something like self-deprecation in his scoff. "That'd be good, since we work together. Being a team, I mean."

"I hope…" She lost her words for a moment, but she gathered them again alongside her courage. "If there's a chance I could return the favor, please let me know, okay?"

He lifted a shoulder. "We don't need to keep things in a balance. It doesn't have to be a competition—"

"No, not like competition. Like, actual support. I'd like to be on your team, Alex."

She held her own vulnerability at bay, tender in it, but adamant to give him some of it. Her resolve squirreled away when he took two steps closer to her, coming to an abrupt stop an arm length away. He remained straight, looking down at her on the sofa.

He stared down at her, his chin still high. "Have I really been that much of an ass, that helping you when you're hurt changes everything?"

"Everything?" Her voice rasped thin out of her throat.

"You're talking to me like you talk to Ana. Even Liam."

She jerked back. "Is that a bad thing?"

"No, but it is new."

She took a calming breath. "You were different today."

"That's my point. Have I been that much of an asshole that the fact I helped you today shocks you?"

"I— Just— at times. But I have been, too."

If her ankle didn't hurt, she would have been up and close to him. The energy in his stance, in his words, it was clear: this mattered to him. It drove her to want to soothe him, as jarring as that was, considering their history.

He barely moved. He dropped his chin to have a better sight line to her. "Look. I know I'm not a nice guy. I'm not someone who will dazzle and charm people into friendship with a smile and charisma. I can deal with that. But I don't want to be someone who's an ass."

Her ribcage didn't seem to want to accommodate her lungs, despite the deep breaths she needed. "We both need to do better. Have more days like today."

"I think the me you've seen today is the real me. Mostly."

She didn't fully understand his statement and it didn't do much to help her. She needed to break the tension.

"Maybe there are some kinks to iron out," she teased. When he raised an eyebrow, she relented. "From both of us."

"We all have things we can improve, always. I'm not worried about that."

"Okay. Well— yes. Maybe we can both do a better job at actually saying what we mean."

"Sure."

"And I really am grateful."

There it was again, the tiniest smile in the world. "No problem. See you on Monday, Elena."

When he closed the door behind him, she stared at it for a long time.

Liking him was a slippery slope.

Chapter 23

A LEX CAME TO THE office late on Monday, having made room for a therapy appointment. A travel mug in hand, he nodded to Celeste in greeting and again to the three teens sitting in the waiting area, phones in their hands. One of them lifted their hand in a military salute to Alex, and Alex went as far as to wave his hand at hip level back to him.

Two other group participants crossed paths with him as he walked down the hall towards his office. They smiled at Alex and continued muttering to each other as he opened his door.

Alex frowned. A ripple in the air hinted that something was going on. Something strange. He left his door ajar to monitor things.

Having young people in the office presented some challenges; they could get loud and some people found they brought Jump Cannon's professional image down. Alex didn't mind having the teens around, generally. While in the stage of the youth program where they came to the office in large groups, Alex could go elsewhere for meetings and move things around. That Monday, when they kept on chattering in loud whispers, they annoyed him for the first time.

He needed more coffee if he was going to concentrate on work.

Alex grabbed his travel mug and went into the kitchenette to rinse it and make himself a dark roast. Celeste popped in to fill her water bottle.

"The teens," he said in her direction. "What has them all acting weird?"

After more than two months working together, she seemed unfazed by his tone. "It's the social media thing. You know, the post with lots of activity?"

Alex placed his mug under the coffee machine, inserted a pod, and ran it; he nodded at Celeste like he knew what she was talking about. "Thanks."

"For sure. See you later." She stepped away, leaving Alex to fret alone in the tiny kitchen.

Elena's laughter reached him from nearby. "Oh my god. Stop it."

Alex didn't know who she talked to, but he willed the coffee machine to hurry the fuck up so he could go check in with her. About the social media thing, of course.

Someone murmured to her.

Her voice continued to come clear enough to him. "Oh, this cane? Sandy gave it to me. His fashion sense is superb, don't you think?"

She'd texted him on Sunday to say thanks again and that she was doing better.

Alex scoffed and shook his head at her, even if she couldn't see it.

The coffee was finally done, and he rushed to throw the pod into the recycling bin and make his way to Ely.

She stood with Clarissa and Tania in the hallway.

Alex joined them with as much aplomb as he could, like he did it every day. "Glad you *are* using your cane, Ms. Castillo."

She gave him a look up and down, but didn't otherwise remark on his sudden appearance. "Of course. First, I wouldn't want to ignite your wrath. Second, I think it goes soooo well with my outfit."

She modeled for him with the cane across her torso and a hip cocked to the side. He let himself study her body, mostly following the curve of her waist and the round, generous curve of her hips, down to her legs. Fuck, she wore skirts all the time, he shouldn't react like that to the simple dark green pencil skirt and flowery, soft blouse. And he shouldn't think of what he knew existed beneath.

The cane did clash with the pattern of her blouse, and he shored himself up in that fact. He raised an eyebrow with all the challenge he could muster. "I don't see a problem."

Tania giggled, and for a second Alex panicked that the teens could interpret their little interaction as flirting.

They would be wrong, he hadn't flirted. Or hadn't meant to, in any case. Whatever. It's not like he could correct them.

Elena hooked the cane around a forearm and crossed her arms. "Any other opinions on the matter?"

"No," he replied. "But I do need to talk to you."

She nodded and turned to Tania and Clarissa. "Do you mind corralling everyone into the boardroom? I'll be there soon. Just get everyone to fill out the worksheets on the table for now, okay?"

The young girls walked away and Elena and Alex turned to each other.

"What's up?" she asked.

"I need to know more about what's happening." He sipped from his coffee. Elena shook her head, signaling confusion. "Celeste said there's something going on in social media."

"Oh." A grin split her face. "That."

He nodded and stared at Elena, waiting for her to offer more. He held his lips closed with the cold of the metal mug on them. Like a shield.

Her eyes dropped to the mug and came back up to his eyes. "Sandy. You really don't know?"

"I wouldn't be asking if I knew, Elena."

"It means you don't follow our social media accounts. Or at least not the one the Youth are running."

Alex raised an eyebrow. "I don't have social media accounts."

Ely gasped. "Are you real?"

He glared at her and her wide-open, brown eyes of molten incredulity.

She shook her head as if giving up on him, a hand in the air like she wanted to make him stop with his ridiculousness. "Anyway. There's a picture from the picnic with both you and Liam. Let's say some fans found the picture... and are very interested in the lesser-known McMillan brother, all of a sudden."

Elena's hands and eyes disappeared from Alex's consciousness. His blood had turned dense and heavy and had dropped to his feet, leaving his hands cold and clammy. "Please don't tease me. And don't be cryptic. What the hell does that mean?"

Ely raised a half-incredulous, half-irritated eyebrow. If Alex had been in less of a panic, it would have stolen a smile out of him. "You know you can go look for yourself, right?"

Alex remained immobile, waiting for her to connect the dots, hoping she would.

"Honestly, Sandy." She grabbed him by the arm and started on her way to her office. She limped and aimed to unhook her cane from her arm to use it, but Alex took it from her.

Without words, Alex secured her hand around his elbow and changed his gait, so that Ely could rely on him. It helped; they walked slowly but she limped less. Once in her office, he helped her sit on her sofa before he sat next to her. She stole a glance at him but he was too impatient to interpret it.

"C'mon," he said. "Please."

"Okay, okay." She handled her phone, tapping away on it until she found what she was looking for. She gave him her cell with the typical sparkle in her eye.

The picture framed Liam and Alex as if in a standoff. They faced the group sitting on a picnic blanket, and the sun shone on them so that every detail stood clear on their faces, including Liam's smile and even Alex's eyes rolling. Whatever camera had been used to take the photo and whatever filter they'd applied, it highlighted the resemblance between them.

"This is not terrible." His stomach settled a notch.

"The picture's good. It's the comments everyone is discussing."

She leaned closer to him, scrolling down from the picture with a single finger— her nail polish was a very interesting shade of orange, and her smell distracting— until a few comments appeared on the screen.

Wow. Delicious!

I could McEat him right now

Liam Lite, 100% the flavor, 100% the yummies

If I had known what @liammcisacting 's brother looked like, I'd've chosen the grumpy one for sure.

Commence the sleuthing! Where can we find this guy?

"Fuck." Alex rubbed his lips with a cold hand, the chill reaching out all the way to his throat. A small spark of warmth appeared in response to Elena's barely suppressed giggle-snort. He cut his eyes to her, nothing else changing. "You find this funny."

"No. Not at all." She pressed her lips together, amusement clear in her eyes. "This is an atrocity."

He rolled his eyes and scrolled down the profile, seeking more comments but catching sight of another picture from the picnic instead— one of him and Ely.

"So that's what happened," Ely tried, reaching for her phone. "C'mon. Give me my phone now."

He blocked her hand and trapped it under his, on top of his leg.

"Alex!"

"I want to see." And having her hand on his thigh wasn't bad, either.

"There's nothing to see—"

It was a bluff. In his opinion, there was plenty to be seen in the second photo. In it, Elena grinned with utter joy or excitement or both, eyes as shiny as he'd ever seen them, as she talked to a group of teens out of focus. She glowed, and Alex stood next to her, gazing at her as if hypnotized by her light.

"Huh." He kept reading. The caption, written by one of the kids in the program, read *Mom and Dad*.

Interesting.

Ely pulled her hand from under his and grasped her phone. She took it away, and he let her. "You didn't need to see that. It was the other picture that everyone's talking about."

As much as he would still need to use some grounding techniques later to deal with the panic that those comments brought, the current situation seized his attention much more.

"You didn't want me to see that picture. Curious," he said.

"Nothing intriguing at all—"

"Fascinating. Perhaps because you're radiant in it, and I'm looking at you adoringly."

She stared at him like a deer in headlights. "Sandy. No."

"Does it make you uncomfortable?" He tracked every little change on her face.

"No."

A lie. Or at least not a full truth. "Huh."

"Stop that. There's nothing to *huh* about." She stood and straightened her skirt. "I'm late for the workshop."

He got up as well, standing to his full height. "Do you want me to help you get to the boardroom?" He wouldn't stay back in her office alone, anyway, and he still held her cane.

"Nope." She took the leopard-print metal rod from him and walked out of her office, with Alex close behind. "I'm fine, thanks."

He didn't think so, but he wouldn't corner her about it just yet. He had a few things to figure out himself.

Chapter 24

F IVE DAYS LATER, ALEX sat at one side of the boardroom table corner, and Elena on the side perpendicular to him. Slightly across from each other, they looked at the files for each teen that participated in the first round of the program, and decided who got to go on to actual placements in the field and who didn't.

Alex couldn't keep his eyes off her. She'd done something to her eye make-up that made them glitter more than usual, which was to say a lot. Her dress today had a geometric design at the waist, accentuating her silhouette. The dress wasn't particularly revealing, but it made you wonder what was underneath... and he remembered what was underneath.

He gulped. He'd been working on finding the line between depression and sternness. Today, he was forced to ask, what was the line between neutrality and attraction?

That damn birthmark on her breast was shaped like a tiny diamond. It haunted him.

"So," she said, distracting him from his reverie. "Jonah. I think he'd be a great fit. He made his application look like a short film!"

"Yeah." He cleared his throat, taking Jonah's file and moving it into the *accepted* pile. "Rodrigo seems good, too. Both of them participated actively in discussions. Didn't miss a thing."

"Yes." She skimmed Rodrigo's file quickly and added it to the *accepted* pile. "I think John isn't quite ready yet. I'll write the letter to explain what he needs to focus on if he wants to apply again next year; he'll still be in the age range." She placed his file in the *rejected* pile.

She carelessly ran her fingers across her clavicles. It was mesmerizing.

"What about Tania?"

"Mh?" When he looked up from her clavicles, she stared at him with a raised eyebrow.

"Tania. She had more of a business proposal; she wants to shadow producers. I liked what she wrote, but I suppose you have the final say as you're our numbers guy."

He took the file from Elena's hand and checked his notes. "Yes. Tania would be a great fit."

"Okay, last one." She took another file from the pile. "We might need to finish tomorrow. I need to leave in five minutes."

"Networking event?" he asked, though he doubted it was the case. She hadn't pestered him to go with her.

"No. Date."

He picked up another file, pretending to read it and be uninterested. "Oh?"

"Yeah. He works in the building. Funny guy and he seemed sweet. Smart, in any case. It took him an elevator ride to make me laugh and invite me out."

"Sounds like a great match for you." He kept his eyes glued to the words inked on paper in front of him, even if he processed none of it. "Now, if we can finish work. What about Clarissa?"

"I love Clarissa. I think she's a yes. And you've been looking at me the whole hour, but let's pretend it didn't happen, shall we?"

"It's the make up," he half-lied. "Your eyes look different with that... long line..."

"Winged eyeliner."

"Right." He cleared his throat.

"Well, I'm leaving my cane in your custody." She laid it on the table. "I don't need it as much and it would kill my style, otherwise."

"We wouldn't want that." He shook the foot resting on his knee.

Elena organized some of the folders in front of her and stood with a mild scratching sound from her chair. "Do you mind taking care of these? I gotta go."

"I can do that."

"Thanks, Sandy. I like us so much better when we're amicable." With a wink, she left, leaving the mildest scent of her perfume in the air and the weight of a rock in his stomach.

Chapter 25

ELY AND THE TEAM— Alex, Ana, and Liam— had just finished an afternoon of work at the office and were packed in the elevator on their way down to the city. They had all been present for a series of interviews for producers they might contract for some of their projects. Three hour-long video conferences and one long debrief meeting later, they were all hungry and wanted to get to the nearest restaurant.

A sigh escaped Ely as the elevator reached the lobby. They had discussed Jump Cannon's upcoming plans for a few hours while Sandy took notes non-stop— she didn't know why he felt the need to write everything down, or why he now used pen and paper rather than his laptop. In any case, by the time they were done, Ely felt a little faint from tiredness and hunger.

The team stepped out of the lobby into the balmy LA air. They were only a block away from the restaurant they'd chosen, so it surprised Ely when the first flash broke the falling darkness.

Shit. She suspected someone in their office building liked to note when Liam visited because, for the second time since they'd moved in, photographers showed up to wait for him. Three paps were busy taking pictures of him and Ana and, by the time they were halfway to the restaurant, the number of flashes had multiplied.

Ana and Liam huddled together as they walked hand in hand, marching fast and trying to ignore the cameras, but not really fighting them much. Apparently, as much as they could be a plague, Liam wanted to keep as much of a decent relationship with them as he could, as instructed by his publicist. It was one of the ways in which he stayed in people's minds, and things had changed for him now that he was at the helm of Jump Cannon.

She didn't understand why he needed to, considering he was one of the most famous of the famous actors, but as she didn't have enough training as a publicist, she didn't question it.

Flashes burst all around and she blinked hard to block the light; she hated the flashes. They overwhelmed her and, in combination with hunger, brought a wave of dizziness to her head. She slowed down, hoping to create distance between her and the cameras.

Alex seemed to notice she fell behind from the group. He waited for her and, when Ely stayed in her place on the sidewalk, he came to her.

He leaned down to gaze at her face. "You okay?"

She looked away from the cameras, hiding from the strobo-scopic lights. "Not really. The flashes are bugging me."

He put his hand on her back. She startled at the gesture. She looked up at him and, to her complete shock, he smiled at her.

"Let's fall back a little. They can follow Liam."

She blinked twice. He'd told her before he didn't see himself as dazzling, but that smile had proved him wrong. "You're letting your brother be a decoy?"

Another smile. The hell?

"Yeah." His grin brought a certain... something to his eyes.

"You okay?" she asked him, echoing his words from a minute earlier. He was. Grinning.

He shrugged. "Annoying moths, that's all they are."

"Yet... you smile?"

His smile disappeared, replaced by a frown— that was more like Alex. He blinked twice himself, before turning to check how far Liam and Ana were. They'd made it into the restaurant.

Despite the knot on his brow, there was a hint of a smile suppressed on his lips. Not that she was looking at his lips or anything.

"I don't know what that's about," he said, eyes still targeting the restaurant. "Shall we?"

The paparazzi had dispersed by the time Alex and Ely made it into the restaurant. Alex kept his hand on the small of her back as they walked, and was in the process of helping her through the door when they had to stand to the side, to make way for people coming out of the building.

"Ely?"

She hadn't realized who was in front of her until he'd called her name.

"Max?" Ely's face warmed. If she had anything in her stomach, it might have turned under the threat of her discomfort.

"Hi!" Max watched the people he was with walk past him and wait for him outside. He turned to Ely and gave her an awkward smile. "Nice to see you."

Alex took his hand away.

"I... sorry I haven't texted. I've been super busy."

She waved dismissively. "We're good! I haven't texted either."

Alex squirmed next to her.

"Maybe we should... could go out again sometime? Unless..." Max pointed at Alex with a mix of a chin gesture and shifty eyes.

"Oh!" Her whole body tensed up. "No— It's not like that— well, he's—"

"Alex." Sandy's voice was deep and short, but he gave Max a quick nod.

"My colleague," Ely added.

Max gave Sandy a look that ended in a double take. "You look like Liam McMillan. I just saw him come in..."

"They're brothers," Ely explained.

Alex crossed his arms. They were all in silence for a moment, Max's eyes shifty, and Alex fixed on Ely.

People approached the exit from the restaurant; Ely, Alex and Max needed to move to make room for them.

This was her chance for an escape. She smiled at Max. "Well, it was nice seeing you again. Maybe I'll see you again?"

"I'll text you. Bye, Alex."

Alex didn't say anything.

"Take care!" Ely nodded at Max and went into the restaurant.

Alex walked by her side, silent.

She wasn't sure why she wanted to explain herself to him, but she did. "He's the guy that works in our building that I went out with, that time."

Alex didn't say anything. Her stomach rolled again, but she didn't say anything else.

They found Ana and Liam and walked to them in silence.

Ana leaned close to Liam and he did the same, meeting her in the middle, talking about something. They held hands on the table and, despite the small gesture, it gave Ely's heart a pang. She'd always wanted someone to love and who would love her back. Although she typically was patient in waiting for the moment she'd meet her person, sometimes the longing attacked her out of the blue.

Ely approached her seat, a wave of yearning pulling down on her heart. Sandy surprised her by helping her get seated, taking charge of her chair until she sat comfortably. All without saying a word.

"Thank you," she whispered, and he gave her a tiny nod.

She took the menu and skimmed the options. She had to believe that one day she'd find the person with whom she could find the kind of intimacy she wanted for herself, someone who could take her energy and sass as well as her moments of need. It was a good thing she had a hopeful nature; by the time they got their drinks, she'd managed to comfort herself in the trust that it would happen for her, one day.

Chapter 26

ICE HIT ELY'S GLASS with its usual sharp clatter, the fridge's motor kicking into gear to replace it. She glanced around Ana and Liam's house, with its multiple paintings on concrete walls, and many wooden elements that leant warmth to the cold, modern look. The sweet man had invited Ana and Ely's friends, Maggie and Christina, to visit from back home as a surprise for his beau's birthday. Ely could see them all chatting and laughing on the other side of the kitchen, thanks to the open space design.

Ely topped her glass with water and gulped some of it down, before filling it up again. She had a personal rule to take turns between alcoholic drinks and hydration that served her well, and she wouldn't change the rule just because it was Ana's party.

Glass in hand, Ely rounded the marble island and made her way to the living room; Ana and Liam sat next to each other on the big sectional, and Maggie and Christina to the other side of Ely's best friend. With a grin for all of them, Ely joined them and sat in the empty space between Alex and the rest.

Awareness of him scraped down the side of her body closest to him. He leaned forward, elbows on his knees, not quite engaging but doing nothing else either. Aloof, but not antagonistic.

Ely tried to join in the conversation among everyone else, but Christina's gaze at Alex distracted her. Ely frowned. Christina had tried flirting with him a bit, soon after she'd arrived, which had irritated— scratch that, *discombobulated* Ely somewhat. Alex had been cordial, and Ely couldn't help but wonder if that was Alex's version of flirting back. It would be so weird if he accepted her advances and somehow, someday, it led to them being an item. It wouldn't happen tonight, not when Maggie and Christina were in LA only for a couple of days for Ana's birthday, but it could happen. Then both Ely and Christina would know what it felt like to be with him.

To have his hands on one's skin. How he seemed to concentrate when he kissed, with a deep wrinkle between his eyebrows and quiet determination.

She reached for Ana's glass of white wine on the coffee table, stole a sip, and blamed it for the warmth on her cheeks.

She was saved from entering into a fight with her memory banks when her phone dinged with the notification she'd set for Clarissa. The student had been having some problems in her shadowing placement, and Ely had told her she could call if she needed it. Excusing herself, she walked to the patio and, resting on the railing overlooking the city, she answered the call.

She wasn't sure how long she'd been on it when Alex appeared to her side. He rested his back on the railing, arms crossed, head turned to her.

"Clarissa?" he mouthed to her. When she nodded, he did too.

"No, you're right," Ely said to the phone. "You shouldn't have to do work for him outside of your shadowing hours. You can absolutely tell him no. In fact, we encourage you to."

"Tell her I could call him right now and help, if she'd like that," Alex offered. She'd told Alex about Clarissa's situation already, and it pleased her he was willing to help.

"Clarissa? Alex is here. He wants to know if you'd like him to call Mr. Johnson and remind him of the limits of this set up? I could stay on the call with you."

Clarissa said no, but asked to be put on speaker.

"Thanks, Alex, but no," the young woman said. A stray thought undermined Ely's attention; while she'd asked the youth to call her by her first name to keep it a bit more casual, she wasn't sure if Alex had done the same but they called him by his first name regardless. Whether he was okay with that or no, he didn't flinch and didn't seem to care. "This is a hard, tough lesson for my first opportunity," Clarissa continued, "but Ely said that I might come across people like this in the future if I stay in this industry and I want to know how to handle it myself."

"That sounds good to me," Alex responded. "As long as you know Ely and I are here to support you, you can make the call on how to proceed for now."

"Thank you." Clarissa's voice seemed determined. "I'll text you two later to tell you how it went."

"Good luck!" Ely said, and they hung up. She stared at her phone for a couple of seconds and pursed her lips.

"You okay?" Alex frowned at her.

"Yeah, I just... ugh! I'm so annoyed at that guy."

"He's a pain."

Ely put her phone in her pocket and leaned on the railing. "And poor Clarissa. This is not the experience I wanted for her. Not for anyone else, either, of course."

"This is the first time we're actually running this program. We're bound to find a few bumps."

A breeze played around them. Ely closed her eyes briefly and took a deep breath. "We need to vet the industry people differently in the future."

"Yeah. We'll tweak where we need to." He continued to gaze at her, ignoring the sight of everyone in the living room across the patio. "The good thing with how this whole thing is set up, this company you and I are leading, is that it gives us the freedom to continue perfecting it."

"I know. It was different in old jobs; needing to answer to a board of directors and all the members had all that political pressure to it, too. Justifying the budget, for things that didn't work, all of that— it's weird, being on a team where my bosses have my back like this and let me make all decisions. Liam and Ana just assume we're doing well." The breeze tickled her face with her hair, and she pulled it behind her ear. "It's scary, sometimes, but good-scary, I think."

He turned to face the city; their arms touched. The fabric of his shirt was soft on her skin. "I suppose you're right. Where I used to work, I would have never made an offer like I just did— call someone to tell them to bring it down a notch, so I could help the person they were mistreating. That's so personal. I was meant to do my work and that included managing people, but it was never like this."

She turned to study him. They mirrored each other. "And is it good? Is this better? Or do you miss the anonymity, the distance of it?"

His eyebrows lifted in big arches. He blinked at her a couple of times. "I can't say that I miss much of it."

His face, so handsome, remained motionless, except for his eyes. Those irises looked light brown in the early night light, and they traveled all over her face.

Ely wasn't a shy person, but a flutter of it nestled in her stomach.

She compacted it all into a tiny speck to be digested and disposed of, and gave him a teasing smile. "Having actual relationships with people you work with can be tough, too, just in different ways."

It took him a second to respond, his eyes finally still— first on her lips, then on her eyes. "I'm learning that."

She turned away toward the city. Lights glittered all around, except for where the ocean lived. "Have you regretted it? Coming back?"

"Not yet." His voice changed to a low, deep tone. Secretive. "But don't tell Liam."

She chuckled. "C'mon, Sandy. What will it take for you to give it a try with him?"

"That's a good question." He lifted the shoulder next to her, the fabric of his shirt a caress against her arm. "We're doing well enough."

"Things have changed, though. Would you agree that things are better? Between us—" she bumped his shoulder with hers— "among all of us."

He smirked. "Sure. It was a bit of a steep learning curve. I'm still learning lots of the inner intricacies of this industry... but I feel much clearer. That's better."

A chuckle escaped her; the wind picked up and she shivered. She turned to her side to face Alex, shoulder to the railing. He imitated her. Somehow they ended up standing closer together in the process.

She shook her head at him. "You misunderstand me and I suspect it's on purpose. I'm talking about the quality of the time we spend together."

He squinted at her, but there was some humor there. "I suppose some things have changed."

"I can help with examples." She bit her lip not to smile. "One, you don't growl as much."

He scoffed. "Elena..."

She counted examples on her fingers. "Two, you look people in the eye now."

"Elena." His tone had turned firmer. Harder. Trying to get her to stop.

She persisted, three proud fingers now up. "Three, you're easier to talk to."

"Ely."

Her fingers and throat froze for an instant. "Woah. You called me Ely."

"Yes." He rolled his eyes. "Things are better. I might still growl, if you keep adding items to that list."

She allowed herself a small smile. His admission settled warm on her shoulders. "Oh, we wouldn't want you to stop altogether. We might start to miss it."

"We?" He raised an eyebrow. "Who's we?"

Her heart beat faster. Her smile faltered, but she fueled it to hide her reaction. "Fine. I might start to miss it, if you stop completely."

He nodded, satisfied. "Not to worry. I'm still easily irritated. Now that I know you secretly like it, I can express it more."

"No, no." She waved a hand in between them to deter him. Her fingers grazed the fabric of his shirt, barely missing the accidental touch of his chest. "This is the right spot."

He stole a glance at her, the humor had left him. Maybe her words had resonated within him the same way they had for her. She'd said them to him before.

In a different context, when they'd been naked. When he'd changed the angle of her hips and stroked the right place inside of her.

Her body responded to the memory, zero to a hundred, unbound and without her permission. Heaviness appeared in the bowl of her hips, a buzzing tension that wasn't welcome. Couldn't be welcome.

She frowned and shifted to face the living room. Warmth radiated from the home, her three friends and Liam laughing in a cozy scene. "And I don't secretly like it."

"Sure you don't." His words reached her in a perfect mix of challenge and tease.

She cleared her throat and mustered a cold look up to him. "We should probably go inside."

He held her gaze for a second, two, an infinity, before nodding and pushing away from the railing. They didn't talk as they went back indoors.

Chapter 27

ALEX'S COORDINATION WAS OFF. His attention blurred. "I'm going home."

He drank more than he should have. That, or his doctor's warning that his alcohol tolerance may decrease while on medication had been right.

"I don't think you should drive," Ely said.

Christina and Maggie were going to stay at Liam and Ana's house, and he thought Ely would stay longer, but he was ready to go. He'd been social enough.

He hadn't realized Ely had been paying attention to him, but she evidently had.

"I don't think I should drive," Alex agreed.

Liam frowned at Alex. "Get a cab and come pick up the car tomorrow."

"I'm going to get a cab." Ely peered at him. "We can share."

So she wasn't staying longer. She chose to leave with him. It gave him the first warm fuzzies he'd felt in ages, but that could be the alcohol, too.

Pity he couldn't take her up on her offer. He shook his head, closing his eyes to keep his brain from getting dizzy with the motion. "I have that meeting tomorrow morning— I need my car early."

"Expense the cabs tonight and tomorrow morning," Liam added.

Alex shook his head no. He wasn't sure why he was arguing, and he was sure that if he was confused about not wanting to leave his car in Liam's house, everyone else would be, too. Despite it, no one was fighting him too much. Interesting.

"You won't be hungover tomorrow for the meeting, will you?" Ely said.

Maybe not arguing with him, but still suspicious of him.

He rolled his eyes. "No. I'm not drunk... I just shouldn't drive."

"Can you drive?" Ana asked Ely.

"Yes. I just had a couple glasses of wine a while ago. Lots of water since then, and that coffee."

Ana shifted her eyes between Ely and him. "You could drive Alex home and then take a cab from his place."

"That works for me," Alex said.

Ely gave him an exasperated look. Like the one she'd given him on the balcony outside, when he'd insisted she liked his new brand of grump. "Of course that works for you!"

Alex pressed his lips together not to smile at her indignant comment.

"Flex time in the morning," Ana insisted, mostly to Ely. "That way you get a good night's sleep."

She sighed. "Okay, okay. Fine. All for that team spirit. I'll escort Alex home."

Alex watched her hug her friends one by one. He followed her, shaking hands with Maggie, then Christina. The latter had made an effort to talk to him but had relented when he'd been his grim self and had failed to engage with her in a friendly manner. She was giving him and Ely an odd look now. He didn't know what to make of it, so he said goodbye to Ana and Liam with his usual casual nod, wishing Ana a happy birthday again.

They left the house and reached his car. Alex got into the passenger seat and Ely on the driver's side; he chuckled at Ely's maneuvers to fix the mirrors and move the seat forward.

His head lolled to the side on the headrest. "You're length challenged."

"I'm not!" She adjusted the wheel to lower it. "I'm average height. You're taller than me, that's all."

The corners of his lips went down. "I'd say you're in the twentieth percentile."

"Ugh. Shut up. I'm doing you a favor."

"Right. Thank you," he added as an afterthought.

"Where to?"

He tapped on "Home" on the GPS map on his car's screen. Ely made no comment but he was sure she'd rolled her eyes.

She started driving, checking over her shoulder as they made it outside of Liam's house. "I can't believe that was the first time I've ever heard you chuckle. Teasing me about my height. I'm not even that short."

He smiled, face forward now but still resting his head on the headrest. He closed his eyes. "I'm sure you think that, coming from me, that chuckle counts as a full belly laugh."

She snorted. "Close to."

"You have a great laugh. You're generous with it, too."

She didn't say anything.

"Does it get tiring?" he asked. "Always being in a good mood."

"No. Not for me, anyway." Some time went by. "Though I'm not always in a good mood."

He lifted a heavy shoulder. "I guess. You've fought with me enough. I suppose you're not all rainbows and unicorns."

"And you're discovering that just now?" The sound of the turning indicator filled the car.

"No. I pay close attention to you." He crossed his arms, the need for sleep descending on him. "I'm drawn and... I think I've gotten to know you."

She didn't respond right away. "If you were any other person, I'd be super curious to know your opinion."

He opened his eyes and dropped his head toward her again. "Why would you want to know what others think? What they think isn't necessarily true. Even if it's me, and I'm an accurate people-reader."

She scoffed. He smiled. He liked winding her up. "You're not. And I know that; I'm not asking in an effort to take their answers like they're the results of a standardized personality test. I just like to know because it says something about people, what they think of you. And it's interesting what other people notice, and what they miss."

"But you don't want to know what I think about you."

She could have stolen a peek at him, but she focused on the road. "I like the state of our relationship these days, Sandy... but it's still fragile. Wouldn't want to ruin it before it began, you know?"

He shook his head. "You have such little trust in me."

She said nothing again, but it could have been because she was driving. It was relatively late and there was less traffic, but driving in this city still required focus.

They didn't talk again while on the way to his place. He'd started to doze off; he didn't realize she'd parked his car.

"Are you sure you're not too drunk?" she asked him.

"I'm sure. I'm just mellow."

"Mellow." Humor infiltrated the word.

"You know me."

"Exactly." She scoffed. "Give me your keys. I'll take you to your apartment and make sure you make it okay."

"I won't get lost," he argued, but let her come with him.

She got into his place with him, putting his keys on a side table.

She found his kitchen and rummaged there. He let her; he focused on taking off his jacket and unbuttoning a couple of extra buttons at the top of his shirt.

"Drink this. All of this," she said, appearing next to him and giving him a pint-sized beer glass full of water. "Do you have stomach issues? Ulcers?"

"No." He took the glass from her.

"Then where is your ibuprofen?"

"I don't need it." He drank half of the water in big gulps.

"Preventative measures. If you don't tell me I will look for it myself and— woah."

He hadn't realized he'd closed his eyes, but opened them at her expression. She walked towards the... canvases. All six of them. She was looking at them. Studying them.

He scrunched up his face. "Fuck."

"You're painting again."

"That's too generous for what I'm doing."

"There's a non-zero amount of canvases here with paint on them, Sandy." Her voice was suddenly full of wonder.

"Non-zero?"

"This is amazing." She sighed.

The awe in her words grated against a vulnerable filament of his soul, yet managed somehow to pluck it like a harp and make it vibrate. His breathing picked up.

She walked from one canvas to the next. "This is just the color of my favorite blanket!"

He took two big steps to her, grabbed her forearm with firm fingers, and led her away towards his bathroom— not forceful, but definitely insistent. She followed.

"What are you doing?!" she asked.

"I don't want you looking at my paintings."

"Too late?"

He rolled his eyes, maneuvering her into the bathroom. "Ibuprofen is in the cupboard."

He left her there and, glass in hand, walked to his room right next door.

She found him standing at the foot of his bed after a minute. "Here. Take this." She scanned his room while he popped the pills in his mouth and drained the glass. "Somehow it makes me glad to see you didn't make your bed."

"Never bother, unless someone's coming and, well... I wasn't planning on having someone come evaluate my place tonight."

He could see her raised eyebrow and scowl from where he stood. She did a three-sixty from her spot, assessing his bedroom. When she faced him again, her eyes zeroed in on him. "Your room is... plain. Very."

"I haven't gone to the trouble of decorating. I wasn't looking to make my space special and haven't cared to, either."

She gave him a long, contemplative look. "Why not? You're not still planning to leave, are you?"

"No, no, not that." He leaned back on the beige wall in front of his bed and crossed one ankle over the other. He put the empty glass on top of the dresser to his side, and put his hands in his pockets. He shrugged. "Just... disinterest."

She stepped closer to him, peering into his eyes, like she wanted to study any and all signs he gave her. "But your paintings— what I could see of them— there was color and abstract movement and... use of the canvas—"

He moved his head to one side, then the other, in the smallest shake possible. His eyes never left Ely. "That's just practice. I've never been one for abstract art. That's my mom. I'm a more realistic artist."

Her face softened, awe back in her eyes. "So you did those paintings in Liam and Ana's house?"

He nodded. She took a step closer to him; placed a hand on his arm in a warm, reassuring gesture. He straightened up.

"Wow," she said. "You really are talented."

He stared at her, unmoving. His heart made itself known, drumming against his ribcage.

"What happened?" she asked.

He continued to stare at her, time elongating, his heart in his throat trying to run away from him, until he shook his head once again; left, right, center.

"Don't want to tell me?" Her voice had lowered to a whisper. If Alex was not mistaken, there was a hint of hurt in her voice. He didn't like it.

"I can't. I'm still figuring it out," he rasped. "Don't have all the words for it, yet."

"If you knew, would you tell me?"

They wondered at each other. She gazed at him with clear, open eyes. She didn't smile, yet her face remained patient.

Something anchored behind his navel, hooking itself into his guts like it never planned to leave.

"I think I would now. Yes."

The admission cost him less than he would have wagered, and her resulting smile balanced the scales.

Her eyes shone. "I'm glad to hear that. We had a rough start but maybe we can take this a step forward. Not just an armistice, but friends. I think we're becoming friends, finally."

He arched an eyebrow, his heart gone from him. "Is that what's happening?"

The slant of her grin turned cheeky. "Of course."

"Friends who've had sex. Who used to fight."

Her grin faltered. If he wasn't mistaken, a soft blush made its way beneath the gold of her tawny skin. Barely visible, but he was looking closely.

She gulped. "Is this your way to tell me you're not interested in friendship?"

The anchor in his belly twisted and dropped, pulling down on him and wrecking his defenses. He buzzed from the exposure of their conversation, a swarm in his brain.

He lifted a hand to caress her face. He ran his thumb over the arch of her eyebrow. Her lips parted at the gesture.

Ely's eyes opened wide and a faint gasp broke free from her. He lifted his other hand to echo the movement and hold her face, but her eyes became heavy with sadness.

"Don't," she said.

He dropped his hands. Her lips pressed together, tight.

His eyes jumped between hers. "Holding back words isn't a look I know on you." The words had come out hoarse; his throat had tightened up.

She shook her head, silent.

She turned away and left the room. He sat on his bed, elbows on his knees and head in his hands, and waited for the front door to announce her departure. It took all of five minutes, but it finally closed behind Ely as she left him to ponder what the hell had just happened.

Chapter 28

"HI, CHARLES." ALEX SAT on the couch in his therapist's office, a metal travel mug full of coffee in his hands.

"Hello, Alex. What's been on your mind today?"

"A few things. Where should I start?"

Charles adjusted his glasses. "Doesn't matter to me. Anything that appears louder than the rest?"

Elena had been present in his mind more than anything else, but he didn't want to start there. He needed to build up to it.

"I had a couple of drinks a few nights ago and they affected me more than I thought. You said that could happen, right?" He drank from his decaf dark roast. He'd decided to eliminate any influences on his nervous system for this conversation.

"Yes, we talked about how that might happen. Can you tell me a bit more?"

"What I said." Alex shrugged. "I drank a bit more than two cocktails and it affected my coordination. I decided not to drive home, just in case... but I wanted to check in with you about it."

"Yes, antidepressants can do that sometimes. Try not to drink but if you do, track what happens. We'll monitor and see, and I'll consult with your doctor if we need to. Thanks for telling me."

Alex nodded. "It also made me feel relaxed."

"Right. In a good way?"

"Yeah, it felt good. Unfamiliar."

Charles had the decency to try to hide his smile. "I see. Definitely talk about that with your doctor, but let's work with it. What did *relaxed* feel like?"

"Like I didn't have to rush. Like I could just go with the flow more." He frowned. "Like when I used to paint."

"Oh, that's great!"

"How do I go back to it? Without the aid of alcohol, that is." Alex shook his foot across his knee and stared out the window at the building across from them.

"We're in the process of doing it," Charles said, taking notes on his pad. "Helping you rewire your brain back to what it used to be like, when you could relax and go with the flow. When you had trust in yourself, and in your life."

"Depression being a bad view of myself, the world, and the future." The warmth of the coffee didn't make it through the metal of his mug; its surface remained cold.

"In general, yes. For you, it may be that the past few years distorted how you thought of yourself and the world, and it showed up as irritation. Then that irritation made you more likely to withdraw and get defensive. Like it can happen for people sometimes, especially if they've been socialized as men.

That's what we appear to have figured out. Does it still seem accurate?"

Alex nodded but gave Charles a cheeky high eyebrow. "To summarize."

"Yes, that's the abbreviated version," Charles laughed.

"Skipping over a few facts." Alex went as far as to chuckle.

"Alex, you're joking."

He scoffed, this time, but it still carried humor. "I'm sure you'll note that as a sign of progress."

"You're correct." He made a show of writing that down on his legal pad. "But let's talk about your future."

"What about the other things on my mind?"

"That's the thing. What you think and feel today tells you something about your future."

"How?" He stared out of the window again. He could barely make out what happened in any of the offices in the building in front of them.

"It helps you figure out what you want." Charles reached for his glass on the coffee table and drank some of his water.

Alex didn't touch his water, happy with his coffee. "Wait. You're not implying that my future will be good if I get what I want."

"No, no. Your perspective of the future will be better if you believe you can get what you want, if you work for it and the context works with you in it."

"The two sides of the coin. What I do and what the world does."

"That's right. So, what do you think about? What do you want?"

Elena.

Alex looked down to his lap. "I think a lot about people."

"That makes sense. It means relationships matter to you. We've been talking about investing in relationships, too."

"So if I'm thinking about people, it means I want them in my life?"

Thinking, he'd said, like the single, simple word could encapsulate the depth of feeling surrounding the many ways in which Elena lived within him.

"Not quite— that's oversimplifying it," Charles continued. "It does mean that there's something about your interactions with that person that shows you something you want."

He knew he wanted, he knew he felt, he knew he thought— his whole self engaged when contemplating the issue of his colleague. His... friend. Whatever Elena was to him. "The question, then, is what do I want when I'm thinking of someone."

"Yes. That's the question."

"What if I want something the other person doesn't?"

Putting the question into words chilled the back of his neck, the cold of it dripping down his back bone. It lit up something inside of him, as if to fight the ice with fire.

"Well, that'd be a problem, wouldn't it?"

Chapter 29

ELY HAD DONE A great job at one thing and one thing only since Ana's birthday: avoiding Sandy.

For the past seven business days, she'd crossed paths with Alex in the office a few times. She'd used each time as an opportunity to evaluate his mood; each time, he'd nodded at her casually, no pressure or frown. She'd decided he'd simply been more drunk than he'd let on, and it had been the alcohol that had fueled his out-of-character moment with her. Maybe he didn't even remember looking at her with fiery hazel eyes, or caressing her face as if he were just about to break and kiss her.

Anyway, better to try to forget about it. Every time she caught herself remembering the moment, her gut twisted when she acknowledged she might not have had enough sense to stop him, if he had tried to kiss her. The only solution was to tie the new realization to something heavy and throw it into deep waters, and move on.

She mostly managed to. That night, Ely worked late without a care about Sandy, focusing instead on her call with Clarissa. The student continued to have problems with the producer she shadowed for her placement, and Ely coached her through the problems as best as she could.

"Thanks for telling me, Clarissa. Do you feel you have what you need? A good plan?" A knock on her door disrupted their goodbye. Ely ignored it for a second. "Let's do that, then. Call me again tomorrow if you need to, okay? I'll talk to Johnson tomorrow and try to get him in line. Gotta go now."

She placed the headset on its cradle and called the person in. "Yes? Come in."

The door pushed inward and Alex appeared through the opening. Not surprising; at this time in the evening, most people would have left.

He leaned on the doorjamb, hands in his pockets. "Celeste left a while ago. Will you be done any time soon?"

"Yep. Just need to write a few quick notes about my call with Clarissa. Swear we won't work with that producer again? The poor girl is having a hard time."

He nodded. "He's still giving her trouble, then."

"He's using her as an assistant. That's thoroughly different from shadowing a producer."

"What a jackass. We don't need him. We won't work with him again if he doesn't change things with Clarissa. Do you want me to call him tomorrow?"

"I can handle it." Her face hardened and she bit the inside of her cheeks to counteract it.

"Relax, Elena." His eyes remained fixed on her. "It wasn't a dig at your ability. It was me trying to help. Join forces. Show a united front."

There was a time where she would have laughed, had anyone told her Alex would say all of those words together in a sentence. Presently, she bristled. "Also he might listen better if a man is telling him to chill."

"If he does, it just goes to show just how much of a jerk he really is. Misogyny is kind of outdated." He cocked his head to the side.

"What about it being mixed with a healthy dose of racism? I'm brown, Clarissa is black. You're white."

"Right. If you do want me to call him, I'll make sure to bring that into the conversation."

"Safer for you."

"Yeah."

They stared at each other. He waited for her decision with a slightly raised eyebrow; she considered while clicking her nails on her desk and rocking on her chair from side to side.

"Okay, yeah, call him," she decided. "It shouldn't be necessary to join forces in the first place, but it might help. I'll tell Clarissa."

He nodded. She began organizing her desk to close shop for the night, and tried not to show surprise when he sat down on one of the chairs across from her.

"Good," he said. "Do you want to have dinner? It's late. We could order in and eat it here."

She leaned back in her chair and crossed her arms under her breasts. She went back to rocking in her chair. "Casual dinner at our desks, after work?"

"We could also sit on the sofa over there instead. It has a nice view of the city—"

"Don't get smart with me. You want to have dinner together now?"

He squinted. "Why do you have to sound so suspicious all the time?"

A siren came close and ran past their street, its noise echoing among the buildings.

Ely flattened her hand on the cool surface of her desk. "Because for the longest time, you kept people at a distance by barking one-word answers."

"Barking?" His lip curled in a reluctant smile. "I thought it was growling."

She shrugged. "Barking, growling, potato, tomato."

"That's not how the saying goes." The glint in his eyes intensified. "And I thought I was doing better."

"Totally, but I guess I'm still waiting to see if it sticks."

The corner of his lips pulled down in a dismissive gesture. He leaned back on his chair, elbows on the armrests and hands steepled. "I'm pretty sure it'll stick."

"How come?" She couldn't help her curiosity, the words leaving her lips without much notice.

"It's an unintended consequence of work I've been doing in other areas of my life."

Ely kept a wall clock for aesthetic purposes nearby; she heard its tick tock in the seconds that passed. "Well, if you're going to leave me hanging..."

"Yes to dinner? No to dinner?"

She laughed, eyes to the ceiling. "Are you really holding the conversation hostage?"

He smiled. She blinked twice at the view; she was still caught by surprise every time he grinned in front of her. It punched her right in the diaphragm, seizing her lungs each time.

"Okay, let's order something." Ely ignored the upheaval that her concession brought into her chest. "You'll have to tell me more about this *work in areas of your life*, though. It's the price to pay for my excellent company."

"Deal."

He got his phone out and they ordered food while she took a few notes about her call with Clarissa. While they waited, she made tea for them— she wouldn't risk him getting *mellow* again. When she came back to her office, she found him waiting for her already, sitting on the sofa.

"Thanks." He took the offered mug and she found a comfortable position.

"So. You were saying?" She sipped some of her peppermint drink.

He left his drink on a small side table she had placed there for precisely that function. "You've said a few times that you think I'm grumpy. That much is true."

She half-rolled her eyes. Talk about an understatement. "It was never a question."

"But I'm also coming out of a depression. I've been in therapy almost since I moved to LA, and on medication as well. I suppose it's been helping."

She opened her eyes wide, realization clicking into place in stages. A hundred pieces of a domino train falling in a chain reaction. "Oh."

He watched her process his statement, and she did her best to hide any reaction she might show on her face beyond what she'd already given him.

"That's it?" he asked. "That's all you're going to say?"

"Well, can I ask more?"

"You can ask more. If I don't want to answer, I'll bark." One of his arms landed on the back of the sofa, and he circled the fabric of the couch with the tip of his forefinger.

She tore her eyes away from his hand and gazed at him instead. "It's a lot of information to process."

"What, that I said I've been depressed? My therapist assures me most people will go through it at some point in their lives." He folded a long leg on the sofa so he faced her a bit more directly. His arm opened wide to reach the warm mug; he sipped from it and rested it on his bent knee.

"Yes, of course. I guess— I never thought that could be happening." Mint taste coated her mouth, and she inhaled the drink's scent in a long, deep breath.

The way he rubbed the couch's surface in circles hypnotized her.

"In the past I would have heard that and believed it was proof of how little you thought of me, or your ignorance, or something else altogether, but likely negative."

It was getting late, and yet Ely could still see several offices with lights on in the building next to them. Not much of her sight out the window was occupied by them, a bunch of shorter constructions lived nearby, giving her a nice look at the city, full of sparkling lights.

She crossed her legs in such an angle that she half-faced him on the sofa, and studied Alex. "But it would be fair, wouldn't it? To think negatively of some of my statements. For a while I didn't think very highly of you. You know I was attracted to you when I met you—" at least half of her brain screamed at her for bringing that up, but this conversation mattered, so honesty mattered— "but I also thought you were a bit of a douche. And I was ignorant. I still am. I don't know how much of being somewhat of an ass had to do with depression and how much to do with a personality trait. I do know... I think you've changed."

"The way Charles— my therapist— explained, the depression likely exaggerated my least favorable traits."

"But they're still your traits."

"I'd say *I'm afraid so*, but I don't mind them too much."

She looked out the window and spied into the offices still alight in the nearby building, tracking the few people she could see in them. A cannonball had lodged itself at the base of her breastbone and she wasn't sure why it had appeared there, but it came with a memory that guided her to the answer.

"I asked you once," she said, speaking as she stitched her thoughts together, not fully sure what connections she was making, "if there was something going on to explain why you were the way you were. I guess there was something... and I don't feel very good about any of it. My question, my assumption, my need to blame it on something."

"I suppose you were confused. You had a hard time believing I was who I was."

"But you weren't who you were back then, either. Right? You're you now, but back then you had been going through a rough patch, and lived with depression."

He cocked his head. "You think we're ourselves and a mental health illness is... like a virus? Something that makes us sick?"

"Well, if you fracture your femur you're not the fracture. Though maybe a lot of mental health diagnoses are just labels we use for normal human diversity. I don't think it's as clear an answer... or maybe I just need to educate myself more."

She gazed at him again. A deep wrinkle lined his eyebrows and he ran his fingers up and down his mug, as if caressing it.

"I think for me it was a fracture," he said.

She nodded and they sat in silence for a minute or two. Had they ever been able to sit like this, quietly keeping each other company?

She shook her head. "Do you like your therapist?"

"Yeah, he's good." He sipped more of his tea. "He's funny. He's also pushy which I wasn't so sure about at first, but I think it's working. Turns out I respond well to someone insisting on things, if they give me enough room to process."

"That sounds amazing. What kind of things has he pushed you to try?"

"To make terrible paintings. To just dip the brush in paint and place it on the canvas, no other expectations." He seemed to hold the ghost of a brush in his hand, which he slid across the air as if painting on an imaginary canvas.

"Wow. That's why there were so many in your apartment."

"Yeah, I've been doing what he suggested. Right now, we think that I couldn't paint because I was so fucking spent from my previous job, from forcing myself to excel at something I didn't care about, that I had nothing left to invest in my own happiness. But I got stuck there and suddenly I had a horrible perspective about everything. Of my place in this world. Of the future. I would never get what I wanted, so why want? Why be creative?" He sighed. "Only that not doing those things that made me happy was also part of what took me down."

"Right. A bad pattern and a terrible job. Burnout that took you down into the pits."

"Yep. Not everyone who's depressed will feel the same or get there the same way, but it's what it was for me. So Charles forced me to pay attention to what I want and invest in it. It's a double-edged sword, but it's working."

She glanced at the clock on the wall; their food would arrive soon. But she was in no rush, the conversation fit well with her. For once.

"So how's the medication working? My mom has been on anti-anxiety meds for years."

He shrugged and brought his mug to his lips; this time, he rested it on the back of the sofa, holding it with a finger looped around its handle. "It's working. Though it has its disadvantages, like having a lower alcohol tolerance. I noticed you gave me tea, Elena."

She faked innocence. "What? Tea is delicious. Be thankful I made us a warm beverage."

He arched an eyebrow but Ely was saved from answering by the call from reception announcing their food was there.

Soon they had set up to eat and, after swallowing her first bite, continued casually chatting with Alex.

"You've never been this open before, Sandy."

"Well, apparently, close relationships are important. It's not about quantity but quality, don't know if you've heard that saying before?" He rolled his eyes. "Charles said that I don't have to fundamentally change myself to have the things that I want. I can be a grump to most people. For the people I'm closer to I can be a bit less so... for people I care about, I can make more of an effort. The right people will want me around even if I'm not the standard charismatic nice guy."

"So this is you making an effort?"

He scowled. She laughed. They ate in silence for several bites.

Alex moved his food around with his fork, eyes down on the plate. "I didn't want to go home and eat alone, and I thought you and I could take this amicable working relationship to the next level. Was I wrong in trying?"

She gulped and studied him across from her. "No. Of course not."

"Besides, I'm on a quest to find something Charles was wrong about. He told me a while ago that he thought you and I could have a nice relationship if we only changed the way we talked to each other, so, yeah." He looked up at her, with a sassy slant to his lips. "We'll see."

"Hey!" Her fork made a *clank* against her plate when she dropped it with mild indignation. "I'm not an experiment to prove your therapist wrong!"

He laughed.

It was a rare thing. This was him with a belly laugh, eyes crinkled at the corners and all, and it had the power to part heavy rain clouds with a brilliant ray of sunshine on its coattails. Her heart missed a beat and restarted at double its normal pace.

"Okay, okay. I also like you a bit more nowadays." He wasn't laughing anymore, but a soft, one-sided smile still clang to his lips.

She sat immobile, her body surrendering to him, to the high speed impact of his laugh. He gave her an extra long look, just long enough that it changed. His one-sided smile turned into a confused slant, then into a knowing smirk. Like he'd read her thoughts or had detected the race her heart ran in her chest, somehow.

She cast her eyes down to her plate, taking on his lesson in playing with her food. She breathed in, out, begging her heart to calm the fuck down.

It was amazing what time and effort could do to a rocky relationship. When she met Alex, she would have mocked anyone who suggested that they could be sitting so comfortably with each other. Chatting with him now, peaceful enough that she could drop her defenses and let him in a tiny bit closer—not having to tease him, and smile, and exaggerate her affable personality to keep the moment pleasant, like she so often did with anyone not in her inner circle, but enjoying a sort of homely warmth between them instead, because it was natural and authentic—well, she was forced to admit she liked him. As he was.

She had to take another long, deep breath to come back to her senses. She liked him, sure, as someone who could become a friend. One day, maybe. Right now, they were still just coworkers, and they had too messy of a past.

Sure, they'd been attracted to each other once upon a time, but they had also exploded in each other's presence like a poorly balanced chemical reaction.

She brought the conversation back to work, to the parties coming up the following week. Maybe it was better that way. Taking a break from true connection.

Done and done, Ely. Done.

Chapter 30

TWO PARTIES IN ONE week, and only one hour into the first one, Alex worried he'd end up over-stretching himself. Despite the garland lights adorning the hall, the swaths of shimmery fabric hanging on the walls, and planters full of vibrant greenery and flowers, his artistic eye wasn't interested in the overall success of the décor. There were too many people around to lose himself in his aesthetic sensibilities, and his business colleague looked far too enticing for him to be truly interested in anything, or anyone else.

Elena wore a gold, silk-like dress. It hugged her every curve and Alex couldn't seem to stop staring at her body. He told himself he was studying its shape for artistic reference; how the light reflected on the fabric draping her waist and hips. How the light caught around the dip of her navel, on the curve of her belly. Or at least, that's what he'd say if she called him out on it.

Or, maybe he'd go ahead and tell her the truth. See where that took them.

She stood in front of him, an arm's length away, and turned to wave at someone nearby. She glanced back to talk to Alex over her shoulder, without fully gazing at him. "You know, we'd probably be more successful if we didn't spend the whole night together. You always stay with me."

He stepped in closer to her. To talk to her without other people overhearing, of course. "I can't be left alone in a place like this. I need your charm to obscure my growling."

"You say such pretty things." She looked at him this time, still over her shoulder, batting her long eyelashes.

He leaned in even further. "I thought I said I have an unfriendly vibe."

"Yes, you did, but you also said you need my charm. Anyway— we need to work on your networking skills; be more strategic. Especially at that big party on Friday. We can come up with something, especially since Liam and Ana will be there, too. That is, if you're willing to perform a bit."

"Perform."

"Yeah. Like you're more sociable than you are."

He rolled his eyes and she chuckled, before turning to the person approaching them. "That's not in my job description," he mumbled, but didn't know if she heard him.

He stayed in his place right behind her.

"Hi, William! It's good to see you again." She kissed him, once on each cheek. "Have you met Alex McMillan yet? He's our operations manager."

Alex shook the man's hand, barely moving out of his position to stand slightly to her side but just as close. William gave him an odd look.

"A pleasure, I'm sure," William said. He seemed like a sleek man. About Alex's height, with blue eyes and dark hair and a charcoal suit, his hair was combed back in what would look out of style for many people. On him, perhaps it worked.

Alex nodded but said nothing. He studied Elena's reaction to William instead.

"Don't mind him," she said to William. "Alex is a serious guy. Numbers man, if you know what I mean."

William laughed good-naturedly and proceeded to completely ignore Alex. "I knew it would work in my favor to come tonight. I hoped I'd see you."

"You did?" Her eyes fully engaged with William, shiny and alert... but that was standard for her. She tended to give people her full attention.

"Yes. Your presence has made these parties so much more bearable."

She laughed. Alex's nostrils flared. Getting Elena's full attention made one feel things, so he got why William wanted to flirt with her but... no. Not okay. He hated every second of having to witness someone else courting Elena. For reasons. Reasons he'd have to work through in therapy.

"You flatterer," she said. "And here I thought you were going to offer an internship for my program."

William's smile overflowed with slime. "Of course, that's already in motion. But perhaps we should discuss the details sometime? Over a meal, to make it more... amenable."

Alex dropped his head to stare at the ground and hide his eye roll. The new field of vision drew his eyes to the way Elena's fingers traced patterns on her belly, shifting the fabric of her dress back and forth slightly, creating ripples of movement down to the floor... and through the floor up his legs and into his gut.

"We absolutely should talk more about it." Her voice remained friendly and open. "I'll call you from my office tomorrow and set something up with your assistant."

"I could give you my number, if you want."

Fuck. There it was. Unmistakable. He gazed up and stared at William— who continued to ignore Alex— and gave him the blandest look he could muster.

If Ely accepted William's advances it would be one thing, but, seriously. The guy had gall.

"Your direct number at your office? It's fine." Ely shook her head, her wonderful smile still in place. "I'm sure it'll be easier to coordinate with your assistant for a work lunch."

Whoop, there she was. That told Alex— and William, if the man had any working brain parts— enough. Relief coasted through Alex's chest.

"That way Celeste— our assistant—" Alex said, surprising himself— "she can check both our schedules at the same time as well. We can avoid playing phone tag."

Ely stole a glance, her eyes falling to Alex's lips almost as if by accident, but didn't linger. She turned to William again. She opened her mouth to speak, but William beat her to it.

"What's your role with Ely's side of the company, then?" William gave Alex a good look for the first time. "I imagine you'd spend more time glued to a spreadsheet than at a party like this... or at a work lunch."

William had gotten suspicious of Alex inviting himself, it seemed. Alex liked that, even if he had no right to it.

"I force him to come to the parties," Ely said.

But Alex didn't feel like letting William think that was all there was to it. "We do make an effort to be involved in each other's side of the business. Work as a team. We designed a big part of the youth internship program together and pretty much work in tandem. It's a good thing that I come to parties... and work lunches."

William arched an eyebrow and sipped from his drink. "So, very involved."

Alex nodded and held the man's gaze. "There's a reason why our program participants call us Mom and Dad behind our backs."

Ely laughed. Alex allowed himself to smile, in part because she liked it, in part because of how it seemed to bug William.

"They don't really think of us that way. That was just copy for a social media post." A pause. Ely turned to Alex to give him her full attention, her eyes bright. "Right?"

This time Alex's smile was genuine. He ignored William and stepped closer to Ely; he took her glass from her hands.

"Do you want more?" he said for her only, though if William overheard, Alex wouldn't be too upset. She nodded and bit her lip. "I'll get you some more."

He kept the smile, knowing there was a hint of territorialism to it, when he nodded at William in goodbye.

Alex had decided not to drink at work parties until he re-learned his tolerance levels, talked to his doctor, or went off medication. A secondary benefit was that he could drive and have that kind of freedom.

It also helped that Ely had asked him to drive her home, upon learning he'd driven to the party.

She remained quiet as she climbed into his car.

"You okay?" he asked, turning in between the two seats to throw and arrange his suit jacket on the back seat.

He took a deep breath when her perfume reached him, now that they were close like this.

"Yeah." She leaned away to make room for him. He frowned. "Just thinking."

"You can think out loud if you want." He finished with his jacket. He returned to his seat and handled the seat belt.

She dropped her head on the headrest to gaze at him, a look of concentration on her face. She hooked a thumb on the long band of her seatbelt; after a quick study, it seemed it was because she needed it to keep the contraption in place between her breasts.

"Do you need to adjust the seatbelt?"

She shook her head. "I checked. It's already as close as I could get it to fitting. I'm used to it."

He frowned. That would not do.

"It's fine, Sandy. Let's go."

He didn't fight her. He turned the car on, drove out of the parking lot, and took the road to Ely's place.

They reached the first red light. In the quiet space between them, thoughts of William and dating and Ely occupied his mind.

"I never asked…" he hesitated. A question pushed at the edge of his conscience, seeking answers he didn't have a right to. Yet the need to hear her answer won, despite his scruples. He continued in as friendly a tone as he could manage. "What happened with the guy from the office building? Haven't heard about him since we came across him at the restaurant."

She stared at Alex for a couple of seconds. "What's that to you? It was weeks ago, Sandy. Why does it matter?"

Alex shrugged. "The way William flirted with you made me think of it. You skillfully turned him down, but there are plenty of assholes out there who wouldn't get it and leave you alone." He cleared his throat. "Max seemed shifty when we met him that time. But maybe you're dating, and I'm just out of practice reading situations accurately."

And maybe he needed to know if she was seeing someone, and was grasping at straws trying to get an answer from her. Because his reaction to the idea of Elena dating anyone heated his blood to a slow boil, and he didn't know what to do about it.

"What's gotten into you today?" He could see her squirming from the corner of his eye. "The way you talked to William— how you looked at me— you got me a new drink, for heaven's sake. You were *weird*."

The light turned green and Alex pressed the pedal. "Look, if you don't want to answer about Max—"

She crossed her arms. Another solution to keeping the seat belt in place, he supposed. "I don't want to answer anything about Max—"

"Why is that?" He didn't mean to challenge her so directly on this, but he couldn't help it. It was definitely a real part of him. "Is it because it's none of my business, or because of something else?"

She stared at him with lowered eyebrows. "Didn't go out with him again. Fine guy. No spark. Nothing happened."

"Okay." It seemed that answering why she didn't want to talk about it was worse than telling him there was nothing going on between her and Max. She wouldn't have avoided the question, otherwise. Interesting.

"Now you."

"Now me, what?"

"Answer my question."

He stole another glance at her. "Which question? You haven't asked anything."

"God, seriously, Sandy. Sometimes I feel like I have to archi-tect a conversation with you. What was up with you tonight?"

He shook his head and brought the car to a stop again. "Nothing was up."

"You got me. A drink."

His eyes latched on the red light a few cars ahead. He tapped his fingers on the wheel. "If me bringing you a drink is a sign of the end of times, then I've been doing a very poor job at investing in our relationship."

Silence filled the car as the light turned green and he continued on the road.

"Our working relationship." Ely's tone had turned monotone. "And our relationship out of work— because of Ana and Liam."

"Yes." He nodded once. "That's what our relationship is nowadays."

"Not nowadays— that's what it *is*." Energy returned to her voice. "We only have a relationship because of them. Even our working relationship is only because of them."

It drew zeal out of him. "We're going a bit further than that, I think."

"What does that mean?"

"It means that I think we've gone far."

"Have we, really? If one of us stopped working at Jump Cannon, I don't know that we'd stay in touch. We were so bad. So bad. Except for that— that *blip* in the beginning, Sandy—"

"You should call me by my name when we're talking about us."

She gasped. The words he'd growled at her still vibrated in his vocal cords, the need of them still reverberated.

He held onto the wheel, determined. It grinded on him, that she called it a *blip*. That she called him by a nickname in the same sentence.

She hadn't responded, so he helped her. Pushed her. In for a pound, and all that.

He repeated and corrected for her, "Except for that... blip... in the beginning, *Alex*."

"I'm sorry." Her tone seemed radically different, multiple frequencies all melding into one— awe, shock, nerves. "I didn't realize it still bothered you... Alex."

He pressed his lips together, hands still tight on the wheel. "Most of the time it's fine. For this..."

"It's different?"

He nodded. "I don't like that you think we'd lose touch. I wouldn't want that."

The air in the car changed, heavy now with the words they said, and what was camouflaged among them.

It took her a moment to reply. "I don't know that we have enough to stand on its own. We fought too much. We're not friends."

"Have you wondered why, Ely?"

He parked his car outside her building, and turned to stare at her.

She had doe eyes, dark and open wide as she stared back. "What do you mean?"

"How it was in the beginning isn't what it's like now. Or what it could be. I'd like to think I'm putting in the work."

Her head traveled side to side in a long, slow negation of his offer. Her shoulders seemed to pull into her, tension clear in them.

She took her eyes away from him. With jerky movements, she grabbed her small bag and wrapped a scarf around her shoulders.

"I don't think we can be more than this, Sa— Alex. In a couple of years, maybe we'll have forgotten everything and we'll become friends. But not today."

"I see."

She unlocked her door and opened it. "It's late. I'll see you for our meeting with the youth tomorrow."

He shook his head but let her go. He stayed there and watched her get into her building. He didn't go right away but, when he finally did, he thought the whole way home about her not answering his question.

Did she wonder why they weren't friends?

Chapter 31

ELY STOOD BY THE mirror in Ana's bedroom, straightening her hair and watching Ana being done up by Jonah, Liam's make up artist. Ely's best friend had asked that they get ready together and bribed her with Jonah's skills; he currently painted Ana's lips. For Ely, Jonah had focused on her eyes with a killer smokey effect. Ely agreed with the decision. She looked hot, if she said so herself.

The cerulean dress she wore had a light metallic sheen to it, the fabric textured and glittery in the most deliciously delicate way. Its tight fit hugged her body all the way down to her mid-thigh, the perfect length to showcase her legs. The dress was designed to draw the eyes to them, with a deep V pointing in the right direction. To balance out the sexiness factor, the dress sported long sleeves.

Attending one of the biggest industry parties of the season called for extra effort in one's looks for the night. Ely would never admit it, but she held a mix of nerves and excitement in her stomach at the night's prospects.

The flat iron left silky hair down its path. After a final pass, Ely fluffed her hair. "If this weren't LA and everyone looked awesome all the time, I would think we're the most beautiful people in town tonight."

Ana laughed. "I love you, Ely. Never change."

A knock sounded on the door, quickly followed by Liam. He entered the room, all pinstripe suit, light purple shirt, and open top buttons. He wore his hair curly, and was clean shaven.

"Well, that's a look," Ely said, shaking her head from side to side to feel her hair move around her shoulders, her eyes tracking Liam in the mirror.

He smiled and threw a high eyebrow her way. "If you mean that in a good way, then I can say— you too. You look great."

She straightened her arms in a big, flirty flair by the side of her body, and cocked her hips to the side. "Thank you. I also love that your shirt matches Ana's dress."

Ana barely moved, not to interrupt Jonah's work. "We've gotten into this habit now where we tend to match, and today it's all in the service of his eyes. Oh, if you'd asked me two years ago where I'd be..."

"You're done, lovely." Jonah took a step back to admire his handiwork.

Ana came to the mirror to check the finished results; Ely stepped to the side to make room for her. Ana's dress, a deep purple versus the lighter color of Liam's shirt, had a structured top; v-neck and thin straps on her shoulders, with geometric boning. The skirt consisted of several layers of tulle that dropped loose to just below her knees, letting through a clear-enough view of dark, short shorts, and her long legs.

Ely took a few extra steps away when Liam came to stand behind Ana. The way he looked at her in the mirror's reflection was so intense, so full of affection and lust and possession, Ely had to look away. She pretended to get busy putting away the straightener, ignoring the way he bent down to kiss Ana's shoulder.

Surprising, the flickering in her heart. Ely would have never guessed it of herself, but it seemed there was something confusing, attractive, even powerful about that kind of intensity in someone's eyes. She'd never gotten to experience it and wasn't sure what it would feel like, but a part of her craved being on the receiving end of a look like that.

Whatever spell they'd been under, it had broken.

"We should go," Liam said. "Alex is waiting outside."

Ely went out first, happy to give them some privacy without her in the room. She was still thinking about that look she had witnessed between Liam and Ana when she spotted Alex.

He sat on the back of the sofa, one ankle over the other, hands in his pocket. He took note of her in great detail, his eyes roaming up and down her body. He stood, giving her an opportunity to check him out in the same manner. He wore a blue suit, with a lighter blue shirt underneath his blazer without a tie; his top button was undone. He looked casual and stylish, a step up from his normal office attire, and Ely's steps faltered. Her eyes locked with his and she full-stopped in her tracks. There was something *important* in the way he looked at her. Her heart hammered against her chest, and maybe she had to go to the doctor, because she was pretty sure she'd developed a sudden case of vertigo.

"Look! So funny," Ana said as she walked past Ely. "You guys are matching, too."

Did his eyes become brighter? Did he get taller? Was this suit made to highlight every part of him that was hot and attractive? Every warm blooded woman she knew could appreciate an attractive person in a well-made suit, but the way her blood resembled molten lava right now? That implied an attractive man in a well-made suit was her new kink, and developing such an interest in Alex was... dangerous. She needed rescuing, stat.

"Car's waiting," Liam said. "We're ready."

He held Ana's hand and waited for Alex and Ely to make their way out of the house. Ely came close to Alex as they reached the door; being close to him, she could smell his cologne. Her knees weakened. Something was wrong with her. She really needed to go to the doctor.

Without saying a word to each other, they got out of the house and into the car, sitting side by side, each of them looking out of their window.

———

Life had changed radically for Alex McMillan over the past several months. The second party he and Elena attended that week filled a grand patio with people in expensive clothes and glittery jewelry, most of them likely branded by big fashion labels. A mansion served as the backdrop, with white, large walls that some millionaire actor of the old Hollywood days inhabited, once upon a time. Guests milled about on the large terrace, flanked by large trees and overlooking a manicured garden. More industry people moved down the grand staircase, and chatted around the reflective pool in the middle of the field below.

Alex shook his head at himself. While the social gathering a couple of days before had been a casual, small cocktail party for those interested to learn of new projects that could be produced, tonight's affair was at another level altogether. He hadn't bothered checking the guest list, but he thought there were about five hundred people at this party and, if he was not mistaken, there were several other actors and actresses that were as well known as his brother was. He didn't think he knew any of their names, though.

"Look," Ely said to his side. "I think that's Julia Hunter. Wow."

He looked at the actress' face and, yeah, she looked familiar. "I think I know her."

Ely turned to him in a move full of speed and sass. "You *think* you know her? God, Sandy. She's only the best paid actress in Hollywood, and she's an Oscar away from being an EGOT winner."

He lowered his head to whisper in her ear; he pretended it had to do with making sure she could hear him through the ambient noise. "I only know what that means because of this job."

He remained close to her. She lifted her eyes to him. The glass pressed against her lips as she sipped from it, indenting the soft flesh in an inviting mix of light and shadow.

"Not because of your brother?" She turned away to study the hundreds of people milling about. "A lot of people think he should have been nominated for something already."

He gazed at her profile, her dark eyes, the change to the curve of her hair, now that she'd straightened it. He dropped his survey of Ely lower, to the point where her dress ended and her skin began. The cut was low, he could see a bit of the side of her breast. Not close enough to that blessed birthmark, though.

He looked back up to the tip of her nose. "I don't keep track of what people write about Liam."

"I never used to, not the way I do now. Since Ana met him... things have changed." She sighed. "So much."

He took a deep breath, packing his chest full of her perfume and the hint of alcohol wafting from her glass. "Things have changed over the past few months. The past few weeks, especially. Do you—"

"Hello!"

Surprised by the interruption, he looked up from Ely to find William.

"Hello!" Ely replied, kissing William once on each cheek again. "Lovely to see you."

"You, too." He offered his hand to Alex. "I haven't checked my work calendar. Are we still planning to meet for lunch, the three of us?"

Alex shook his hand and nodded. "I believe Celeste mentioned she found a time."

"Excellent. Are you here with anybody?" William asked them both.

"Yes." Ely's smile was rich and enchanting. "We're here with Liam McMillan and Ana Lira; we're their guests."

"I see." William inspected how close Alex stood to Ely. "And are you here together to party, or for work?"

Alex wasn't going to attempt answering that. He stared at Ely and let her navigate the moment.

"We're here for work." A sudden tension line appeared on the curve of her shoulders. "Will you introduce me to a few people? You know I'm always happy to make connections with those who might be interested in joining my program."

"Do you only think about work, Ely?" William said. "So focused."

"I do my best. This is too good an opportunity to just have fun."

"Okay, all right." William pointed in the general direction of the crowd with a hand. "I'd love to introduce you to a couple of people." He turned to stare at Alex. "You won't feel too adrift without her for a while, will you?"

"A bit."

William laughed, probably thinking Alex had been joking. "I'm sure you'll do fine. Are you single?"

Alex blinked twice. "Why is that important?"

The look on William's face held enough leering to make his sentiment obvious. "It's always helped me to know that while networking for my job, I've met some great dates. I've had lots of fun in this industry, if you get my meaning. I was going to wish you luck; maybe you'll meet someone special tonight."

Alex cocked his head. He was looking for something to say when Ely interrupted.

"Go on, I'll catch you in a bit," Ely said, hand on William's elbow. "I just need to tell Alex something."

William nodded and walked to a group nearby; Ely led Alex to the side.

"You'll be okay, right, Sandy?"

He tried to catch her eyes but she didn't quite look at him. "I thought you wanted me to be more social on my own at these events."

She nodded. "Yep. That'll be good."

"Maybe I'll meet someone special tonight."

Maybe he'd missed the mark in mocking William, because Elena took him seriously.

Elena glanced up at him and bit her bottom lip, rolling it between her teeth. "Maybe... maybe that'd be good."

He couldn't fully hide the jerk of his head at that. "You think?"

"Sure." She lifted a shoulder, but the gesture lacked nonchalance. "If it helps— if you think that meeting someone could... ease you... socially."

He arched an eyebrow. "I thought alcohol was supposed to be the social lubricant."

"And we both know it's not a good idea for you to drink a lot."

"I know my limits. I'm an adult, Elena."

"Yes, and lots of adults have an interest in dating." She took a long drink of her white wine. The well-known spike of irritation showed up between them. "If it helps you… find the motivation to be more social."

"If I'm getting this right, you want me to go and network, and do it as if I'm trying to *meet someone*."

She sighed. "Yep."

"That's nonsense."

Her glance turned hard. "Just an idea."

"A bad idea." Alex scoffed.

"Then do whatever you want. I'll go be social with William, meet a few people myself. You do you."

"See you later," he said as she left him and approached William, and seamlessly joined the conversation with one of her bright smiles.

"What the fuck," he whispered, looking around the room for any guidance as to what he should do next.

In the end, Alex decided to follow Elena's advice.

He'd first walked through the big hall and the patio overlooking the building's gardens, pretending he was looking for Liam to check in with him. In reality, he was busy thinking about what Elena had just said.

She'd encouraged him to meet someone. A person whom he might date. Sure, her idea was bad in itself and, sure, it hadn't been her idea, but the fact that she'd even gone with it was telling.

First of all, Alex didn't need help being social. He could be, he just disliked it. Second of all, he hadn't considered the possibility of dating. He hadn't even asked the question for himself; he hadn't had any interest in dating for a couple of years. All he wanted to know was if what he felt around Elena meant he wanted to date *her*. Those were completely different things.

He'd come to terms with a few things. One, he perceived her to be smart, and caring, and fun— and he didn't even care about fun but, in her, he liked it. Two, he considered her to be one of the most attractive people he'd ever met— but none of that meant that he wanted to be in a romantic relationship with her.

Dating someone else wouldn't help him figure out if he wanted to date Ely... but perhaps *meeting someone* would help him gauge if he could feel the same things for other people. That would collect data for his investigation. So he moved through the room with a loose plan to do just that.

He approached a couple of women and chatted with them a bit, not really feeling like they'd hit it off. Funnily enough, after approaching other people, he met a producer and Alex now was in the possession of an excellent business card. The connection would help Jump Cannon add more placements in the future and potentially contract them for project productions.

Later in the evening, Alex approached Liam and Ana, who were talking to people they knew from Liam's old management group.

"Does everyone know my brother?" Liam asked. "This is Alex. He's the Operations Manager for Jump Cannon Productions."

Alex nodded in response to everyone's greeting.

Liam introduced the people in the group. "This is Michelle, and this is..."

"Cassidy."

"Cassidy," Liam repeated. "They're actors represented by Leanne." He pointed to a third person, who waved at him. "We knew each other from when I used to work with TCA. She's still there."

"Hi, Alex," Leanne said. They shook hands. She was pretty; long blonde hair and big, brown eyes. "Nice to meet you. I'd heard Liam's brother was working with him, but I hadn't met you yet. I've met Ely, your colleague."

"Yes, she's around here," Alex offered.

"You don't attend many of these events, do you?" Leanne seemed to take close account of Alex's face. Interesting.

He gave her a playful smirk. "Not enough, I'm told."

Leanne smiled. "There are a lot of them, for sure."

"Yes, and I'm not the most social of people."

"I know what you mean!" she exclaimed. "I'm an introvert by nature; going out in the world like this is real work. Good thing I get paid for it."

Alex's mouth turned up from a corner, halfway into half a smile. "That's refreshing to hear. Sometimes I think I'm too much of a fish out of water to be doing this job, but I'm learning."

"We had to push a bit to get Alex to accept the position at Jump Cannon," Liam said. "But he did, and we're really glad for it."

They chatted for a bit and, soon enough, Leanne said she needed to go chat with someone and she and the two actresses left.

Alex turned to Ana and Liam.

"You seemed to hit it off." Ana's eyes glittered at Alex.

"What makes you say that." Alex took a sip of the drink he'd been nursing all night. He'd held it as a prop more than anything, and it'd turned warm.

"I don't know. It's the feeling I got."

"She did preen a lot." Liam smirked. "Kept putting her hair behind her ear and her gestures were bigger."

Ana frowned. "I don't think you can know her thoughts just from reading her non-verbal communication."

"Lots of people would disagree," Liam added. "Assessing someone's body cues is a whole business. And, you know. Actors do a lot of non-verbal communication so we know something about it."

Soon they had been joined by other people and, without really trying, he'd gotten another business card.

Yet he thought more about the possibility that Leanne had been flirting with him, and how strange it was that he hadn't even realized it. Stranger still, that he was curious about it.

She didn't seem put off by his rare smiles, or his short answers. So when he saw her later by herself, he approached her.

Chapter 32

T HE PARTY HAD BEGUN to dwindle, and Ely itched to go home. Gallivanting around the place with William had turned out to be more work than fun, and she'd had an extra drink to compensate, and now she regretted it. She was tired, a bit buzzed, and ready to leave.

She found Ana and Liam first. "Hi, guys."

"Hey, Ely. You going home yet?" Liam put an arm around Ely's shoulders for a quick one-arm hug.

"I want to. How 'bout you?"

"We're leaving now." Ana gave her empty glass to a passing server. "We're waiting for our car."

Ely nodded. She was aware there were cars waiting for them; they just needed to text Mo. They had needed the flexibility of it, so they could all leave at different times if needed.

"Have you seen Alex? Did he leave?" she asked.

"I don't think he's left yet." Liam said, letting go of Ely and holding Ana's hand instead. "Last I saw him, he was talking to Leanne."

"Leanne?" Ely frowned. She knew she had drunk a bit more than she should have, but maybe it had been a lot more than she should have. She must be mistaken. "As in, from TCA?"

"Yes," Ana said. Her smile had a certain mischief in it. "We introduced them and I think they hit it off. After the people with Leanne left, she and Alex found each other again and have been talking for a long time."

Ely lifted her eyebrows. "Wow."

"I think he'll be fine," Liam added, a cheeky smile in place. "And he has Mo's number, he can leave when he's ready. Just text him so he knows."

Ely nodded again, though she wanted to shake her head. "I think I'll go find him. Just in case. Then I'll leave."

"Sounds good." Ana hugged Ely. "Come have lunch with me tomorrow? And stay over. We can swim on Saturday. All day."

Ely grinned at her best friend. "Sounds lovely. Let's do it."

"Love you. Sleep well," Ana said, and Liam hugged Ely again.

"See you." Ely watched them go, trying to make sense of the twister in her mind.

She walked around the place, searching for Alex, and wondering how it was possible that she had clung to William's idea earlier, but now her stomach twisted into a gordian knot at the thought of Alex with someone else.

The twist tightened when she saw him chatting with Leanne. Ely came to a fast stop and watched them from afar. Leanne batted her eyelashes and played with her hair and he... and Alex...

Sandy was *smiling* at her. A close-mouthed smile, but a true, full smile nevertheless.

"Here," she called a server passing by with drinks. She took two glasses. She quickly emptied one and put the glass back on the tray; she thanked the server, held the second glass in her hand, and marched to Sandy and Leanne.

"Ely!" Leanne said when Ely reached them. "I'm glad I got to see you tonight!"

"You too!" Ely couldn't look at Alex.

"You hadn't told me Alex was so nice."

Ely wanted to scoff, to challenge her, to question her, but didn't.

She hid it all behind a smile. "He should come to these events more often."

Sandy had his arms crossed, and Leanne put a hand on his forearm. "From what I've learned of him, I get that he avoids it."

"Oh?" Ely took a long sip of her drink.

"We've been bonding over being introverts forced to be social for work."

"That must be so hard," Ely offered, still engaging with Leanne only.

The agent kept gazing at Alex every few words. "I've been doing this for a few years now, so I offered to give him a few tips."

"That would be great, for sure." Ely nodded through the growing knot in her stomach. "Being an extrovert myself, maybe I'm just at a loss about how to help him."

"I think I've done well enough," Alex said.

"You certainly seem to have managed tonight," Ely responded. She glanced at him for the first time; he seemed to be studying her. "Good job."

He squinted at her. She drank the rest of her drink in two big gulps.

"Anyway," Ely said. "I'm going home."

Alex grabbed his phone from his pocket, forcing Leanne's hand to release him. "I'll text Mo to let the driver know we're ready for the car."

She shook her head but had to stop— the room seemed to get less stable when she moved her head like that. "You don't have to leave with me."

She knew it was irrational and probably a sign of how much she'd drunk more than anything, but if this night was teaching her something, it was that she was okay being irrational sometimes.

"It's fine." Alex typed on his screen with both hands. "I need to talk to you about something."

Ely frowned. "You can call me tomorrow."

"Can't." He put his phone away in his pocket again. "I have other plans. We have each other's numbers," he said to Leanne.

"Maybe we can chat some time?" Disappointment shone in her eyes, but she made a gallant effort and played with her hair again.

"Maybe," he smiled. Smiled at her, full teeth and everything. A dazzling. Grin.

"It was great seeing you," Ely said, pushing down her sudden distaste by squeezing her empty glass in her hand.

Leanne had done nothing wrong. No one had done anything wrong. If anything, Ely had been the one to make a mistake. Or several.

Alex and Ely said their last goodbyes to Leanne and walked away together. They had to stop to say bye to a few people on the way— including one of the people Alex had talked to; apparently he'd been quite the popular guy that night— and, when they made it out, their car was waiting.

The car drove for a while with them in silence. Ely looked out of the window, doing her best to ignore Sandy.

"Looks like something's the matter," he finally said.

His voice was breathy. Raspy. Maybe he'd used it too much at the party, talking to *Leanne*.

"Nah." She continued to stare out the window.

"You're not someone to hide what you feel, typically."

She crossed her arms and twisted her torso to stare at him. "I'm not hiding anything."

"I think you're wrong." His face seemed impassive, but his eyes proved there was more to his words than his tone suggested.

And to think that once upon a time, he never looked at Ely, or anyone. She wasn't sure how much better this was. There was so much power in his gaze, and it pierced her skull.

She bristled. "Are you seriously implying that I'm wrong about what I'm doing? What I'm feeling?"

"Thought that maybe you don't know what you're doing, yourself." He had the gall to shrug.

She scoffed, but that was actually close to the truth. "I just drank a bit more than I should have, that's all."

"I noticed. That's why I left with you."

"You didn't have to. Looked like you connected with Leanne, you could have stayed and seen where the night took you."

His voice dropped a couple of octaves. "I knew where the night was taking me."

"And you still chose to deliver me safely home?" She had to challenge him. This whole thing was getting out of control and she needed a bit of room to lick her wounds and organize her ridiculous mind. Her absurd heart.

"Yes," he said. Like it was the obvious conclusion.

She shook her head. "You don't need to take care of me."

"I know."

"I'd've been fine."

"Probably."

"You didn't even know I was tipsy."

"I didn't realize you were feeling tipsy. I just saw you acting weird."

She pressed her lips together. "Then... thanks, I guess."

He nodded. "Did William introduce you to interesting people?"

"He did."

"Was he... pushy? Did he flirt with you again."

"No." She crossed her legs. "He got the message last time. He didn't flirt with me tonight. Though I don't know why that matters. You were in good company."

"It matters because I wanted to make sure nothing happened to make you upset."

I'm upset you were so successful at meeting someone.

But that made no sense. And it was so unfair to him. She'd told him to, she'd pushed him to— she thought that, if he met someone, he'd stop looking at her with blazing hazel eyes, then maybe she wouldn't be so drawn to an attractive man in a well-made suit.

There was nothing between her and Alex. Okay, fair, correct that: there could be nothing else. She'd never, ever be with someone who'd proven to be gunpowder to her spark.

"Why do I feel so..." The words escaped from her and, with them, a deluge threatened to break through. She pushed it into a box then put the box under a rug. She spoke through a clenched jaw. "I don't like what I'm feeling."

"You do sound childish."

Her jaw loosened and she gaped at him, her backbone turning ramrod-straight. "What the fuck, Sandy?"

"You're poking. You're itching for a fight and I don't know why. You're not telling me."

"You're not asking, either!"

"Fine. Why are you so irritated? Why are you itching for a fight?"

"Argh!"

They arrived at her building. She got out of the car; she heard him asking the driver to wait there before she closed the door with more force than necessary. Alex got out of the car and followed her, easily catching up with her before she could get to the building's entrance.

He put a hand over hers on the handle and pried it away from the door. "If you're angry about something, tell me. If we're going to fight, I'd like to know why."

She took her hand away from his. "We're not going to fight. We decided so weeks ago."

"Yet, we're fighting."

"We're not."

"See? Childish."

Her nostrils flared. She fisted her hands at her sides. "Maybe I just don't want to tell you!"

"Then you tell me that." He leaned forward, his face close enough to hers that she could see each one of his eyelashes. His words were clipped, his anger barely contained. "Tell me, Sandy, I don't want to talk about it. Say, Sandy, I'm angry. Then, with as much scorn as you can, tell me, Sandy, I'm scared."

"I'm not scared," she said through gritted teeth.

"No?" He came close to her, his cologne invading her senses, the warmth of him a caress on her exposed skin. "Then you're just jealous."

"Jealous? You mean, like you with William? You with Max?" she spat.

"If I can't be jealous, neither can you."

"Exactly. Jealousy is an ugly feeling. It's sticky, and icky, and—"

"And it has no room in our relationship."

"Our working relationship. Our amicable relationship."

"If that's what it is," he snarled.

"We're not friends."

"Agreed."

"Then we're nothing."

"Wrong."

She shook her head, arms growing more rigid with every word. "We fight too much."

"Are you fighting with me, or with your feelings?"

"I really hate you right now."

He gave her a once over, a scowl on his lips. "I don't think you do."

"I guess you're right. We are fighting right now."

"I'm ready to leave that behind. For real, this time. Are you?" He tried to hold her in place, warm hands on the sides of her shoulders.

She squirmed free. He let her go and put his hands in his pockets. She stared up at him, hoping her gaze reached him as stoney as her stomach felt. "You know, regardless of this... impasse, I admire you. You've done great work. I know you've changed. But neither of us is fundamentally different. I'm still who I am, and you... you..."

"I still call you out on your bullshit?" He arched his eyebrow and his general expression echoed the provocation in his words.

She pointed her chin forward in defiance. "Me not seeing things the way you do doesn't mean what I think is bullshit."

"On this it is. Ask yourself this, Ely. Why push me to meet someone? Why can't you stop for a moment to look at this thing between us and ask what it means, and really look at it, and take the fucking time it takes to figure it out?"

She barely stopped herself from stomping her foot on the ground. "Because I don't want to!"

"Why?" He got close to her again, daring her. "Ask the question, Ely. Why?"

She crossed her arms. "I don't want to ask why."

He scoffed. "I know." He shook his head and took a step away, then one to the car. "We'll talk again when you find your courage."

She choked on her indignation. Her chest wanted to explode into rage; air pushing through her in a loud rush, to insult him, push him. She pressed her lips together instead and turned to open the door; she heard his steps on the sidewalk, the car door closing.

She had nothing to think about. He was wrong about that. She'd made her decision a long time ago: they had moved on.

She just needed to find a way to let it rest, and let it go, and he needed to do the same.

Chapter 33

A WEEK LATER, ALEX was one hundred percent convinced that Ely was avoiding him.

When he'd confronted her after the party, he hadn't been sure he'd gotten it right. He'd accused her of being scared, and had thrown at her that she'd wanted him to meet someone because of it, but it had all been a wild guess. A hope, really. Seeing her react to it and avoid him now made him think he'd probably gotten it right. Potentially. The biggest problem was that, if he didn't get to spend more time with her, he'd never know for sure.

She'd done a good job of staying away. He'd only seen her in passing and she'd never directly looked at him; he recognized the strategy. Today, her lucky strike would end. They had that meeting with William over lunch, and she could hardly ignore him for a full hour and a half.

He waited for her at reception, checking in with Celeste on a few things until Ely surfaced from her office. When she approached the desk, he closed his laptop and gave it to their assistant.

"Thanks, Celeste. I'll pick it back up when we return."

"We?" Ely said, her hand grabbing her purse harder.

"We're meeting William. I don't believe you would have forgotten."

"Of course I haven't. I just don't understand why— what—"

"I've been waiting for you." He invited her to walk out the door in front of him with a wide gesture of his hand. "We should share a car; we're going to the same place, after all."

Ely closed her mouth with a snap. She glanced at Celeste, as if deciding how harsh her answer could be, or maybe whether she'd like to flat out lie.

Their assistant helped his cause, likely by chance. "Minimizing the carbon footprint where we can, right?"

"Right," Alex agreed, serious. "Exactly."

Ely rolled her eyes. "Fine. Let's go."

She passed him on the way out and he put a hand on her lower back by instinct— he hadn't meant to, but his hand had landed there as if drawn like a magnet. She glared at him, pursing her lips and silently demanding he retreated. He did, pulling his hand away as if it were burning.

They got into his car without a word. He started driving, and they didn't talk. His attention split between the road and Ely; she disconcerted him by keeping eerily still.

They were halfway to the restaurant when she broke.

"So you're not going to talk to me?" she asked.

"I thought *you* weren't talking to *me*."

"You were the one who said we'd talk again when I— when I got my courage. Which is complete bull, by the way." She seemed to squirm in her seat.

"Okay." When she didn't say anything else, he added, "But you've been avoiding me."

"I haven't."

"Sure."

"I'm here, aren't I?"

"Because you must. To save face with Celeste— because of the carbon footprint or whatever."

She snorted, crossing her arms. "You're funny."

"Thank you." He bit the inside of his lips not to smile; his fake gratefulness must have irked her.

She didn't speak for a few moments. "I didn't think you would actually come to lunch."

"Why wouldn't I?" He stole a glance at her. She stared forward with a certain intensity that told him she still refused to look at him.

She clenched her teeth. "You invited yourself when you thought William was flirting with me—"

"He *was* flirting with you." He was forced to put his attention back on the road and he clenched his own teeth at the frustration of it; having Ely all to himself in the car had its benefits, but he hated it meant he couldn't track every one of her million gestures. She gave him— anyone— so much with every movement of her face.

Her voice gave him almost as much, energy and assertiveness clear in it when she responded. "One, he can do it. Maybe I liked it, even if I don't want to go out with him. Two, you have no right to care."

"Yet, I care."

"Sandy."

He squeezed the wheel in his hands. "If only as a colleague, who wants to make sure no one is pressuring you with sexist expectations when you try to network for the youth program."

"Right." She rolled her eyes— he couldn't know for sure, but he could see it clearly in his mind's eye. "That's why you care."

"For what it's worth, I do care if that's happening."

From the corner of his eye, he saw her turn to study him for a minute. He kept his eyes on the road. "There's a lot of that in this industry, but so far I'm able to manage."

He didn't respond. He stole another glance at her; she flicked her nail on the edge of the seat belt adapter he'd gotten, in case she got in his car again.

He'd pay to know what she made of it when she saw it. Was she sitting more comfortably now? Did she wonder at seeing it there, and realized he did it for her?

She didn't comment on the adapter, but her tone was much softer when she spoke again. "I do appreciate that you pay attention to that."

They came to a red light. He nodded. "I know I don't have a right to feel any kind of way when someone flirts with you, or if you were to flirt back—"

"I rarely if ever flirt! I am the same with everyone."

"I know, Elena. That's not what I'm saying. I'm saying that if you were to flirt back, that's not my business. I know you wouldn't do it unless you actually had an interest in the person."

"I don't get where you're going with this."

"I'm trying to get to it." He hoped the red light lasted long enough. He wanted to see her reaction in detail.

"Go on then."

Yes. Fire in her eyes. He devoured it.

"What I want to say is that I know shit happens and that there's a culture of expecting things out of women in this business. It was the same in the corporate world. So fucking creepy. I want you to know I know you can handle it— I saw you do it— and that, if one day you feel you need back up, you can let me know."

The fire in her eyes turned into a simmer, and he missed the combustion of her inner flame, but he liked the softening of her, too. It invited him closer.

"Thanks, Alex."

Closer.

His breathing quickened. "Even if we never do anything about us, as your colleague, I'd want to help."

A loud horn from behind them informed him the light had turned green and he hadn't noticed; he drove the car forward, pursing his lips in frustration that he couldn't see her face to guess at anything she may be keeping from him.

"You had to mention that?" A complaint lived in her statement.

He smirked. "I wanted to mention that."

Several beats went by, and he wasn't sure what she'd been thinking, but she let him know— complaint and fire subdued.

"I believe you," she said. "I see it in the way you're helping with Clarissa, how you treat Celeste and everyone else. But please don't think this is earning you brownie points, Sandy. This is the bare minimum. I'm not going to give you a cookie for being decent."

He rolled his eyes. "I'm not asking for a cookie. When have I ever?"

She glanced back to the road again. "Never. You may be a grump but you're not a true douche."

He scoffed. "Thank you. That's praise coming from you, about me."

This time, he meant it.

They fell into silence again. They approached their destination.

"So you want to be flirted with." The words escaped him as he parked the car.

One big scoff left her, maybe in exasperation at him, maybe not. "Of course. By the right people. That makes all the difference."

They got out of his car; he waited for her and they walked to the restaurant's entrance. He helped her inside with a hand on her lower back again; this time, she didn't comment on it. In the narrow hallway, he leaned down to tell her in a sotto voice, "I'm not good at flirting."

She startled and halted her steps. She looked over her shoulder at him. "Are you sure?"

"Pretty sure." He gave her a serious nod, their faces close together.

She raised an eyebrow. "You were flirting with Leanne."

He mirrored her. "I was?"

She started walking again, and he followed.

"You smiled at her," she said.

He grinned. She stared.

The hostess welcomed them and upon hearing of their reservation, led them to their table; William wasn't there yet.

"By that measure," he continued the conversation as if there had been no interruption, pretending to be checking the drinks menu, "I flirt with you the most."

"I thought you said you're not good at it."

He lifted her eyes at her, the menu still in his hands. She hadn't touched hers yet. "You sound somewhat jealous."

She rolled her eyes. "I'm not."

"I haven't called Leanne."

"I didn't ask." She reached out for her menu then.

"Well, you don't have a right to be jealous, either."

"I'm not a jealous person."

"This is new for me, but... I guess I am, right now."

She opened her mouth to reply, but they were interrupted by William's arrival.

They did not talk again about anything personal.

———

Several days later, Ely returned from a quick lunch with Ana to find a busy reception area. Celeste, Sandy, and two teens chatted there, and two things hit Ely in the chest. One, there wasn't much time left for this first round of placements; soon, silence would be back to Jump Cannon's offices... until the next round happened in a couple of months.

Two, Alex was smiling. Again. A closed-mouth smile, not the full grin she'd seen a couple of times, but still. She'd rather he didn't. It made things harder for her.

Okay, maybe it was a good thing that he smiled now, but it did make things harder for her. Her heart didn't seem to be with the program, that she was supposed to feel nothing when his face contorted that way.

Fine. Fine! She didn't need to lie. He looked damn handsome when he smiled. And when serious. He just was gorgeous, period.

Anyway. Not the point.

Ely squeezed into the group surrounding Celeste. They laughed at something one of the program participants said, something Ely didn't hear.

She crossed her arms. "Well, you guys are making me jealous that I missed all the fun!"

"Travis is a pretty funny guy," Celeste said from behind the reception desk. Ely and the other three stood on the other side, near the main door.

"Oh, you know." Travis lifted a shoulder. "Just trying my jokes on a safe audience before I risk stand up comedy."

His words had hit the right note of self-deprecation and honesty that made everyone smile.

"I thought you wanted to write scripts." Alex leaned against the tall desk. "I'm going to guess, comedy scripts?"

"That's the dream!"

"A sitcom?" Ely asked.

"Stop. I'm going to faint just imagining it." Travis pressed his palms in a prayer-like gesture.

"I think you can do it," Rodrigo added. "You have us all laughing all the time."

"If I'm smiling, you know it's good." Alex's lips didn't quite curl into a smile anymore, but there was a tiny hint of it in the slant of his mouth. "We all know I'm the office grump."

"Oh, you're not that bad." Rodrigo shook his head, relaxed—like he really meant it. "It was a bit scary in the beginning, but then it clicked. It's not like you're going to scold us or kick us out of the program."

Sandy dropped his head to the side, pretending to give the matter serious thought. "I would be the one getting kicked out. Out of a job before I could give any of you the boot. Elena would make sure of it." He punctuated his statement with a single nod.

"You're right," Ely said. "I wouldn't let you. But don't worry, you'll get a break from the ruckus soon."

He turned his hazel eyes to her. "I didn't say I wanted a break from the ruckus. In fact, I think I've grown quite fond of it."

"Aww. You're going to miss our first program participants?" she teased, holding his eyes.

Alex nodded. "Seems I have a weak spot for energetic people."

Ely squinted at him. She suspected he had secondary intentions in choosing his words, but she couldn't risk giving it much thought. "It's all good. Soon the office will be quiet again and you'll remember why that is more like your natural habitat."

"Oh, no." His mouth pulled down at the corners. "I think it's too late to go back now. It might have been tough in the beginning, but now I appreciate the energy of it. It fits well with my dark soul. Warms up my cold heart."

Rodrigo chuckled, a drop of nerves in the echo of his voice. "You don't have a dark soul."

"You don't think so?" Alex asked him, an eyebrow high.

It was Travis who responded with a shaking head. "Nah. You're just a bit more serious than everyone else here, that's all. So when you smile at my jokes, it's a huge deal."

"That's fine, boys. You don't have to take care of the grown up here, but that was extra kind," Ely interrupted. Her stomach pinched with discomfort. "But since I'm here, can we schedule a follow up call with William?"

"Sure," Celeste said. Travis, Rodrigo, and Alex left, and Ely stayed to check a few things with the assistant.

Only a few minutes later, Ely left Celeste and stopped at the kitchen to make herself coffee. She was selecting a flavored pod from the cupboard when whispered words reached her from the other side of the wall.

"They were totally flirting," Rodrigo said to someone. "Alex was all like, I like energetic people, and making eyes at Ely."

Ely froze behind the open cabinet.

"No way," Tania responded in the same tone. "They're getting bolder."

Ely closed her eyes but didn't otherwise move; she didn't want to give them any reason to suspect she eavesdropped on their conversation.

"But how do we know they're not together?" Tania continued. "It's not like they've said anything either way."

"I guess it would make sense if they're together, after all," Rodrigo added, their voices growing quieter as they walked away.

Fuck. Ely hadn't been the only one to pick up on Alex's vibes. If the teens were talking about it, then things were worse than she'd imagined. Ely and Alex had bickered in meetings in front of the kids before, but since when did teenagers turn that into flirting? Just because they were obsessed with romance it didn't mean there were romantic undertones to how Sandy and Ely communicated.

Hazelnut coffee seemed like the right choice, to warm up her cold hands. She put the pod in and ran the coffee maker, palms on the counter on each side of the machine. Ely's head hung from her shoulders, the cozy smell teasing her nose as she bit the inside of her lips.

Fuckity fuck fuck, if the kids could see his flirting, then she couldn't stay in denial. Alex certainly seemed to be growing bolder, demanding that Ely confront whatever was happening between them, and what he seemed to want from her.

Coffee filled her mug; she recycled the pod and took her drink to her office. She didn't know what she was supposed to do, if it wasn't to tell him to stop. That his advances weren't welcome. Even if her body disagreed, even if her heart beat a little faster just by being around him. Even if her emotions quaked whenever she thought about him this way.

It would not go anywhere. Best to dot a period on the brief sentence of them both. Before any attempts resulted in a nuclear blast.

Chapter 34

"**I** WANT ELY."

Alex's words seemed to echo off every surface of Charles' office. He gazed around the place that had seen him pull his heart apart and together again, with its wooden furniture, big bookcase, and couple of plants. It seemed even the walls and their abstract paintings knew that his words were far from accurate.

"Want?" Charles asked. Evidently, Alex's therapist knew it, too.

Alex cast his eyes to the desk at the window once more, and chose his next words carefully.

"I... I like her." He tasted the words in his mouth, and they didn't seem right, either.

He washed them away with his coffee.

"Sure," Charles said.

Damn Charles. He challenged him with one simple word.

Alex took a deep breath and stared at the ceiling. "I feel things. Something that feels a lot like... affection."

"Platonic affection?"

Alex rolled his eyes and dropped them to Charles' face. "You're going to make me say it."

"Yes. You don't have to actually say anything, but I wonder if you have the courage to put it into words at all, even if only to yourself."

Funny, that Charles talked about courage, demanded it of Alex and he didn't like it, when Alex had been so comfortable asking Ely to be brave.

"Fine." Alex sighed, then held his breath for a few seconds. "I... I feel love. I'm not in love, but it's similar to it. Like at the start of the journey... or a couple of stops into it."

Charles had a smirk that looked a lot like a smile. "Do you know when you started feeling this way? And, again— you don't actually have to say these things out loud to me, but at least answer honestly to yourself."

Alex flicked his nail on the edge of the silicone sleeve wrapping his travel mug. The answer came easy to him, but it came with memories he struggled to keep at bay.

It had all begun the night they'd slept together, all that time ago. So much in those hours had been simple, no more than a fun release... but there were instants, secret, unspoken moments, where it had been different. Where they had truly connected.

Like seeds, sprouting through the cracks formed by cooling lava, a blackened field after an eruption— a fragile, green little thing had grown from it. Now it bloomed, perhaps too early, forgetting to wait until the stem was strong enough to sustain it.

"Seems like you know," Charles said. "Now the question is, what are you willing to do about it?"

The question clattered in Alex's brain for long afterwards, but he knew the answer. He'd do most anything. He wanted to be with Ely. His mind was made up: he was done and done.

Chapter 35

ELY HAD A NEW part-time job. Avoiding being alone with Alex was laborious enough to qualify.

The need to evade Sandy took root in her stomach, twisting and coiling and starting to explore the edges of her lungs. It got a little harder to breathe, when she imagined what would happen if she confronted the conversation that needed to happen. Maybe she was scared, after all. She'd rather die than admit that to him, and she really planned to talk to him. She actually did. Ely would remind him that they'd agreed there was nothing between them, there wouldn't be, and that they had moved on.

Only one thing needed to happen before she could do that. She needed her heart to catch on, so it didn't take over, stage a coup, and disrupt her plan.

The organ in the middle of her chest was fighting a hard fight, though, and Ely didn't know what to do about that.

Especially on days like this random Wednesday, when the meeting they were in turned into a battleground. He stared at her throughout and, whenever he'd laid eyes on her, she could feel him undressing her with his eyes. At times, she was certain she could feel his eyes hot and heavy on her even if she tried not to look at him. Even though he sometimes looked at her in weird ways, half-pretending to be taking notes— a look at her, then writing a few words. Then staring again, then more note-taking. It annoyed the hell out of her— no matter how he looked at her, she felt it.

When he spoke in the meeting, his voice wormed into her ribcage, echoing in her guts. She would never, ever concede that she felt anything like what was clear he was feeling. If she had gulped every time she felt his want on her skin, it was because she needed to push everything down to be dissolved in the acid of her stomach.

This is why she couldn't be friends with him. Her body was confused and it wanted him. Amicable colleagues had always seemed like the best answer for a reason.

The meeting finally ended. The young people left the boardroom and Ely rearranged the chairs, putting the projector back in its case. Alex helped her in silence.

Celeste popped in to let them know she was going out for lunch.

They were completely alone in the office. Working side-by-side with no words exchanged. The fine hairs on her arms stood on end, betraying her and trying to reach for him.

"You've been keeping away from me again." His voice was low, casual. He stated it as a fact.

"What makes you say that?"

Shit. No. She needed to make her exit. Soon.

"I had to engineer this to get us alone."

She dropped the papers she'd been organizing on the table in front of her and, crossing her arms, turned to him.

Her heart hammered against her breastbone. "You engineered this moment? Sandy— "

He mirrored her. They stood face to face, crossed arms almost touching. Her silly, naive hairs kept on trying to meld to him.

"See? Why call me Sandy right now? You're keeping me at arm's length. Why would you, if you didn't know?"

"Didn't know what? I don't understand you— *Alex*. Don't know what's on your mind. I can't read you anymore."

What the fuck was wrong with her mouth? She'd gotten all mixed up, just because of how he stared at her. This wasn't her typical self. She needed to resolve things and be done with it.

"Don't lie." Alex stepped closer to her, their arms actually touching now, a bare brush against her skin. "I know you know what's on my mind. I can still read your face."

"Okay, let's have it—"

But he got it wrong and interrupted her by approaching her lips, holding back for a second, two, his mouth hovering a breath away— and she wanted it, so she didn't pull away, but couldn't close the distance, because this was Alex— and within the next second, his lips crashed on hers.

She knew his mouth. Her body remembered. His lips still fit warm against her, and when their tongues joined the kiss, the sensation still stormed her senses.

Her arms remained crossed between them, pressed against his chest. His arms surrounded her, enveloping her back, one hand on the small of it, pulling; one hand on the back of her heart, holding.

His warmth radiated into her, it knocked on a closed door between them. He offered to show her something but she was scared; she couldn't open her eyes and look. But she kissed him, and he kissed her, and they swam in the exhilaration of it. She could drown in it.

Her arms wanted to unfurl and hold him. She redirected them and pushed him back instead. Alex released her but didn't go far. Any tiny movement and they'd be touching again.

"Stop. No." She shook her head and resisted rubbing her lips together. "That is not what I want— not what I meant."

"You didn't feel it? Just now?" he asked.

She had. She shook her head regardless. A scream built in her throat, but it carried a *yes* in it and she quieted it. She fought with herself and it cost her. Her no wasn't to his question, it was to what it meant.

She hardened. "I moved away from all of that. What happened— that's in the past."

"Is it? In the past? Because to me it's clear it's here, and it's a new thing, too."

When she failed to respond, he slowly, so slowly, giving her all the time in the world to stop him, lifted his hand and placed it around her neck, thumb on her pulse, fingers in her hair, cradling her nape.

"It's just a physical thing," she tried. He tilted her head up, but she cast her eyes down. "My body— we had sex and now it just— we should have never had sex."

"God, Ely. Stop. You know that's a lie. When we had sex it was just sex. It was good, and fun, and I've definitely had fun, casual sex before. But the closer we get, the more I find myself thinking back to it and seeing it through new eyes. I keep thinking of that damn birthmark— and I know, I just know— if we had sex again it wouldn't be the same. This time it would mean something."

He got closer. He leaned his forehead against hers.

"Alex..." The word came out in a whisper.

"We had something good that night. Remember? We both left it behind. We never meant to hold on to it, right? But now... we're reaching back and bringing it forward. And we have more. We could have it all. Don't you know?"

His voice was softer than she'd ever known it. It trickled without resistance into her heart, through the tiny cracks in it, seizing her throat in the process.

She teared up, but blinked it away. "We've had a horrible start to it. We salvaged what we could to make it work here at Jump Cannon. That's not anywhere close to us actually building something out of that nothing. We've hurt each other. No one should ever go back to something rough and hurtful."

"Don't ignore how we've grown. There are things we need to fix and do better at, but that's true of every relationship. If we want to stick together and we're both willing to hear each other out, work things out, then we can make that happen. I want to be here; I want us to make it better. If you push me away then we can't make it better."

"You pushed me away first with your anger."

"I worked on that. Now you are pushing me away with your doubt."

His words speared her sense of self. He was right; she was working so hard at pushing him away. Pushing her own feelings away. This was not a version of herself she recognized or even liked. She loosened up and lifted her eyes to him.

"Tell me you felt it," he asked. "That you feel it, now."

When she didn't reply, he moved his face so they were cheek to cheek. Chin to chin. Lips to lips.

The gentle touch of his mouth disarmed her. His softness cracked the strong wall of her defenses. Her feelings for him escaped free through the narrow opening, just for that moment, and she threw herself to him, arms around his neck. She kissed him full force; she bit his lip, then licked it, then kissed him once more.

"Ely."

He found her lower back again, forearms across it, and pulled her into him. She was on the balls of her feet and he took advantage of her lessened purchase. He maneuvered them to the frosted glass boardroom wall.

His hands grabbed and squeezed her waist, his full body pressing her against the cold glass. She grew warm, yet goose-bumps covered her, every single hair standing on end, celebrat-ing they'd gotten their way, they were finally close to him. Her mind sparkled with sensations and images. If someone came into the office, they'd see fractured sections of her body flat against the white-sanded material; the shadow of the curls of her hair against it. Their melded silhouettes backlit by the window.

He pulled her blouse from her skirt. Touched the skin of her belly. Traveled against her waist, her hips, and around to her ass, and pulled her up against him. One of his hands caressed the back of her thigh and, hooking onto the back of her knee, lifted her leg and placed it around his hip. Her skirt rode up and he pushed his pelvis against hers in a rolling motion.

They needed to be careful. They were at risk of shattering glass.

They shouldn't do this. Couldn't. She pushed against his chest. He stumbled back.

He rubbed the back of a hand on his lips, back and forth. Ely's hands craved to do the same, to erase the tingling, to hide the swelling. She didn't.

"If this is you telling me to stop, I'm stopping," Alex said. "Show me, tell me you want this or I'll go away. I can't keep on going on mixed signals."

She did nothing. Said nothing. She stared at him, her pulse sprinting in her veins and her blood rushing in her ears.

"Fuck," he said, taking another step back.

Motionless again, they both stood there, not looking at each other, catching their breath.

He still didn't look at her but to the floor; he dropped his hand from his mouth to his hips.

"I'm not going to bring this up again. You know where I stand. The rest is up to you." He finally lifted his eyes to her. "If avoiding me is your answer, then that's your answer."

He stomped out of the room.

Chapter 36

ELY STAYED IN THE boardroom for a few minutes after Alex left. She didn't look for him when she finally pushed herself off the glass wall and out the door; she went to her office and picked up her things. She ran out of the Jump Cannon headquarters, making a quick stop at Celeste's desk to leave a post-it announcing she was taking the rest of the day off.

In a daze, Ely left the building and drove around for a bit. It took her an hour to calm down. When she could finally think, she stopped at a bakery and texted Ana.

> **Ely**: Can I come to your place?
> I'll bring sweet things.

> **Ana**: Of course! Everything okay?

> **Ely**: I'll tell you everything.
> Be there in a bit

Ely's best friend opened the door to her home with a wrinkle between her eyebrows.

"Hey." Ana ignored the box of pastries Ely had in her hands, eyes assessing her face instead. "You okay? I know there's no tonal detail over text, but it felt like something happened."

"You're right." Ely entered the house and followed Ana to the living room, where they sat on the sofa. She left the pastries on the coffee table.

"Do you want something to drink?" Ana asked. "Coffee to balance out the sweets?"

Ely shook her head. "Is Liam home?"

"No. Why?"

Relief slumped Ely's back. This was the moment she bared her soul, and she needed to do it in private. Only Ana held a place that made it safe to pour her heart out, truly, completely. She needed her friend to mirror back the mess inside of her.

"I think Alex and I are falling for each other," Ely blurted out.

Ana startled. "Falling... how? A falling out?"

"No. Falling... romantically. Or... unless it's just lust. What if it's just lust? I don't know, Ana. We have feelings for each other."

Ana's brown eyes stared at Ely, wide, zipping back and forth. In her confusion, she stayed silent.

"Look at my face." Ely waved a hand in front of herself in a big circle. "Go over what I just said again. I'm serious."

Ana gasped. "Oh god. You're serious."

"I have a lot to tell you." Ely stared back at Ana, a whirlpool opening up in her chest. A few tears built in her eyes, announcing the storm building in her mind, but she blinked them away again.

"This is what has been on your mind lately, isn't it? I could see it, when we met, but I didn't push. I figured you'd tell me when you were ready..."

Ely nodded. "I'm not ready, but I have to. And you're the only one I trust with it."

"Oh, friend." Ana reached with a hand on Ely's knee and rubbed. "What's going on?"

Ely gulped. "I slept with Alex."

Ana's hand froze. She didn't even blink.

"Please... say something." Ely closed her eyes. She couldn't keep track of Ana's reactions while also trying to stay afloat her own swirling emotions

"When?" Ana finally asked.

"Months ago."

Another beat of silence.

"Why didn't you tell me?" Her voice seemed calm, non-judging, perhaps even curious.

Ely sighed. Her shoulders were still heavy, but she lifted her head to look up at Ana. "You and I, we've never been the kind of friends to talk about who we slept with, unless it was someone important to us. When it happened, Sandy had just quit. We were alone and we'd been chatting and one thing led to another— at first it was a random night with a guy I thought I wasn't going to see much, if ever, again. You know— he's so attractive, and has that way of looking at me— and if he was going to leave, maybe we could let it happen, that one time. You know, for fun."

"And then?"

"Then Alex returned. We'd be around each other a lot. So we had an arrangement. Nothing was going to happen again. But in these months of working together things have gotten a bit more complicated."

Ana fell sideways onto the sofa's cushion, shoulder indenting the soft fabric. "How long have you been together?"

Ely shook her head. Discomfort tingled in her hands, and she wrung them together to hide the feeling. "We're not together but... we could be."

Ana's breath caught in her throat. "Oh, please, Ely. Tell me you're not asking for permission?"

"Of course not. I just need my friend to help me figure this out."

"Okay, good. I can do that. You want to figure out if you want to be with him?"

They'd completely forgotten about the pastries, and Ely made no attempt to reach for them.

"Yeah... but I shouldn't even care about that, because I can't see us working out together. When he came back he was harsh, Ana. He only thought about himself. He didn't care enough to think of me. But now affection— emotions other than irritation— are involved and it's different."

"Sure, emotions are involved, but why is that a bad thing? Because you didn't get along in the beginning?"

"Yes! But now he defies our agreement, and he dares be less of an ass and is more like a grump who can be quite sweet, like a stern brunch daddy."

"Ew. Do not call him daddy. He's my brother— in a way."

Ely nodded. "No problem, not my kink either. I mostly care about the stern brunch part of it." Ely searched her friend's eyes, and sighed. "I've told him we don't like each other enough but he says we do, if we have feelings for each other. I tell him we need to be more authentically harmonious to make it work, he says we can work to make it work. I say we shouldn't, he says why not."

Ana gave Ely an incredulous look, her lips pressed into a thin line. "Why shouldn't you?"

"C'mon. Really?" Ely's frown was a mixture of confusion and irritation.

"Yes, really."

Ely made for the box of pastries and stopped herself. She retreated from it and shook her head.

She finally settled with her eyes out the window, and away from her friend and her challenging gaze. "Because... because love is supposed to be calm, isn't it? It's supposed to be light, and make you feel like the person you're falling for is the sun."

"And you don't feel like Alex is the sun." It wasn't a question.

"Sandy is not a sunny person and you know it. You also know what it's like to feel you're in love with the sun. I don't feel for Alex what I see you feel for Liam."

"What do you feel for Alex?" Ana's voice had taken a gentle tone, and her question resounded with genuine care.

Spikes pierced Ely's throat as a wave of emotion invaded her. "Alex is— lightning. He's wind I can't see unless it's shaking a tree. When he's sweet, he's the coziness of hearing the rain fall on the roof while you're under heavy blankets. He's been amazing, helping me as I support Clarissa with that horrible producer. He got me a seat belt adapter without asking and without notice and I almost melted right there and then, when I saw. I didn't know he had that in him. He's good with the kids. When he smiles— his smiles are so rare— his grins are like the ray of sun cutting free from the dark clouds." She shook her head, then scoffed. "Just listen to me. I get lyrical over him. I feel too much. It's too intense. What if I burn?"

Ana's hand left Ely's knee, and caressed her face; dropped to her shoulder and squeezed. "I think love can have many different looks. Maybe for you it looks like that. Loving the sun can also feel like you're close to burning, you know. And plenty of people prefer rainy weather."

Tears built in her eyes. "I wasn't supposed to prefer rainy weather."

"You said that he has kindness in him? And that his smiles fill you up. That he can be supportive and has been supportive—"

"I asked him to let me be on his team... and I think he let me. Now he wants to be on mine."

Ana dropped her head to the side. "Ely, I'm almost afraid to say this, but— that's awesome?"

Ely chuckled and one tear broke free. "What do you mean, you're afraid to tell me that?"

"Because you don't seem to want to feel any of these things."

Ely's breath caught, and her sight became blurry.

"You've always been my guiding light when I'm confused," Ana continued. "Remember when I was afraid of all the stuff that came with loving Liam?"

Ely nodded. A sob escaped her throat.

"You reminded me that risk is necessary in love, and that I shouldn't punish him for how people see him." Ana gave Ely a small, sweet smile. "You've always been so clear. You'd go out on dates and be like, *he's trash, forget him.* You've always cared about not settling, demanding they were decent human beings. You're awesome and you'd never be with someone not as awesome as you. I've always loved that about you."

Ely's appreciative chortle was at least halfway to a hiccup.

"So when Alex came back," Ana continued, "he hurt you. And you decided he wasn't as awesome as you. So you moved on. And now you can't wrap your head around the fact you want to go back to him. You can't figure out how he can also be awesome like you, just in a different way."

Ana rubbed Ely's shoulder, staring at Ely with complete tenderness. Her friend put it together because she knew Ely, and loved her, and could see her. Even the parts that Ely had trouble seeing herself.

The tears now flowed freely down Ely's face. "Yes," she said with a thin voice. "That's it."

Ana scooted close to Ely on the sofa and wrapped her arms around Ely's shoulders; Ely put her head on Ana's shoulder and cried.

She wasn't just falling in love with Alex. She was two-thirds of the way there. She didn't understand how that could be; Alex was stern against her joy, introvert to her extrovert, strict with his smiles to her generous ones, selective in his affection to her indulgent personality.

He was also kind, and smart, and committed, and persevering. He was clear, and honest, and knew what he wanted.

If he was critical, so was she. And he said he wanted to invest, and commit to making it work. She needed to decide if she wanted that, too.

Ely continued taking comfort in her friend's arms when they were interrupted by a notification from Ana's phone, indicating that the gate had been opened. Liam was home.

Ely's new-found calm was gone.

"Ana, I'm not ready to tell Liam." She got up in a flurry and grabbed her bag. "Don't tell him."

"Oh, no, no." Ana stood as well and reached to hold Ely's arm. "Please don't ask me that. I can't hide things from him. He'll know within a minute that there's something on my mind that I'm not telling him."

The door connecting the garage with the house opened and closed.

Ely hissed. "Tell him on the weekend. Until then—"

"Ely? Hi!" Liam said, finding them in the living room. "I didn't know you were coming!"

"Just in passing." She stepped away from Ana to receive Liam's hug.

He studied Ely, then Ana. "Everything okay?"

"Something happened." Ely looked up at Liam, that face that was so much like Alex and yet so different. She cared about Liam enough that she couldn't risk his reaction to her feelings about his brother, not until she had a map about what was going to happen next. "But I can't tell you yet. Ana will tell you on the weekend."

"That's... not worrisome at all..." he stated, his eyes continuing to jump back and forth between Ana and Ely.

"Please." Ely clutched her bag closer to her body and tried to convey her need to Liam with her eyes. "You should know and you will know. Just give me a couple of days to figure things out, okay?"

"I... well..." His eyes finally stayed with Ely, and he scanned every detail of her face. "...Okay."

Ely hugged Liam tight, holding on for a minute, and kissed him on the cheek. "Thanks, Liam."

"Are you okay?" he asked. "At least tell me that."

"I think so." Ely nodded. "I will be."

He squinted at her. "Did Alex do something?"

Ely shook her head and walked out of their place with a quick farewell. She was sure her voice had a note of hysteria in it.

Chapter 37

WHEN ELY DECIDED TO take the rest of the week off, she'd planned to treat herself to a massage, do hot yoga to unknot every muscle, and process the hell out of her feelings for Alex. She'd done all three of those things, but she wasn't done with the latter. That Saturday, Ely had gotten dressed with the idea of going to the beach and thinking some more, when she got a text from her favorite student. Not that she'd ever admit she had favorites.

> **Clarissa**: This guy crossed a line.
> Please, I need to talk.

Ely ground her teeth. Rightful, protective anger flared up inside of her. She started typing her reply with resolute fingers but, before she could finish, another text came in.

> **Alex**: Let's meet at the office. I can
> be there in an hour.

Ely blinked twice, eyes fixed on her screen. Clarissa had texted them both, it seemed, which was new. Whatever Clarissa's reasons for adding Alex this time, seeing Sandy's name came with a big *whoop!* in her heart.

> **Ely**: I'll try to rush and make it there
> in an hour, maybe 1 hr 15

> **Clarissa**: Thanks. I'll be there.

Shit.

The universe was conspiring against her, it seemed. First, Ely wasn't done thinking about things, and Ana had said she'd talk to Liam later in the day. If that hadn't put pressure on Ely, going to the office to see Clarissa did. Even though Ely still didn't know what, or how, to talk to Alex about everything, she couldn't think much about it. Going to the office had to do with showing up for Clarissa, and Ely's heart tribulations had to come second.

Not like going in circles in her mind had helped much, anyway.

Ely pulled up her big woman linen shorts— she had planned to go to the beach, after all— and pulled herself up from her sandal straps, gathered up her courage and went to the office.

She entered Jump Cannon's headquarters as silently as she could. It didn't matter, in the end, because Sandy and Clarissa sat in the waiting room. She had a mug in her hands, and he crouched on his haunches in front of her, meeting her at eye level. His eyes didn't waver from the young woman in front of him.

"Hey," Ely said. "I'm here."

She sat next to Clarissa. Alex only glanced at Ely; he appeared to quickly track the details of her face then returned his attention to their student.

"Ready to tell us what happened?" he asked.

Clarissa nodded. Her mug was one of the ones in the office's small kitchen; Alex must have brought her a warm drink.

He sat on the coffee table behind him and waited. Ely would have spent a longer time dissecting his casual look of jeans and a t-shirt, she'd gotten so used to seeing him in business casual— but didn't. She put her attention on the teen asking for their help.

"He got worse this week," Clarissa said. "He stopped caring about my school responsibilities. He demanded I complete all tasks he assigned to me, and left me a voicemail with screams and insults because I'd missed his call— I saved it, if you want to hear it."

"Not right now." Ely tried to make her voice as warm and supportive as she could. "I believe you. But save it, just in case."

Clarissa nodded again. "On Thursday, he said I needed to make a choice about the career I wanted and, if I really wanted this, I was old enough to leave school. He said I didn't need a degree, anyway, if I made my way through experience."

"Fuck him," Alex said. Ely would have smiled at any other time; the response was very much Sandy, and also unprofessional. Clearly he didn't care and, honestly, Ely didn't, either.

"That's not all." Clarissa cast her eyes down to what smelled like chamomile tea. "He wanted me to skip school yesterday. I didn't. Then he wanted me to go to his house to finish a couple of tasks and I... I said no. It wasn't pretty."

"Did he hurt you?" The tendon in Alex's jaw bulged with the force with which he clenched his teeth, but his tone had been calm enough. Like his first priority was Clarissa, too.

The student shook her head, but it didn't seem to be enough to convince him.

"You don't need to give us any details," Ely offered. "Just tell us if he hurt you in any way, so we can help."

"Not physically— he called me names and told me I'd never amount to anything. He just... he did lift his hand as if he was going to slap me with the back of it, but didn't."

"That's too far, already." The rage in Alex's voice was barely contained. "He's gone too far, too many times. You don't need to accept this anymore, Clarissa."

"I'm proud of how hard you have worked to try to handle it but, honey..." Ely bit the inside of her lips, wishing she didn't have to say the next part, but she pushed through. "I think at this point we need to make sure you're safe and end this placement."

Clarissa nodded yet again, but disappointment and frustration were clear on her face. Her eyes were full of unshed tears.

"I haven't talked to Alex yet, but..." she stole a glance at him, and he stared back. His face was impassive, perhaps unsuspecting of what Ely planned— and fairly so. She hoped he would be okay with it, regardless. "I wonder if it'd be okay to plan for you to participate in the next round of the program, too. You deserve to have a good placement experience. We don't want what happened with this guy to be all you're left with."

"Really?" Clarissa lifted her eyes to Ely first, then double checked with Sandy.

"Of course," he said. "The good thing about running this place is that we can do whatever the hell we want."

Clarissa laughed at that. Ely smiled.

"He has your phone number, right?" Ely asked. "Not your address or other ways to contact you."

"Only my number," Clarissa confirmed.

"Good." Alex gave her an encouraging nod. "Don't block him, in case we need evidence, but also don't answer his calls. Let it all go to voicemail. I'll go call him in a minute."

"Don't get in trouble," Clarissa said.

That made Ely grin; Alex's lips curled up on one side. He stole a glance at Ely, but looked away within a second.

"I won't get into anything I can't handle." He leaned forward with elbows on his knees, and peered at Clarissa like an over-protective papa bear making sure his cub was all right. "Okay. We have a plan."

"Why don't you go home and do some self-care?" Ely said. They all stood. "Call a friend, watch a movie."

Alex put his hands in his pockets, his pose fully relaxed. "Everything will be okay. We'll figure it out. I'll go call him right now. I'll text you later if anything major comes up but, if you don't hear from me, know that it's because it went well. We'll talk again on Monday."

Clarissa sighed. "Thanks, Sandy."

Alex startled. Ely covered her mouth with a hand and giggled.

"I'm so sorry!" Clarissa said. "I've heard Ely call you that sometimes, it slipped. I didn't even realize..."

Alex exhaled a quick breath, and a hint of humor escaped from him in the sound. "It's okay. Just try not to. Only Elena calls me that."

"I'm sorry," Clarissa said again.

"We're good." Alex dipped his head in acknowledgement of the young woman's discomfort. "We'll talk on Monday."

"Thanks, Alex," she added.

"Take care, Clarissa." He waved at her with a casual move of his hand and, without looking at Ely, went to his office.

Ely walked Clarissa to the door. "You okay?"

"I will be."

"Yes, you will be. We're here to help."

"I know. You both have been amazing. This program was my dream. I didn't want to ruin this."

"You haven't, I promise." Ely took Clarissa's half-full mug from her hands and left it on the reception desk. "You're great, Clarissa. As crappy as all of this is, there is one good thing. I'll be lucky enough to see you again for the next round."

Clarissa smiled.

"Would you like a hug?" Ely asked. "It's totally okay to say no."

"I'd like one."

They hugged for a minute and Ely imbued the gesture with as much reassurance and warmth as she could. Ely closed the door behind the teen and, taking a deep breath, she leaned against the wood.

The tenderness in her heart was quickly replaced by a narrowing of her attention; she could hear Alex on the phone across the big space, quiet as it was with no one else there.

She walked toward him with slow steps, paying attention to his words.

"No, you listen. We don't owe you anything. We're not indebted to you. This is not a favor you're doing for us. This is not free labor for you. You didn't enter into a working relationship with Jump Cannon; we're not producing anything with you and, frankly, I don't think we ever will. This was a social program. Your cheap, abusive ass just ruined your name with us. We never needed you. Now we don't want you."

Alex had left his door ajar. She pushed it open with two fingers and studied him; he leaned forward on his desk, with an elbow on it while his hand held the phone to his ear. His other hand held on to his hip, arm jarred.

Ely linked her hands in front of herself and waited.

Alex laughed. "Sure. Just write that down and send it via email. We'll only do written communications with you moving forward, and good luck avoiding evidence that way, asshole."

Alex hung up, the sound of plastic rattling, the force of it punctuating his words. "Fuck him."

Ely didn't say anything until he lifted his eyes to her, serious, nostrils flaring.

"I kinda love that you called him an asshole," Ely said.

"He is one."

"What did he say at the end?"

"Mostly libel and empty threats. I doubt he can follow through with any of it. We'll just log any interactions with the guy and, if necessary, pursue legal action." He shrugged. "No big deal."

"No big deal, huh?" She grinned.

He arched an eyebrow and gazed at her, up and down. He leaned back in his chair and crossed his arms. "I thought you'd've made your exit by now."

She took a deep breath. "I deserve that."

Cocking his head, he considered her. "What do you want, Elena?"

"I'm not sure..."

He sighed, got up, and strolled to her. "Let me know if that changes."

He made to walk by, but she stopped him with a hand on his arm.

"Wait."

He turned back to her, hiding his hands in his pockets. He looked a bit different today; his eyes were not aflame, but hazel embers.

She took a fortifying breath. "I've been thinking a lot about... things. Us. I talked to Ana, too. She helped me answer the why. You know, the question you wanted me to ask?"

He nodded.

"I'm worried we're not meant to be together." She gulped. "And I've never in my life, ever, looked twice at something— or someone— I thought wasn't right for me."

She saw the hurt her words had caused him, but he didn't move; his gesture didn't really change. "So you think I'm not the right person for you."

"I want you to be, but— I'm afraid you're not. This wouldn't be a small mistake in my life. I'd go all in and if we get together and we fail, my life— my heart— I just—"

He came closer to her. It was becoming a habit; whenever they talked like this, he sought to be closer to her. Closer. Her heart lodged itself in her throat.

"Look, I know I'm not the standard nice guy." His voice came out gruff, a swell of emotion resonating in it. "They wouldn't write one of those romcoms Liam acts in about someone like me. But I'll always tell you the truth, and I'll challenge you, and I'll be next to you. Fiercely. I know that once I fall in love I'll be in it— forever. What I lack in romance I make up in loyalty. Devotion, Ely. If you want it."

"What do you even want from me?" She stared up at him, her face contorting in her angst. "How can you come back from where we've been, and look at me and say, 'You. You are who I want?'"

"I don't think anyone knows. I could give you a list of things I like about you— and things I don't, for that matter— but it's not about balancing two things. A person is more than the sum of their parts. A couple is more than the sum of the partners. And you and me... it adds up to something I crave. When I look at you, I know it— you're the one for me."

"Alex..."

"We've already overcome so much. We came back to each other after we dealt with things people break up over."

"How can you trust what we feel like this? I haven't fully figured it out, myself. How do you know?"

"I'm pretty sure of it. I've talked a lot about this with Charles."

"You have?"

He nodded. "I needed to know if what I felt for you meant I wanted you in my life like this. I do." He lifted his arms to cradle her head in his hands. His thumbs caressed the curve of her jaw, down her neck. He angled her head up, aligning their lips but not touching. "I want to be the right someone for you."

"What do you want from me?"

"I want you to want me to be the right person for you. To challenge me, tell me the truth, even bicker with me when I get grumpy. Call me Sandy when you're annoyed, or want to tease me, then whisper my name as an apology. As a promise. I want you to work with me and build something together that—"

He didn't get to finish. Ely's wall had broken down into sand and what had been inside the fort came out of her like a broken dam. She kissed him, hard, hands clutching at his t-shirt.

His shock lasted only an instant. He recovered fast, and kissed her back with as much might as she gave him. Another second, and they'd become entwined, arms around each other, hands grabbing and pulling and holding.

He walked her back to his desk and he pushed the stuff on it away so she could sit there.

"Oh god. That goes straight into the fantasy bank—" Ely tried, but it was her turn to have her words interrupted by a kiss.

He settled between her legs and devoured her lips.

"Tell me you want this," he said as his hands traveled up her torso, underneath her shirt. "Tell me you want me."

"I do. I want you. Alex, I want you to be my person."

"Fuck." He kissed her jaw, down her neck.

"I want you to challenge me and help me be right for you." She ran her fingers through the back of his head, relishing in the way the short hair there brushed against her hands. "I will not let you settle— we will not settle."

"Done deal. We're together now."

"Done."

His hands went up her naked leg. "God, Ely. I have got to kiss that birthmark again."

"Here? Now? I mean, it's kind of sexy—"

He chuckled. "No. At least, not here today. I thought we could—"

Ely's phone rang. She would have ignored it, only that it was Ana's ringtone.

"Crap. That's Ana," Ely said.

"Do you need to answer? We're kind of busy here." He put his hands on the desk on each side of her.

"Yes. She told Liam today that I have feelings for you. That we may be falling for each other."

He gazed deeply into her eyes. "You told her you have feelings for me?"

"Yeah."

He dipped his head. "I'm past the halfway point."

She smiled. He sighed and dropped his head to her shoulder, resting his forehead against her neck.

"I want us to have this talk with Ana and Liam." Ely rubbed the back of his neck. "They have a part in this, both as our friends, your brother, our employers. We need to make sure we're all on the same page."

It took him a second to respond. "Fine. Let's get it out of the way."

The phone had become silent a long while ago; when Ely checked in, there was no voicemail. Ana had texted Ely instead.

> **Ana**: Liam would like to talk.
> Can we chat sometime soon?

Alex pulled back from his position, and took his phone out of his pocket.

"That's a text from Liam," he said. "He wants to talk."

He looked at her; his eyes were hooded with want. He sighed.

"Okay, then." He started typing his reply. "We can meet at my apartment. If we're going to have this conversation, it's going to be where I am comfortable."

Chapter 38

A LEX KISSED ELY DEEPLY one more time, indulging in it— she wanted him. Him. Then he guided her out of the office and into each of their cars.

They drove to his place separately, but rode up the elevator hand in hand.

He opened the door and let her in, before closing the door behind them.

"Wow, Alex." She approached the canvases. "There's more than last time, and... so many colors!"

He came to her and hugged her from behind. "I'm still in experimental mode, trying to find my art again. I think I'm close."

Still in his arms, she leaned her head back and kissed his cheek. "Can't wait to see."

"Help me put them away. I don't want them to see any of it."

"Why?"

Despite her question, she helped him pick up a canvas and take it to his bedroom.

"Too personal."

She didn't argue; she just helped him.

The buzzer rang right as he closed the door to his bedroom. He took Ely's hand in his again; he wanted her close when facing Liam.

Having his brother come into his place with Ana was a bit of a Western standoff. The four of them moved into the living room. He didn't have much furniture; he'd saved most of the space for painting. He led Ely to sit on the couch; Ana sat next to her. Alex moved the small armchair closer, so he could be within distance of his... girlfriend, he supposed. Liam sat on the sofa's arm, a hand on Ana's shoulder. Ely placed a hand on Alex's thigh, and he put his hand over hers.

They sat in silence.

"This is awkward," Ely said.

"Liam wanted to talk." Alex let them fill in the blanks. *He can talk.*

His brother's hand tightened on Ana's shoulder. He talked to Ely first. "Why did you feel you couldn't tell me about this, Ely? When I saw you at our home the other day, you asked me to wait."

"I didn't want to tell you because I needed to know what to tell you. I hadn't made up my mind yet."

"And you have now?" Ana asked. While Liam's eyes were hard, Ana's sparkled as she looked between him and Ely.

Ely nodded. "Just a couple of hours ago. I decided— we decided—"

"We're together," Alex said. Liam and Ana looked at Ely as if wanting confirmation. Alex scoffed. "I'm not lying."

"I hope you get that this comes a bit out of the blue..." Liam lifted his free hand to scratch at his eyebrow.

"What did you tell him?" Ely asked Ana. "This has been in the making since we met."

Liam jerked back. "Since the beginning?"

Ana patted Liam's knee but talked to Ely. "I told him that you said you were falling for each other, but were still figuring things out. That you were worried about how much you two used to fight, and whether you were suited for each other."

"Suited for each other." Liam laughed, but it wasn't a very humorous sound. "Not a term you hear much anymore."

"Why does that matter?" Alex said. "And why do you have a say? This is between Ely and me."

Liam arched an eyebrow. "I think we've managed to entwine our lives enough that talking about things like this is important."

"If you mean that we are your employees," Alex countered, "then this is about business, not our romantic relationship."

"You don't need to tell us anything private or personal," Ana said. "We're here to figure out the boundaries between work, friendship, and love."

"I get it," Ely said. "The relationships we all have together overlap a lot. We need to talk to make sure where one begins and the other ends."

Ana turned to Liam. "We always knew that getting Ely and Alex to work for us brought an extra layer of complexity to our project. We were okay with it."

"I didn't expect them to start dating!" Liam chuckled.

"Ely's amazing. You didn't think I'd notice?" Alex squeezed Ely's hand on his thigh.

"I know you guys have your problems still," Ely said, squeezing Alex's leg in turn. "You may not be aware, Liam, but your brother is great, too."

Liam's mouth hung. "Of course I know. First thing I told you about him— he's a good guy."

"Because I love you, Liam, but I'll fight you if I have to," Ely added.

Alex pressed his lips not to laugh. He took the chance to lean into the warmth spreading in his chest at her words, nevertheless.

Liam also seemed to be suppressing a smile. "I don't want you to fight me, Ely. Thanks. I've seen you two; I'd rather not get on that side of you."

"You have seen us, and that's the only reason why I think it's important to have this conversation with you both about our love life. If you were just our friends and brother, we'd probably still share the news and you two would probably still have questions. I get that. But you're also our employers. I don't want you to think I'm failing you."

"You don't need to apologize," both Liam and Alex said. They stared at each other, and Liam's gaze held as much suspicion as Alex felt.

Ely smirked. "I'm not apologizing. I'm explaining I understand why this conversation is important. If I were you, I'd wonder what it would mean to the business if we were to keep bickering and fighting and things didn't work out. What happens if we break up?"

"We won't." Alex surprised himself; he didn't realize he'd let those words out.

Liam's eyebrows shot up in two big arches. "Okay, then. Though I'm not worried about that. You've already been at odds and disliked each other. You never let it affect your work."

Ely reared back.

"What?" Alex said to her. "It's true. We've dealt with a break up already and we kept doing our jobs, and did them well."

"You call what happened a break up?" Ely turned to him.

"You… broke up?!" Liam exclaimed.

Ana called her partner down to provide more details, but Alex focused on Ely.

"It was a break up of sorts," he said. "When you told me you were done with me. Don't you agree? And I believe it's as close as we're gonna get to breaking up in the future. If I didn't think so, if I thought we would really break up again, why would I be bothering with this conversation? With what I said earlier."

Ely studied him for a second, before she nodded and a smile appeared on her lips.

"Huh," Liam said. "So you two really have been into each other from the start."

"I thought she was beautiful. And dangerous." Alex lifted a shoulder.

"And I thought he was hot. And annoying," Ely added.

Liam laughed. "Well, I guess you two resolved your issues."

Ely stared at him again. She reflected back the same mix of joy and hope and awe he felt.

"I've never seen you look at someone like that, Ely," Ana said. "And I've waited, and I've hoped. Remember our conversation? You do look at him like he's the sun." Ana waited a second, and Ely turned to her best friend. "I'm happy for you guys."

Liam released a gust of air. "I do want you both to be happy. If you've found that with each other, then... that's awesome. It is."

"We won't let it affect work," Ely said. "We're on each other's teams, we want Jump Cannon to succeed, too."

"I know." Liam smiled. "Ana and I obviously think that it's possible to work with someone you're in a relationship with."

"Okay. So do we have any problems?" Alex asked.

"Yes," Ana said. "Liam and Alex."

Alex studied his brother with a twist in his gut. He wasn't sure he was ready for this talk, especially on top of the discussion they had already had. But he got where Ana was coming from, and he knew what Ely would want. He could give this a try.

Ely's hand hadn't moved since the start of the conversation, but she tapped his leg now. "Would you like Ana and me to give you and Liam some privacy?"

Alex interlocked his fingers with hers and shook his head. If he was going to have this discussion with Liam, he wanted her presence and support.

"Please stay." With effort, and in a show of his good intentions, he turned to gaze at his brother. "If that's okay with you."

Liam watched him and Ely, then turned to Ana. They shared a small smile, before Liam gazed at Alex again with a decision on his face.

"I'm okay doing this in front of them," he said. "I'll tell everything to Ana, anyway, and I could use her support the way you want Ely's. And I adore Ely."

Then there were no reasons to delay. Alex sighed, and threw himself into the conversation.

He unclenched his jaw. "Okay, then. Let's do this. Let's drop the masks."

Liam frowned. "What masks?"

"These masks." Alex pursed his lips and shook his head. "We've been stuck in this relationship for so long we only know one way to interact with each other."

"I thought it was better."

"Marginally."

Liam scoffed. "I guess we can agree I'm the optimistic one of the two."

Alex glanced at Ely, and she gave him an encouraging smile.

"We are different," he said. "My therapist had a hypothesis about that."

"Funny. My therapist also had some thoughts about it." Liam crossed his arms and challenged Alex with a stare.

Alex had no problem with that. "Charles says we're probably in a vicious cycle of contempt and defensiveness."

"Your contempt."

"Your defensiveness."

Liam squinted at Alex and thought for a second, before adding more. "Doctor Linda thinks that the way I want to pull away and renounce you every time you say something that makes me angry makes you angry."

"We both push each other out of our comfort zones. I refused to be pulled anywhere... then struggled when I was pushed down."

Alex jiggled his leg. If nothing else, the fact he was having this conversation was a sign of his growth, but it didn't mean he enjoyed it.

"And I couldn't understand why you wouldn't just go for it. Take the risk," Liam added.

Alex nodded. "Ever since we were kids... You'd want to go for it and I'd resent you wanting me to go with you. Then resent you when you did it anyway without me."

"I wanted you around." Liam shrugged. "I also wanted you to do it my way and, when you didn't, I resented you."

Alex took a good look at his brother and smirked. "I guess I got tired of it all."

"I'm sorry, Alex." Ely grinned at him. "I don't think Charles was wrong about this, either."

Alex smiled in return.

"So what do we do with all of that now?" Liam asked.

"I've been learning to not say no to opportunities just because they were offered," Alex said. "Learning that someone proposing something to me doesn't mean they're pushing me."

"And I guess... I need to learn that you may choose not to go where I'm going. That you may not want to follow."

"That although you're the older kid... I'd rather be your equal."

"God, Alex." Liam stood and took two steps in Alex's direction. Instinctively, Alex got up from his armchair to be at his eye level. "I've always thought we were equals. I've always wanted you by my side."

Alex shook his head and crossed his arms. "I didn't know how to be by your side without growling for my space. Not that I'll never growl... but maybe I can actually talk to you when I disagree with you."

Liam smiled, and it seemed genuine, this time. "And I can let you choose not to go for something if you don't want to."

Alex allowed a tiny grin to take over his mouth. "I know you've wanted us to be closer. I think I'm ready to figure out what that looks like."

Liam opened his arms in a silent request, and Alex took it. They hugged.

"I'm glad that out of anything I've tried to get you to do, you tried therapy," Liam said while patting Alex's back.

"Sure," Alex rolled his eyes, even if his brother couldn't see it. Maybe because of it. "Just don't forget that one thing is to give me a referral. Another to do the work. And I did that."

"You did. I have, too."

They let go of each other. Alex put a hand on Liam's shoulder. "You saying you'd been in therapy for a while helped. I'll give you that."

Alex turned to the side, searching for Ely. He stretched his hand to her and she came to him, and took his hand.

"I like working at Jump Cannon," Alex added. "It's a good balance for me. And Ely makes it better."

"So you want to keep on going," Ana said. She'd also approached them and put her hand around Liam's waist. Liam surrounded her with his arm. "You're still invested in this."

"I am."

"Do you think you're going to paint again?" Liam asked.

Alex hesitated. Ely put her free hand on his stomach, encouraging. She looked up at Alex with confidence in her eyes.

"I have been painting. I hid it all before you got here." He gazed at Liam and smirked. "Go on. I know you want to ask."

"Can I see?" Liam said.

Alex sighed. "Sure."

They all moved to his room and checked the paintings hidden there. Alex studied the canvases as an spectator; so much color, like Ely had said, and so much of his old art shone through... but they were different, too.

Liam studied each picture with what seemed like appreciation. He went back to one of the first he'd admired, and held it at arm's length.

"This is amazing, Alex."

Alex didn't say anything at first, but responded when Ely squeezed his hand. "Thanks."

"Can I have it?"

"Don't push it, Liam."

His brother turned to him and smiled. "I mean it. I've always liked what you do. This one is..."

"It would be perfect for that spot in our office," Ana said. "It's really amazing."

"You should sign it." Ely patted Alex's stomach. "And let them have it."

Alex rummaged in a drawer and found a permanent marker. He signed it in a corner, *AMcM*.

"Thank you, Alex."

They walked back out to the living room, still so open without the paintings.

"So you fell for my partner's brother," Ana teased Ely.

"I don't know if it's a good thing that you already met the parents," Liam said to Alex.

"I don't think I made a good impression." Alex pushed his lips to the side.

"You didn't," Ely said. "But I changed my mind. They will, too."

"Alex and Ely. I would have never guessed..." Liam shook his head and let out a gust of air, as if still getting used to the idea.

"I like to surprise you, Liam." Ely gave Liam a friendly punch on the arm.

"You sure did," Liam said. "Maybe we'll get to be one big happy family after all."

Ana and Ely hugged each other goodbye, while Liam and Alex smiled.

"I'll need to grovel to your parents, Ely, won't I?" he asked as Liam and Ana left.

Liam left Alex's place laughing.

Chapter 39

A LEX TOOK A DEEP breath, closed the door behind Liam and Ana, and turned to Ely. She stood in the middle of the room, expectant.

A few seconds went by. He took a step closer to her, another, another, until he could smell her perfume.

"The way I see it," Alex said, "we have two options. We can take this slow. Or..."

"Or?"

She blinked up at him. He put a strand of her hair behind her ear, and dropped his hand to her neck in the same movement. Her pulse under his thumb signaled what her choice might be.

He wet his bottom lip. "Or we can jump right into it."

"Jump," she breathed out.

He pulled her head to him and he crushed his lips to hers. Her arms wrapped around his neck, and he walked her back. She hit the wall and he pressed his body against hers, rubbing himself on her. He nibbled on her bottom lip.

"Alex." She bit back. "Are you going to tell me how you want me, today?"

He kissed her neck, and licked the spot where it connected with her shoulder. He cupped a breast, getting reacquainted with the fullness of them.

"Desperately," he confessed. "I want you desperately. Completely."

"Oh god." Ely pulled at his shirt and up and away from him it went.

His hands returned to her in an instant, doing the same to her blouse. She ran her fingers down his chest, nails scraping down his front. The burning sensation pierced him all the way down to his cock.

"Fuck." He took a step back, only so he had the room to turn her body around, front to the wall. He pressed back against her, pushing her forward.

"Sandy! Shit. It's cold."

He gripped her hands and pressed them against the wall, sliding them up above her head in a wide arch.

He bit her earlobe and spoke into her ear. "You'll survive."

"Depends how hot you make me."

He ran his hands across the front of her body and unbuttoned her shorts. He slid a hand into her underwear, teasing the spot where her flesh parted into her labia, the other holding her firmly from her soft belly. "So hot you're gonna beg me to make you come."

She whimpered. "Show me."

He dipped a finger into her hot sex and rubbed her clit in a lazy circle. She buckled; he pushed his cock into her ass, but his jeans blocked the sensation.

"Use your hands." He nuzzled her ear. "Get me out of my clothes."

He didn't make room for her, and it pleased him that she didn't seem to have a choice but to strain with her arms back, unseeingly using her fingers to unbutton his jeans. She managed to open up his zipper and stroke him over his underwear, his ministrations on her never stopping, until she had his dick free from obstruction.

With nimble fingers, she palmed him and rocked against him, keeping his cock pressed to the curve of her still-fully dressed ass. They rutted against each other like this for a minute, her breathing picking up speed, a moan escaping out of her throat.

He left her stomach and slid the hand between her breast and the wall. He kneaded her. "Again. Make that sound again."

"Make me."

"Elena."

He left the wet heat of her sex and her breast, and started to push her clothes down her legs, but stopped when she tried to help him. He left her clothes half in place and grabbed her hands; he pushed them flat against the painted sheetrock.

"Do not move. Your hands stay on the wall. You hear me?" When she didn't respond, he pushed two fingers into the spot where her clit was, over her underwear. He rubbed the side of his face on her ear, and spoke coarsely to her. "Tell me you heard me."

"Yes. Yes. I'll keep my hands on the wall."

"Good, Elena. Condoms?"

"In my purse."

He finished pushing her clothes down. With a firm hand, he guided her feet out of her shorts, then placed them back on the floor at what seemed like a good distance apart. He scrambled out of his clothes and found her purse on the entryway table; the same two condoms he'd left behind last time remained in the inside pocket and he took one of them.

He walked back to her slowly, rolling down the condom. He checked her pussy, confirming the wetness he'd felt there before, careful not to touch anything else. She moaned and he smiled; he'd gotten the sound out of her again.

He grabbed his dick in his hand and pushed into her with no warning.

"Fuck! Alex." She wiggled her ass on him. "Yes."

He adjusted his height and gripped her hips, starting a slow movement in and out of her. "Love how prepared you are. Condoms in your purse. So wet for me."

She gasped, the sound raspy. His heart beat strong and steady in his chest, and he closed his eyes to focus on the feeling of her around him, the sounds of his pelvis hitting her ass, of their breathing harshly cutting the air.

Only when the sounds had engraved themselves into his memory, he opened his eyes again to do the same with the way her soft body jiggled with each pump of his hips.

Ely's hands slid down the wall, her forehead now resting on it. He slowed down his thrusting and left her hips and pushed her hands up the flat surface; he interlocked his fingers with hers and continued his slow rhythm in and out of her, in and out.

"Alex," she moaned. "God."

Close to her now, most of their bodies touching, he kept the teasing motion of his cock and bit her shoulder.

"You take me so good," he groaned into her neck, the smell of her intoxicating. She curved her back to change the angle in which he entered her, and it was his turn to moan. "Ely."

He let go of her hands. He cupped one of her breasts and rubbed her clit with his free fingers once more.

He heightened his pace.

"Alex. Yes. I'm gonna come."

He stopped.

"Sandy!" She pushed her ass back toward him, but he kept himself away.

With a hand flat on her back, he kept her there until she stopped squirming. Her body still again, he unclasped her bra and helped her out of it.

He stepped in closer to breathe into her ear. "I still need to kiss that birthmark. And you still need to beg. Let's go to my room."

The first thing he did once she lay on her back on his unmade bed, was to settle between her legs and hold her breasts in his hands. He kissed the small dark brown diamond next to her areola, sucked on it, then licked her nipple.

"I've been waiting to do this again." He kissed the birthmark again. "But I have more planned for us."

He crawled back on the bed until his face aligned with her labia. After a quick rub of his nose against the coarse hair on her mound, he darted his tongue out and licked the seam in front of him.

Her fingers threaded through his hair and latched; he released a gust of air on her when she pulled at the strands, and smirked when she guided him to get to work.

He readjusted his position and did as instructed.

It didn't take long for her fingertips to dig into his scalp, and for her sounds to brand his heart. He sucked and licked and used his fingers until his hips pushed on the mattress out of utter desperation, and until she twisted and buckled to the point he had to hold her down to the bed with a firm hand on the squishy flesh below her belly button.

"Alex. Fuck! More with your fingers."

He curled the fingers inside of her. "You want to come?"

"Yes. Please. Yes!"

"There it is." He pushed those three fingers knuckle-deep into her, sucked her clit into his mouth, and flicked it with his tongue.

She'd asked for it.

"Alex!" she screamed, and she trembled, and she quivered.

After her climax subdued, he kissed the inside of her thighs and gave her a second to recover. He trailed more and more kisses up her body.

"That sound you made," he said. "I've been hearing it in my head for so long. I needed to hear it again."

"I want to hear you come." Her voice sounded breathless.

He came up to nibble on her clavicle, suckle on her neck. "Tell me more."

She raked her fingers through his hair, this time gently. "I want to see you look at me like you can't hold back."

He paused on his way to play with her earlobe, locking eyes with hers for an instant. "What do you remember."

"You let me in."

He hovered over her for another moment, then kissed her. "Tell me what you want."

"I want you to have your way with me." Her eyes were hooded yet bright, her smile feline. "C'mon. I want you inside me again."

He lifted himself onto his hands, arms straight and long. He looked for every sign he could find of what she felt as he pushed into her, and unadulterated joy and pleasure spread from his heart out, permeating every corner of his soul.

She gazed at him like she was all in. Like she trusted him.

She moaned. She pushed her head back into the pillow, elongating her neck.

"No," he said. Begged her, if she could hear it in his voice. "No. Show me your eyes."

He continued the rolling of his hips, speeding up when her dark brown eyes fastened to him with unguarded openness.

"Alex." She placed a hand on his heart. "Let go. Lose yourself in me."

The coiling tension built and sprung into spasms deep in his abdomen, and his breath sputtered out of him as he came.

She'd become a home to him.

Her warm hand caressed his face.

"You were right," she said. "It was different this time."

―――

Alex disposed of the condom in the bathroom and came back to bed. Ely stretched and turned to her side, cuddling to him. They were both gloriously naked and Alex melted into the bed, spent.

She traced a random pattern on his chest. "We should probably talk about sex."

He smirked. "When two people are into each other, sometimes they want to do erotic, physical things for the purpose of pleasure; sometimes connection, too. That's what we call sex. Would you agree?"

"Ha, ha. Yes, I agree."

"Excellent."

"What I really want to know, is how long it's been since you had sex."

He frowned. He looped his arm closer around her, pulling her to him. He rested his head on his free hand. "That would be a few months ago, with you."

"Sandy, I can't believe I'm going to say this but, this is not the time to joke." She flattened her hand against his heart.

"Elena." His lips curled into a small smile. "I'm not joking. I don't know where you're going with this."

"Right." She went back to charting a pattern on his skin. "I suppose you could have had sex with someone else after me."

"Yeah. I didn't."

"I also didn't. No moral judgment attached to that; I just didn't like any of the people I met."

"I'm not the one asking about it."

The A/C cooled him down fast, now that he wasn't so physically active. The point where his body touched Ely's remained warm and, as he enjoyed the sensation— the contrast between the heat of them together and the cold everywhere else— he didn't attempt to cover him and Ely with a blanket.

"In any case," Ely said. "What about before me? When was the last time you had sex?"

"A year or so. Why?"

She lifted her head and rested her chin on her hand, palm to his pec. She gazed at him. "That's a while."

He arched an eyebrow at her. "I was depressed. It affected my desire to want to go out and meet people. My libido probably went down, too. I didn't care enough to seek partners, in any case."

"I've heard antidepressants can also cause diminished libido."

With the arm holding her close, he snaked a hand into a different position where he could grab a handful of her plentiful ass. "Not a problem at the moment."

She smirked. "Have you got tests done? I do it every few months. I do have casual sex sometimes. Always protected, but I like to make sure just in case."

He nodded his agreement. "I got one done with my physical last year."

"You got a physical but the doctor didn't ask anything about mental health?"

He shrugged. "They didn't. And I hadn't realized what it was, either."

"Well, now we know." She rested her head on the crook of his shoulder, and wrapped her arm around his stomach. "And we're helping it."

He took a deep breath. "We, as in you and me?"

"Yes. Well, and Liam, and Ana, and Charles..."

He kissed her forehead. "Were you asking me about sex because you're worried about my libido?"

"No!"

"Because I think you should give it a chance first. We should do it a few times before we establish if frequency needs to be discussed..."

"Stop."

"We could schedule a check-in meeting for next month—"

"Sandy."

"Fine." He smirked. "Then?"

"I was making my way to ask you whether this is exclusive or..."

He turned his head to better study her gestures. "Is this why you wanted me to meet someone? You don't want monogamy?"

"I happen to want monogamy, yes. I'm checking if you do."

He couldn't see her properly. He detached from her, grabbed the sheets from the bottom of the bed, and cocooned them both. They lay face to face now.

He looked into her eyes. With his free hand, he caressed her face, then smoothed the hand down her body, inviting her to put her leg around his hip.

"I do," he said.

She gave him one of her small smiles and a soft kiss. "Then we're exclusive?"

He nodded. "I'm sure you'll be plenty to handle."

She rolled her eyes but made no comment on his quip. "I wondered if maybe you'd want to meet other people, too, now that your libido is back and you're deciding what you want."

"Nah, I'm good. I know what I want, and that's you. Is this why you wanted me to meet someone that day?"

She shook her head as if she was exasperated with herself. "No. I thought that if you met someone, you might shift your attention from me to them. And I thought it would be easier, to not see you looking at me like you wanted me. Then I saw you with Leanne."

His lips stretched up at the corners. "And?"

"And I hated it."

He grinned. He brought his hand back to her face. "You're in love with me."

"Oh my god, Sandy." She slapped a hand on his chest.

"You don't agree?"

"I've only known you for a few months."

"Your point being..." He arched an eyebrow.

"Fine." She scoffed, but placed a hand on his chest, this time with much more care than before. "I'd say I'm... halfway past the middle point."

Without saying another word, he kissed her again.

———

Alex got the food he'd ordered from the door and returned to the sofa, where Ely sat. She'd put one of his shirts on plus her underwear, and her legs were fully available for his admiration. Things still so very new between them, they distracted him as he did his best to find each of their dishes in the paper bag.

"It's okay, Sandy. Take your fill of my legs, but I'm not going anywhere. You'll get another chance with them."

Her sass stole a grin out of him, and he turned it into a smirk. "I'm taking notes, for when I'm bored in a meeting, and you're wearing one of those tight skirts."

He passed her a fork and she arched an eyebrow at him as she took it. "Do you spend a lot of time thinking about me naked while in meetings?"

"No. Not always naked. I try not to get boners while at work."

She laughed, the sound loud in the space, the vibration changing the DNA in his heart cells. This time he didn't hide his grin, he smiled.

Her eyes glittered when she looked at him. "Oh, but now I think I'm going to try to give you a boner when we're alone in the office, late at night."

He'd forgotten his dish on his lap, but now he grabbed onto it a bit more firmly. "Under those conditions, I might be okay with it."

"And only once in a while, when we're in a meeting full of adults, I'll misbehave and tease you."

"God." He closed his eyes. "I knew I was getting in trouble wanting to be with you. You're going to make me suffer, aren't you?"

"But you're going to love it. What's the worst that can happen? You don't take as many notes as you typically do?"

Huh. Seemed she hadn't figured that one out yet.

He pursed his lips, excitement and nerves blooming in his chest at the prospect of what he wanted to show her. He put his food and cutlery on the small side table next to the couch, then took her food container and fork and put it next to hers. They could always microwave it all back to the right temperature later.

"What are you doing?" she asked, but he signaled her to stay on the sofa while he got up to find his notepad. He found it in the kitchen, and brought it back to the couch. "Isn't that your work planner?"

The gray and navy high-end binder opened easily, the magnetized latch giving way without resistance. He ruffled through the pages until he found what he sought.

He gazed at the drawing for a second, butterflies in his stomach, and gave it to her before he could second guess himself.

She took the planner and stared. She placed it on her lap and gasped. "Alex..."

"Doodling helps me to concentrate. Charles-approved strategy." He bit the inside of his lip.

She flipped through the pages, taking note of the little sketches he'd made, many of her— Ely in profile, Ely standing and leading a meeting, Ely sitting across from him on the big boardroom table.

"This is more than doodling, Sandy." She gazed at him, her eyes shining with awe. "You're really good." She looked down at the lineart he'd chosen to show her; she traced it with a finger. It was one of the most detailed ones, where she looked like she was stealing a glance at him. "Is this what you were doing, when you would keep looking at me, then writing, then looking at me again?"

"Probably. I couldn't get enough of you, Ely. Can't get enough of you. This was... this is one of the ways I tried to bring you into me, I think."

"Wow." Without letting go of the binder, she snuggled closer to him on the sofa. She curled her bare legs under herself and leaned into him; he put an arm around her shoulders. Her fingers went back to following the lines of blue ink on paper. "I think you're in love with me, too."

He laughed, the seed of it rooted in his gut.

"Holy shit, I love that sound," Ely added.

He kissed her temple. "You know, you didn't get me out of my depression. But knowing you really helped."

"Yeah?" She turned to better gaze at him. "How?"

"For one, you shine too hard to really avoid it. But I think what really pushed me was when you called me out for my bitterness."

She winced. "I'm sorry about that. I didn't know you had depression."

"I did have depression. It was also true that, in my case, I had the chance to do something about it, and about my bitterness. You were mostly right about me, that night. I was struggling and didn't know it, and also I have so much privilege and hadn't looked for my agency."

"You had, though. You'd started therapy by then, right?"

"Yes, I'd started therapy and medication by then. But I wasn't fully involved in therapy."

She leaned her head against his shoulder, eyes still on him. "Maybe that was depression and not you. You're less of a jerk than you give yourself credit for."

"Oh, yeah?" He wrapped his fingers around the generous curve of her hips.

"Yeah. Depression is its own weapon. It takes away your agency and it numbs you down and it... flops you."

"It flops you."

"Yeah. You go limp. You're empty. No one chooses to feel that way. Maybe you didn't choose bitterness; maybe depression took you there. I don't think anyone would do that to themselves. But if there's any room, any tiny space where you can escape that nothingness... you have to grab it, hang onto it, and do what you can to get yourself out of it. And you did. I'm proud of you."

His chest grew several ounces lighter with her words. With a small smile in place, he kissed her. "I'm going to have to talk to Charles about that, but... thank you."

Later, he packed a small bag and they went to sleep at her place.

Chapter 40

T HE WEIGHT OF ALEX'S arm on her waist anchored Ely to the bed, and she allowed the bliss of the moment— both of them in her bed, him spooning her, cozy blanket over them— to permeate her marrow.

They had agreed they'd go to sleep, and were dressed in their pajamas and lying in the dark, but she wasn't ready for it yet.

"I want you to know," Ely said, "that although I sleep on the left side of the bed, I'm aware I'm on the right side."

"Noted."

"Do you know what that means?"

"No." He nuzzled the back of her neck.

"That I'm letting you make a claim to my bed."

"Okay."

"It's a big deal." She tried to turn around to face him, but he held her in place. She relented, and stayed put.

"If you say so."

"Well, if you're not grateful for it, then we can change back and restore the proper order to this chaos."

She imagined he smiled. "Elena, I'm grateful. I'm sharing your bed." He moved a hand to cradle her breast. "I'm cuddling with you."

She closed her eyes and grinned. He massaged her breast, slowly, lazily, as if he'd been doing it for hours. Years.

A sigh released from the warmth in her chest. "Give me the list. Of things you like."

"List."

"Yeah. You said in the office today that you could give me a list of things you like about me. I want to hear it."

He chuckled; it tickled her neck. "I also said I could give you a list of things I do not like."

"I know, but I don't want to hear those."

"Got it." Humor infused his words. "Only the positives."

"You can start whenever."

"I like your hair." His hand left her breast and roamed on her body. "The curls are so big and round. The way they catch the light— it'll take me years to get it right."

She moved her ass into his hips and burrowed into him.

"Talking about light... I love the way your eyes sparkle." He was getting a little breathless. His hand now traveled all over her, as low as it could go down her leg, as high as her neck. "Granted, they also drive me wild when they shine because you're challenging me, but it's growing on me."

"Many things are growing," she said, and pressed her butt against him.

He stilled the roaming hand on her hip and held her in place as he rubbed himself on her ass.

"Your sass is one of those things I hate a bit and like a lot."

She reached back with her hand, making a try for his skin. She dipped her hand under his pants and explored everything she could reach. "What else?"

"I like how loyal you are. Caring. Working with the youth, it's so clear how much you care. Your heart is beautiful."

"I didn't show my heart much to you."

"I could see it, anyway. And the day you asked to be on my team... that's when my heart finally opened up. When there was space to fill with good things, to balance out the bad stuff."

"We all need that."

"I want you."

"You can have me." He pulled her pajama shorts and underwear down on the same movement, then held himself and teased her.

He teased her as if wanting to make her pay for the bickering but, without words exchanged, with no demands, he pushed into her and drove into her until they were both spent.

Later, after they'd both re-arranged their clothes, she turned to her other side to burrow into him again, nose against his chest.

"Tomorrow we'll have a good day," she whispered, warmth surrounding her. Sleep finally called. "Then on Monday, we'll meet in the office. I'll stop by yours on my way to mine, and kiss you, and we'll work. In the evenings, we'll find our rhythm."

She fell asleep content in his arms, comfortable in the knowledge of what they were about to build with one another.

Epilogue

THE BOARDROOM IN WHICH Ely and Alex sat with a handful of managers and producers seemed completely nondescript. She had imagined that the meeting space for one of the biggest movie production companies in Hollywood would be a lot more glamorous than it was, with its mid-range wood tones and pleather furniture. Ely could hear Alex's comment in her mind, if he knew what she was thinking; he'd probably say it was a smart business decision to spend their money on one of their multi-million dollar productions, rather than office chairs.

Ely smirked. His voice sounded so dry and clear in her head, that a burst of love for him popped into her heart.

She kept listening to the conversation happening around her, but studied her partner sitting several spaces away from her. He nodded at the right times, made comments and asked questions as appropriate, but he didn't glance at people much. His eyes seemed glued to the paper in front of him, where he appeared to use one of his favorite concentration techniques: doodling.

Maybe he was making a light study of the room they were in. Maybe he was doodling her.

A tingle always appeared in her stomach when she waited to see what he'd drawn.

He stopped scribbling. He placed his pen on the table and, in the same movement, grabbed his phone. He nodded at something one of the managers said.

"Yeah," Alex said. "That makes sense. But we'll have to schedule well in advance, to coordinate among the many groups involved."

"But only after our financial team prepares the projection numbers, and you review them."

"Yes." Alex woke his phone up and tapped into it. "I'm going to ask our assistant to send us the spreadsheet I've been preparing for that."

The conversation around them continued, and Ely's phone vibrated in her pocket. Upon checking it, she found a new text from Alex, sent less than a minute before.

Alex: stop looking at me that
way. It's very distracting.

Ely bit her lip not to smile at his text. She stole a glance at Alex; he continued to ignore her. He put his phone on the table, screen up, and took his pen and continued doodling.

Ely: YOU are distracting. Too
hot for my own good.

His screen lit up, but he didn't take his phone.

"But you said the preliminary goal would be to have a summer release for the movie, right?" he asked of the man currently talking.

She texted him again.

Ely: Are you drawing me naked?
From memory?

She put her phone back in her pocket, and re-engaged with the meeting as best she could. Alex had asked her to be there because he'd wanted to discuss the social program as a part of this potential production agreement; that conversation had ended twenty minutes before, and Ely was now here mostly for moral support.

Not that Alex needed it; he tended to be quite the rockstar in meetings like this. Chances were, Jump Cannon productions logo would be joining some pretty classic ones on the big screen soon.

It took several minutes for him to reach for his phone again. He unlocked it; shook his head. Typed on it again, and the tingling in Ely's stomach turned into a heavy pull deep in her core. She loved the way her body woke up when they teased each other like this.

Her phone vibrated again, but she didn't get it right away. It was a good idea to pause for a bit.

Alex put his phone back on the table. "My assistant got back to me. You should all have the documents in your inbox."

The meeting continued around Ely. She even managed to make a couple important comments, as if she'd been paying full attention to the men surrounding her, before she checked her phone again.

> **Alex**: I always knew you were dangerous,
> but I'm glad I didn't heed the warning.
> It means I get to draw you naked soon.
> Maybe use you as my canvas.

Ely's insides jolted, images flooding her mind of herself sprawled on the sheets, Alex dipping a brush in paint— or maybe chocolate— and then painting a stroke down her neck, over her nipple, down her belly— she almost lost her grip on her phone. She caught it just in time; the woman sitting next to her gave Ely a judgemental look, and Ely decided to put her phone in her purse for the time being.

Alex sat on the sand and placed his coffee to his side an inch into it, so that the cup wouldn't fall. He took his shoes and socks off, and sighed when his toes dug into the warm, flowy substance.

Ely, who'd done pretty much the same thing, leaned into him and hooked her arm around his. She gave him a soft kiss on the lips. "Thanks for playing hooky with me."

"You know I can rarely tell you no."

"Oh, lies." She chuckled. "You can say no to me quite easily. But today is such a beautiful day, you had to tell me yes."

"Yeah. I had to. You were very convincing."

"You must like me very much, because all I said was that we could make something up and tell Celeste we'd be back in the office later, and come to the beach for a little bit of a break."

"I suppose I like you a little. A lot. I like you so much, I doodle about you in meetings. Text you when I shouldn't."

The smile she gave him shone brighter than the California sun, competing with the ocean itself for his attention. It won easily.

"What were you drawing in your planner today? It *wasn't* me naked, was it?"

He snorted, even as his heart expanded. And his cock twitched. "No. That's for a lazy Sunday afternoon, not for a meeting."

"Yeah?" She bit her lip, and the sparkle in her eyes told him she did it on purpose, to tease him. "Afraid you're gonna lose your train of thought and embarrass yourself?"

He leaned closer and held her eyes, halfway to a kiss but not near enough. "Wrong. Just making sure I don't say fuck it, get up with a tent in my pants, grab you by the arm to pull you out of the meeting room, and have my way with you in the first secluded corner I find."

She laughed, loud in the open space, obscuring the roar of the waves and grabbing his heart in its power. Her arms went around his shoulders, and she kissed him with forceful lips, like she couldn't contain the flood of affection for him.

He melted a little every time she did that. He put his hand on the side of her face and kissed her some more.

"Oh, Sandy. You still can't get enough of me, can you?"

He gave her a long, suffering sigh, even as he could feel the corners of his eyes crinkling in barely-hidden humor. "Cannot. I don't really expect it to change, at this point. I'm used to it now."

She squeezed him in her arms and shook her head, a chuckle escaping her. "Such romantic words."

"As long as you still love me." He dropped his forehead to hers, time suspended like every time he waited for her words back.

"And I do. I love you."

He breathed through her words and smiled. "Good. Then I don't feel ridiculous showing you my doodling."

"Oooh." Her eyes opened wide. "Show me!"

He reached into his pocket and took the folded piece of paper he'd hidden there before. He held it in front of her face between his index and middle fingers.

She reached for it like it was her birthday gift, glee all over. Nerves fluttered in Alex's stomach, but he focused on her and tracked every detail of her reaction. He wanted to see the exact moment she found the secret message, concealed among a study of the bold flower pattern of her blouse.

He'd played with the proportions and design of the drawing on purpose. He'd filled the page with flowers that echoed and stretched the design of her blouse, using the blue ink of his ballpen to etch texture into them. In between the flowers, more etching, designed to both bring the flowers forward and mask the words he'd written there.

"This is gorgeous, Alex. It's better than my blouse." She brought the page closer to her face. "You wrote something here?!"

Alex couldn't help it, he kissed her temple. "Look closely."

"I love you... aww, I love you too. You're irresistible..." she laughed. "I love that you feel that way."

"Keep looking. Follow that same path among the flowers."

Her eyes traveled down the simulated river lines between two small buds. "One year together... I want more..." she sighed. "Move in with me. Let's find our own place."

"Yes. I accept."

Ely laughed and bumped his arm with her shoulder. "Sneaky. I wasn't asking. I was reading what you wrote."

She turned her face to look at him. Her eyes shone like they ever had, bright and full of her inner light.

He'd been thinking about it for weeks, since he realized his lease was up for renewal. The more he imagined them fully living together, no more duplicate toothbrushes, one for each of their places; no more plans for who slept where or those nights they spent apart— no nights apart at all— the more he wanted it.

To walk the next stretch of life, maybe all of it, with her.

"When is your lease up?" he asked.

"A bit over a month."

He nodded. "That should work."

"Ask me, Alex." She leaned closer to him. "Ask me with your whole chest."

He lifted a hand to her face and she leaned into him. Warmth spread through his torso. "Move in with me. Let's find our own place."

She kissed him. "Fuck yes."

Her enthusiasm powered the smile that appeared on his face. "Live with me and let me be with you everyday. Give me your every night."

"I will give you my every minute," she said, her kiss as much a promise as her words.

THE END

———

I love these two SO much! If you'd like to see them another year into the future, **there's a sweet story of them at work and... somewhere else**. If you're curious, go to https://www.leonorso liz.com/dnd2ndep and check it out!

Chapter 42

Thank you

A S ALWAYS, I'D LIKE to thank my husband and our little family, for all the support (particularly in patience, time, and labor) you've given me. From correcting prepositions to listening when I'm having a confidence crisis, you make it possible for me to pursue my dream.

I would also like to thank my friends, in particular Beth and Chantel, for reading this novel and helping me make sure it told the story I wanted to share with the world, and for squeeing at all the right moments. Your feedback truly made a difference. I'm also forever grateful to my Coven, as well as Sara and Janelle, who continue to support me in different ways.

My gratitude extends to my online friends as well. To the amigues in the Council's Chambers, eterna gratitud for your friendship, support, and advice. To every Discord server I'm in, thank you for your generosity, companionship, and understanding.

Finally, I'd like to thank booktok and bookstagram people, for making me feel like there's room for me and my stories.

Chapter 43

About the Author

LEONOR WROTE HER FIRST Meet Cute at eight years old and never really stopped. After many years of practicing and dreaming, she took the plunge and wrote a full-length romance novel. Then she wrote some more.

Her stories are written for comfort: love as it can be. Writing love for today means diverse characters with emotional depth and wisdom. Her characters are doing the work, folks.

Leonor is a Latina living in Canada, working as a therapist during the day and fitting as much writing to her life as she can. She's also a multi-crafter, trying her hand at watercolor, jewelry, and anything else that strikes her fancy.

YOU CAN CONNECT WITH ME ON:

www.leonorsoliz.com

hello@leonorsoliz.com

TikTok: https://www.tiktok.com/@leonor.soliz.author

Instagram: https://www.instagram.com/leonor.soliz/

Twitter: https://twitter.com/leonorsolizz

Facebook: https://www.facebook.com/leonorsolizz

Chapter 44

Upcoming Series by the Author

LATINE BILLIONAIRES

Watch out for **my next series, starring the Sotomayor family and the eldest son Gabriel's friend group, all pseudo-adopted by his parents.** So far, these are the stories I have planned:

- *Gabriel and Lina:* fake relationship

- *Jake and Violeta:* brother's best friend

- *Max and Eva:* marriage of convenience

- *Javier and Nora:* Daddy Long Legs modern retelling

LAGUNA ISLAND

Max and Eva's story is also going to be the first book in a **Small Town Series** that I'm still planning, but let me reassure you: I am not suffering for book ideas!